She belonged to him

From the first time her eyes had locked with his, Chase knew. He might not understand it, but he'd always known Samantha Kincaid was his. His for the taking, but not for the keeping. Her father had made that very clear. And the way Chase felt about her didn't invite just the "taking" part.

He stepped back. Maybe that was the key: Drive her away and do what was right—what he knew was right, no matter how wrong it felt.

"What are you doing here?" He made himself ask.

"You know better than to ask," she said.

"What I know is that you could have any man you want. No matter how rich or powerful or smart. And yet, for some reason…"

"You know the reason." Samantha took a step toward him, and in that one movement, all of Chase's resolve vanished. He knew the reason. She was his. She'd always been his….

Dear Reader,

Although we were both born and bred in Alabama, my husband and I were fortunate enough to live for several years in West Texas, very near the Rio Grande. Accustomed to the fertile black soil and virgin forests of the Appalachian foothills, we were both surprised by how quickly and passionately we fell in love with the border and the desert. The truly unique blend of cultures and the unhurried pace of life there enchanted us as much as the magnificence of the country that surrounds the river. We have always vowed to return, and now, in this HOME TO TEXAS trilogy, I have in some small way fulfilled that vow.

The three heroes in this trilogy—the McCullars—are strong men who love the rugged, desolate land they've inherited with the same passion I felt for the desert. With roots deep in the land they love, they choose to fight the increasing lawlessness that threatens both the ranch and the people they love. I think you'll find that the women who stand beside them are well matched with these lawmen heroes. And I also hope you will see a reflection of your own family in the sense of family strength, pride and unity I've tried to instill in these three books.

Thank you for allowing me to show you the McCullars and the border country I still consider a second home. I sincerely hope you enjoy these stories as much as I enjoyed creating them for you!

Much love,

Gayle Wilson

Ransom My Heart
Gayle Wilson

Harlequin Books

TORONTO • NEW YORK • LONDON
AMSTERDAM • PARIS • SYDNEY • HAMBURG
STOCKHOLM • ATHENS • TOKYO • MILAN
MADRID • WARSAW • BUDAPEST • AUCKLAND

For Dianne
"Rare as is true love, true friendship is rarer."

ISBN 0-373-22461-3

RANSOM MY HEART

Copyright © 1998 by Mona Gay Thomas

This edition published by arrangement with Harlequin Books S.A.

® and TM are trademarks of the publisher. Trademarks indicated with
® are registered in the United States Patent and Trademark Office, the
Canadian Trade Marks Office and in other countries.

Printed in U.S.A.

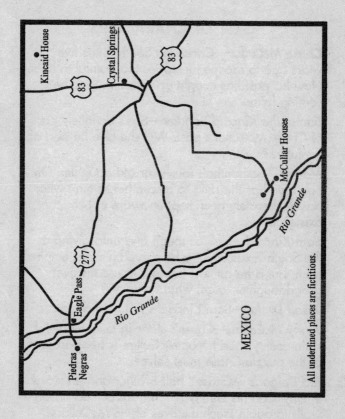

Kincaid House

Crystal Springs

83

83

McCullar Houses

Rio Grande

277

Eagle Pass

Rio Grande

Piedras
Negras

MEXICO

All underlined places are fictitious.

CAST OF CHARACTERS

Chase McCullar—Chase left South Texas five years ago to escape memories too painful to bear. Now his past has caught up with him, and he's coming home.

Samantha Kincaid Berkley—She's definitely part of Chase McCullar's past. Will she also be part of his future?

Mandy—Samantha's four-year-old daughter. Only one man has the skills to rescue her, a man who has deliberately been kept unaware of her existence.

Sam Kincaid—He's as tough and unforgiving as the South Texas country he carved his vast empire from, but is he ruthless enough to use his own granddaughter to get what he wants?

Jason Drake—Sam Kincaid's right-hand man.

Jenny McCullar—Chase's sister-in-law, widow of slain county sheriff Mac McCullar. Is her past part of the puzzle Chase must solve?

Rio Delgado—Chase's half-brother and his worst enemy. Can his enmity reach from behind prison walls to again touch the lives of the McCullars?

Rosita—She knows all the Kincaid family secrets, including those that should never be told.

Prologue

Coming home always brought back the old hurts. Always reminded him of the raw places in his soul that he thought he had forgotten. Or had learned to ignore. Or of those he sometimes foolishly tried to alleviate with a temporary panacea.

Chase McCullar blocked those memories, concentrating instead on soothing the aches he could do something about. He hunched his right shoulder, easing tired muscles under the spray of the shower. He slowly rotated his body, allowing the wet heat to relax the long day's stiffness across the back of his neck, and then shifted position again to direct the pulsing stream onto his left shoulder.

Despite the demands of his job, despite the fact that he knew he'd have to be back on a plane bright and early Monday morning, Chase had never even thought about refusing when Mac had asked him to come home this weekend. His brother didn't like asking for favors, but Mac's instincts were usually right on the money, especially when they concerned the stretch of the Texas-Mexico border he was responsible for, a stretch that encompassed the ranch where they had both been born.

If Mac thought something was going on down here, then Chase was willing to stake his life he was right. Not that anything that melodramatic would be required. It usually wasn't, in law enforcement—not unless somebody did something stupid. And neither McCullar brother was noted for his stupidity.

Deciding he'd gotten about as much therapeutic value out of the hot water as possible, Chase cut off the shower and took the top towel from the stack on the bathroom shelf. In trying to convince him to spend the night at the big house, Jenny had warned him that everything out here would be musty. Although it had been a long time since he'd been home, Chase had known better. His sister-in-law looked after his small house with the same care she took of her own. He knew the sheets would be clean, as were the towels, fresh and sweet because between his infrequent visits, Jenny stored them with sprigs of dried lavender in his grandmother's cedar chest, which stood at the foot of the iron bed he would sleep in tonight.

Enjoying its subtly pleasant aroma, Chase used the towel on his body, bending with an unthinking grace to rub drops of moisture from the long muscles of his legs. He wasn't conscious, of course, of the masculine beauty of his powerful body, which had first grown strong through hard physical labor, the unending, backbreaking work of ranching. His father had considered his sons men at sixteen, old enough to carry their share of the ranch's workload, and the twelve years since then had only made Chase tougher. He had witnessed a lot of mankind's greed and cruelty, and he fought the cynicism he had seen ruin too many law-enforcement officers.

When his body was dry, he used the same towel to wipe the fog off the mirror above the sink. The face that appeared there was as completely masculine as the body, its angles and planes too strongly defined, perhaps, to be called handsome. The pale blue eyes had seen too much during the last few years, the muscles of his jaw were almost perpetually tight, and his skin was weathered from its lifelong exposure to the Texas sun.

Chase ran considering fingertips over the late-night stubble on his cheeks. His whiskers were as light in color as his sun-bleached hair, which still had a slight tendency to curl. That was the only boyish thing about the reflection that stared back at him.

As he turned his head to examine the beard, trying to decide whether to shave tonight or in the morning, a thread of white scar caught the light. It ran from the middle of one eyebrow to disappear into the fair, close-cropped hair at his temple. He watched in the mirror as long brown fingers lifted to touch the silvered line, and the unsmiling lips flattened. Another of those painful memories. He had never forgotten the night he'd acquired that scar. Sure as hell hadn't forgotten the beating it had resulted from.

To say that Sam Kincaid had not taken kindly to his daughter's infatuation with a McCullar, a family rich only in pride and stubbornness, was a serious understatement. And in all fairness, Chase couldn't blame him. The straight line of his mouth moved upward a fraction with that admission, and then Chase pulled the short chain that hung beside the mirror, cutting off the bathroom light, deliberately destroying his own reflection.

He wrapped the towel around his narrow hips, more from habit than for modesty's sake. There was no one here to shock with the sight of his naked body. No one nearer than Mac and Jenny, a good three miles away by road, probably already curled together in sleep in the warmth of the ranch house his great-grandfather had built with his own hands. Just as Chase had built this one in the year before Mac and Jenny had married. This was smaller, of course, and simpler, but his. Living in it had suited him just fine until Sam Kincaid had issued his ultimatum.

Still trying to erase the thought of Kincaid from his mind, Chase walked into the shadowed bedroom, broad, bare feet making almost no sound on the heart-pine boards of the floor. He had already reached for the overlapped edges of the towel he wore, preparing to discard it and to crawl nude between the sheets of the bed he'd turned down earlier, when he became aware that he wasn't alone.

A breath. A movement. Something. Maybe just a feeling crawling around in his gut—lawman's instinct. He might not be sure what had given it away, but he knew there was someone else in the room with him.

This was always the worst. The unknown. The psyche could deal with danger far more easily when it had been identified. Until then, the primitive instincts got in the way of clear thinking, instincts like raw fear, making the hair lift and the mouth go dry. He turned his head slowly, surveying the black that gathered in the corners of the bedroom. His eyes were just beginning to adjust after the comparatively bright light of the bathroom.

"Chase," she said softly, her voice drifting out of the lavender-scented shadows.

And he reacted to that sound. Just as he always had. It didn't matter how many other women had whispered his name in the darkness through the years, only one voice had ever had the power to stir him so that sweet hot need jolted through his body, overpowering every other consideration. As it did now.

"Samantha?" he asked. Asked it as if he hadn't recognized her voice, as if that slight Texas accent weren't embedded in his heart as surely as the scar her father's hirelings had given him was etched forever on his face.

"Jenny told me you were coming home," she said. "That Mac had asked you to."

"I thought you were still in school," Chase said carefully, working at control. His hands fell away from the towel, and he wasn't surprised to find they were trembling. He curled the long fingers into his palms, hoping Samantha couldn't see any better than he could in the darkness. She was only a shape standing in the shadows, a slim silhouette wearing something light, something that diffused the occasional shaft of moonlight filtering in between the high clouds outside.

"At Wellesley," she said. The word contained amusement, almost a joke, private, meant to be shared between the two of them.

He had known that, of course. Despite the size of the state, despite the gap that yawned between them, he always knew what she was doing. County gossip accounted for most of his knowledge. Or Jenny. Or the newspapers. Maybe he knew because he needed to know so badly.

He had made the promise Sam Kincaid had asked him for. He had made it for Samantha's sake, just as her father had insisted he should. Not because he cared about Sam's opinion or because he was intimidated by his power, but because somewhere deep inside he was as convinced of the rightness of Kincaid's arguments as Sam himself was.

Chase McCullar wasn't the man for Samantha Kincaid. He was too old for her. Uneducated. Definitely unpolished. Far too many of the things Sam had thrown at him that night four years ago were true. He was not the man Samantha Kincaid needed or deserved. Certainly not the man she had been groomed to marry. He knew that. Understood it, even. His body had just never quite seemed to get the message.

As a teenager, she had even spent a year in Europe being "finished," whatever the hell that meant. It had always seemed to him that Samantha Kincaid had been born finished. Perfect. But not for him.

"You like it?" he asked. Talk about college. About what she was studying. About anything except why she was here, more than a thousand miles from where he had thought she was. About anything except the effect that was having on him.

"No," she said calmly, "but I graduated early—all those summer hours—and finally Sam had to let me come home."

Home, Chase thought, the forbidden images the word conveyed fighting against his control. *Not home to me. Never to me.*

"That's good," he said. His hands were still trembling

and he could feel his arousal pushing against the just-laundered roughness of the towel. That sensation wasn't helping the situation. Not that it really mattered. He'd never found much help for this particular situation.

Just thinking about Samantha Kincaid usually sent him to find something to take his mind off her. Off the dreams he'd once had. Not the kind of dreams he still had about her. Those were the ones he had learned he couldn't control, just had to endure. Those wake-up-in-a-cold-sweat kinds of dreams, his groin as achingly hard as it was now, dreaming he was making love to her.

At the beginning he hadn't comprehended the reality of the gap between them. After all, it seemed he had always been aware of Samantha Kincaid. He had seen her occasionally shopping in Crystal Springs, riding in shows, and taking part in other activities around the county. He had watched her grow up, watched her mature into a beautiful and highly desirable young woman, but always he had watched from a distance. Until the summer she turned seventeen. Then everything changed.

It was Mac's policy that either he or Chase always be in town on Saturday night—not really on duty, but just to make sure everybody stayed out of trouble. Suddenly, surprisingly, Samantha Kincaid was always there, too—at least on the nights Chase was in town—and she always managed to end up keeping him company. He eventually realized that those seemingly casual meetings had been carefully orchestrated by Samantha, but Chase certainly hadn't been averse to them or to the developing relationship that followed. Only, he hadn't known that her father knew nothing about what was going on. And when Sam Kincaid found out…

Although he had certainly been a man at the time of that meeting with Samantha's father, Chase had been forcibly made to realize the other dreams he'd had about her were the stupid adolescent kind, the kind that kids in love had.

At least until adults like Sam Kincaid pointed out exactly how unlikely they were to come true.

Those dreams you replaced with something else. Booze if you were inclined that way, which Chase wasn't. Other women, which he'd tried—tried a lot, he was ashamed to say. Or work, which seemed to be the only slightly effective solution for the endless agony that was Samantha Kincaid.

"Jenny says you're working yourself to death," Samantha's voice offered from the darkness, echoing what he'd been thinking. The slender silhouette finally moved out of the shadows, coming nearer to him.

He could smell her now, the expensive perfume she had always worn replacing the dry hint of lavender that hung in the air. He had thought his body couldn't get any harder. He discovered he'd been wrong.

"Lots of bad guys out there," he said, injecting a note of humor into the disclaimer. "More of them than there are of us. Ask Mac."

"How is Mac?" she said conversationally. She sat down on the edge of the bed, and it creaked slightly under her weight.

He eased in a breath at the sound. Samantha in his bed. Those slender, milk-white limbs relaxed and waiting for him to touch them. The fragrance of that red-gold hair spread out on his pillow. He wiped out that image as quickly as he had the one in the mirror.

"What are you doing here, Samantha?" He didn't know how much longer he could play games. He should cut to the chase and get her the hell out of here before he said or did something he'd be sorry for.

"I came to see you."

"You shouldn't be here," he said, taking another slow breath. *I came to see you.*

"Because Sam says so?" she asked. There was no defiance in her voice, and no amusement. She knew her father too well to doubt that he could make a grown man stay away from her. Too well to make childish judgments about that man if he did.

Sam Kincaid was a ruthless old bastard, as hard as the country he'd carved his multimillion-dollar empire out of. His great-great-granddaddy had given him a head start, buying up Spanish land grants from people who no longer wanted them when Texas became a state.

But Sam Kincaid had protected the legacy he'd been given, had even added to it, despite the shifting economic realities of falling oil prices and droughts and unexpected freezes through the years. The Kincaid ranch was bigger and richer than when the old man had inherited it. And that was very rare these days.

"Or because *you* don't want me here?" she added.

He could lie, he thought, but he wasn't sure he was that skillful. The bed creaked again, and then the bedside light came on, illuminating all the shadowed recesses of the room. His eyes found Samantha, her slender body leaning backward, propped gracefully on one elbow, her hand still on the switch of the lamp. Her gaze was focused on the front of the damp towel he was wearing.

"No, I guess *that's* not it," she said, and her green eyes lifted to meet his. She smiled at him. "I thought you'd never get around to asking," she said, her smile widening slightly. Not taunting his blatant arousal. Not teasing him. Just smiling at him.

He didn't know why she was so beautiful. The features themselves weren't spectacular. There were even flaws. Her mouth was wide, making her smile almost too generous. The right eyetooth was the tiniest bit crooked, and there was a minute dusting of freckles across her nose. But she had won every beauty contest her daddy had entered her into until, somewhere around age fourteen, she had put her foot down. She was through parading around on a stage in front of a bunch of horny strangers, she'd told him. The comment had been repeated for a couple of years by those who delighted that someone had finally stood up to Sam

Kincaid, even if it was only his daughter and about nothing more important than a beauty contest.

"Samantha," Chase said softly, the word almost a groan.

"What do I have to do?" she asked, the question tinged with resigned amusement. "I really believed I *could* leave you alone—and I did try. You have to admit I've tried, except…somehow I've always known…"

She hesitated again, and he didn't bother to fill in the blanks. He'd always known, too, from the first time her eyes had locked with his, her interest in him somehow clearly expressed in their green depths. He might not understand it, but he had always known Samantha was his. His for the taking. But not for the keeping. Sam Kincaid had been very explicit about that. And the way Chase felt about her, had felt about her for what seemed to be his entire adult life, didn't invite just the "taking" part.

He wanted what Mac and Jenny had. That oneness. That rightness. The till-death-do-us-part stuff. Only, he knew it would never work for the two of them. Her father would never let it work. And he knew he couldn't make her happy. In bed, maybe he could. He'd love to try, but he knew that wouldn't be enough, not for the long haul. The gap between them was way too wide. It seemed he had always known that, too.

"Go home, Samantha," he said. He fought to keep any inflection out of the command, to keep the raw, aching need from showing in his voice. "Get out of here."

"I'm not a child anymore, Chase. I'm twenty-one, fully capable of making my own decisions, and I don't think you're too old for me. Or too anything else Sam told you." She smiled at him again.

"I don't think your father would agree with you."

"I didn't plan on asking him for his opinion. Or are you afraid Sam'll have you beaten up again for touching me?" she asked. Her eyes held his challengingly for a moment, and then they softened, knowing as well as he did that wasn't the truth of why he'd stayed away from her.

"It's no good, Samantha. You know it and I know it. Just go home. Save us both a lot of grief," he said, his voice as carefully controlled as before.

He picked up his jeans from the foot of the bed and carried them with him into the small bathroom. But once there, he laid them across the bowl of the freestanding lavatory and gripped the porcelain rim of the sink with both hands. He put his forehead against the cool glass of the mirror and closed his eyes. He held them closed, fighting against the thought of going back into the bedroom, fighting against the strongest temptation he'd ever known in his life.

He jumped when her palms slipped over his shoulders and down his upper arms. The bare skin of his back shivered in reaction. Her warm lips brushed along his spine, the ringed column of bone made prominent by his forward lean. They trailed slowly downward, caressing and tantalizing. Gathering every ounce of resolve that hadn't melted under the heat of her mouth, Chase straightened.

The effect was not quite what he'd anticipated. Samantha's arms came around him, her fingers laced together over the hard, contoured planes of his abdomen, and she laid her cheek against his back. When she breathed, he could feel the small movement of her breasts against his skin.

"You slumming?" he made himself ask. "Is that what turns you on about me? They say some women are like that. They get turned on at the thought of crossing barriers. Is that why you're here? Just a little sorority-girl experimenting on the other side of the tracks?"

She released him then, stepping back, breaking the almost-unbearable contact, and he swallowed hard in relief. Maybe that was the key. Drive her away. Keep his word. Do what was right—what he knew *was* right—no matter how wrong it felt.

"You know better than that," she said.

He turned around to face her. She was still standing close enough that he could see her features clearly, despite the lack of light in the small room.

"Or maybe sleeping with me is just a way to get back at your daddy? A way to finally declare your independence. Is that it? Because other than that, I really—"

"Don't," she protested. "You *know* better than that," she said again.

"What I *know* is you can have any man you want. No matter how rich or powerful or smart. Men that Sam would find highly suitable. And yet for some reason—"

"You know the reason," she interrupted. "You've always known the reason. It's always been the same. All these years it's been the same."

Her voice was different, the surety that had been there before, faltering in the face of his accusations.

"Hell, Samantha, you just got an itch, and you picked me out to scratch it," he said harshly, crudely. "That's all it is. All it's ever been. Even Sam understood what was going on."

The words were brutal, and she reacted. Her face changed, her mouth opening slightly as if to offer a rebuttal to what he'd claimed, and then it closed, but her lips trembled as if she were on the verge of tears.

"So why don't we just get it over with, just do it, and then maybe we can both get on with our lives," Chase suggested harshly. "I'll give you what you came here for, and after that, you leave me the hell alone. I'm getting a little too old to be your daddy's whipping boy."

Now, he thought, watching the shimmer of tears invade the wide green eyes. Now she would leave. He'd done everything else he could think of to keep his word to Sam Kincaid. He'd practically exiled himself from his own home, from his family, and he'd never contacted Samantha in any way, trying to pretend that what was between them didn't exist. It hadn't worked, of course, but maybe this would.

If he could finally destroy whatever image she had of him. Destroy what she felt, or thought she felt, about him. Destroy the possibility that she'd ever seek him out again,

ever offer the temptation she had offered tonight. *And in
the process, destroy myself,* he acknowledged bitterly.

"All right," she whispered. "Maybe you're right."

It took his breath. That wasn't what she was supposed
to say. Was not the way someone like Samantha Kincaid
was supposed to react to the suggestion that she become a
one-night stand. Damn it, he realized, she had called his
bluff. She knew as well as he did that it wasn't that way
between them. It never had been. He loved Samantha Kincaid. Had loved her for years. Probably since the first time
he'd seen her, pigtailed and preadolescent gawky, riding in
some local horse show, easily controlling one of the magnificent horses the Kincaid ranch was famous for.

And loving her was a sickness he had never gotten over,
despite the years of separation, despite Sam's arguments,
despite everything. He loved her, but God knew how much
he wanted her, too. Had wanted her far too long for his
body not to react to that whispered agreement.

He watched her fingers lift to the top button of the shirt
she wore. Watched unbelievingly as they unfastened the
first and then the second, his eyes following as her hands
moved downward. Breathing suspended, he watched her
shrug almost awkwardly out of the garment and drop it onto
the tile of the bathroom floor. She wasn't wearing a bra
and her small, perfect breasts had peaked with the touch of
cold in the night air. His hands tightened into fists, fighting
the urge to enclose, to make her body warm and soft and
wanting under their touch.

Her fingers had already dealt with the metal buttons of
her jeans when he became aware of something besides the
beauty of her breasts. She moved, sliding the denim down
over her hips, allowing the jeans to puddle on the tile beside
the light shirt, another small mound shadowed with the
darkness. His eyes had followed the drop of fabric, and then
they lifted, slowly, tracing the line of slender perfection
upward. Long legs, beautifully shaped by years of riding.
Hips almost boyishly slim. Slight convexity of her belly

centered by the darker circle of her navel. Slender waist leading upward to the breasts where his eyes had begun feasting.

This was not what he had intended. Not what honor demanded. Not what he knew in his soul was right, but there was nothing he could do about the rush of desire that seemed to consume him. Even his hearing was affected, the sweep of blood so strong in his ears that it was as if he were standing in a vacuum, as if this were one of the endless dreams he'd had. Not real. It couldn't be real.

She took a step closer, the small thrust of her nipples touching against the mat of hair on his chest. His body jerked with the depth of the breath he took, and he was surprised that in the soundless vacuum of dead air that surrounded him he could still hear that gasp. Not a dream.

"I don't have anything, sweetheart," he said, his voice hoarse with need. "Nothing to protect you. I didn't expect—"

"It's all right," she said. Her fingers found the end of the towel, and she pulled it away. The terry cloth fell to join her scattered clothing on the floor. Released from constraint, his arousal seemed to leap upward, making contact with her body. Then it was far too late for reason. Far too late to remember that this was the last thing he'd ever intended to happen. Far too late for any shred of sanity to interfere with what they had both wanted for more years than they could remember.

He wasn't even aware that he had picked her up, cradling her against the strength of his chest as if she had always belonged there. Unaware of the short journey to the lavender-scented bed. Too unaware of the stark reality of what they were doing.

Despite the all-consuming force of his desire, he didn't forget that this was Samantha, and he didn't forget what he had dreamed about making her feel. His big hands were shaking, but they were infinitely tender, practicing a restraint that he wouldn't have believed possible as they

moved against her. Not possible except for the fact that he
loved her so much. Had always loved her. An eternity of
love, which he intended to demonstrate slowly and carefully. Using all the skills he had learned while trying to
forget her. All the things her substitutes had taught him
about lovemaking, he finally was allowed to show to the
woman he had pretended they were.

Through the years he had never allowed himself to wonder if Samantha had done the same. If she had sought release in the arms of other men. That didn't bear thinking
about, although he wasn't chauvinistic enough to believe
that it was right for him and wrong for her. It was just
something he couldn't face, and so he had locked the question from his consciousness.

Until tonight. Until her body was moving under his trembling hands and worshipping lips. Arching into his touch.
Reacting to his whispered avowals. Shatteringly responsive
to his every caress.

She had told him she was protected, so that must mean…
It didn't matter, he realized suddenly, if he weren't the first
to make love to her. He was in no position to make demands, not given the fruitless attempts he'd made through
the years to destroy in the arms of other women the hold
she had over him. What mattered was that this was the
memory that endured, erasing whatever had gone before.
Making all others meaningless. Forgotten.

Finally, he knew she was ready. As wanting as he. As
empty. She had whispered the words and her body's re-
sponses had spoken to him even more clearly. Chase was
certainly experienced enough to read all the signs. It was
time, and so he allowed himself to push into the sweet, hot
wetness he had so carefully created, that he knew was waiting for him.

The barrier he encountered was a shock, but not enough
to prevent the completion of what he had begun. Nothing
could have prevented that. But he felt his eyes sting with
hot moisture that had nothing to do with the sensations that

grew with each small surge of her hips beneath his. Samantha was his. Only his. He was surprised to find how much that meant. Despite the long years, she had waited for him. Only him. Despite her father's wishes and his own lonely exile, Samantha had waited.

As he thought that, the control he had exerted spiraled away into the darkness and his need exploded inside her, the hot seed of his passion pulsing into her building response. He thought briefly that he had left her behind, too moved by what he had discovered to wait for her. Then she joined him, her body moving as convulsively as his. He held her, hearing his name gasped into the darkness as if it had been waiting on her lips through the eternity of their separation. His, he thought again. She was his—she always had been—and to hell with whatever Sam Kincaid thought about it.

WHEN THE PHONE SHRILLED into the predawn darkness, Chase awoke instantly. It took him a moment to deal with the fact that the slender contours of Samantha's body were pressed against his side. Not a dream, he realized with the same wonder he had felt in the bathroom, watching her undress. Reality. A remembered reality of her body moving under his. Several times.

Maybe that was why his brain felt like sawdust. Maybe that was why he couldn't move to answer the phone until the second ring. Maybe...

"I got a call," Mac's voice said in his ear when he finally managed to pick up the receiver and mumble into it. He was aware that Samantha had shifted, moving closer to him. He listened with half his mind, the other half occupied by what was happening to his body—something that, given the number of times he'd made love to her through the night, shouldn't be happening.

"A call," Chase repeated, trying to clear his head.

"A tip. Something happening at the Sanchez ranch. I'll pick you up in ten minutes."

"No," Chase said. The denial came out too sharply. But Mac was nobody's fool, and Chase didn't know where Samantha had parked her car. For some reason, he didn't want Mac to know she'd spent the night here. His brother wouldn't say anything to anyone except Jenny, but still he didn't want anybody, not even them, to know. Not until he figured out what to do. Not until he'd talked to Sam Kincaid, confessed that he'd broken his word and that he couldn't let Samantha go, now that she was his.

"No," he said again, concentrating on controlling his voice. "I'll come there. Jenny can feed us breakfast when we get back."

Mac hesitated for a moment, perhaps sensing that something else was going on, but the need to check out the tip he'd received precluded argument.

"I'll give you ten minutes," Mac offered and hung up. Another man of few words.

Pushing off the covers, Chase sat up on the edge of the bed.

"What is it?" Samantha asked. "What's wrong?"

"Mac got a tip. He wants me to go with him."

"A tip about what?"

"Drugs," Chase said, standing. At least, that was why his brother had asked him to come down here. Unofficially, of course. Chase knew a lot about running drugs across the border. He ought to after three years with the DEA. That was why Mac had sought his advice, not because he wasn't capable of taking care of his county.

Mac had been sheriff here for almost six years, and he knew just about every secret folks didn't want anyone to know. But they'd been lucky so far with drug smuggling. There were easier places to bring it across, places closer to major U.S. highways and closer to the Mexican cities where the stuff from South America was flown in.

"Here?" Samantha asked. The same doubt was in her voice that had been in his own when Mac had first broached the possibility to him. Not here.

"Maybe," he said. If he looked down at her, he knew he would never make Mac's deadline, never pull himself away before he had touched her again. And if he touched her...

"You be careful," she said softly.

Almost against his will, his lips lifted. She sounded like Jenny. Like a wife. This, then, was what it felt like. This sense of loss, this separation. A tearing at the oneness they had created last night.

"I will," he promised. "I'll be careful."

HE HAD DRESSED IN THE darkness of the bathroom, and when he recrossed the pine floor, awkwardly on tiptoe, his boots had sounded too loudly, echoing in the dark stillness. They hadn't spoken again. He wasn't sure what to say. Not yet. It was far too new. Almost fragile. Too easily destroyed.

He stepped out onto the small porch, closing the door to the house behind him. The clear December air was sharp in his nostrils, replacing the scent of her body that somehow had clung to his as he dressed.

He drew in a deep lungful, fighting the urge to go back, the urge to let Mac check out his informant's tip alone, as he would have done if Chase hadn't agreed to come home this weekend. Fate, maybe. Instead of wondering about how that one simple decision might change the future, he stepped off the porch and down onto the first of the two wooden steps.

"You give your brother a message." The voice spoke from the darkness across the yard, raised only enough to travel to him through the chill of the Texas night. "Maybe save his life."

"What message?" Chase asked. Although it had been years since he'd heard that voice, he had no trouble recognizing it. A familiar bitterness tightened his throat.

"He doesn't know who he's dealing with."

"And you're going to tell him," Chase mocked.

"Pesos or bullets. *You* tell him."

Chase laughed, loudly enough that he knew the sound would carry to the figure in the shadows. "That's supposed to scare Mac off? You don't know my brother very well."

"*Your* brother," the voice repeated. The comment was somehow taunting. "Tell *your* brother what I said. His life depends on it."

"You go to hell, you bastard," Chase said. He descended the remaining steps and paused for a moment, looking into the darkness where the warning had come from. "And get off McCullar land. You don't belong here. You've got no right to be here."

He felt like a child, shouting into the darkness. All the old regrets of the past were encroaching on the present tonight. *Coming home.*

The cloud that had obscured the moon drifted, and the horse and rider it revealed seemed to waver out of the darkness, briefly illuminated against the backdrop of shadows. Although his mother's slender beauty was clearly stamped on the rider's near-perfect features, underlying that perfection Chase could see the other half of the speaker's heritage. The half he shared. The McCullar half. Then horse and rider turned and disappeared, the sound of their departure lingering in the stillness longer than the shifting patterns of moonlight and shadow.

"Who was that?" Samantha asked.

Her voice came from the doorway behind him, but Chase didn't turn around, working still to control the anger and the hurt child's bitterness.

"No one," he said softly. "No one who matters."

Without another word, he climbed into the rental car he'd driven down from San Antonio. When he started the engine and turned on the lights, he could see her. She was wearing only the light shirt she'd taken off last night, and her hair was loose, tangled in curling strands over it. His hands had done that. Chase sat in the darkness for a moment, just watching her, and then he put the car into gear, backing across the yard and then turning down the narrow road that separated the two McCullar houses.

MAC WAS ALREADY SITTING in his pickup when he got there. Chase knew if he had been a minute or two later, his brother would have done exactly what he'd threatened and gone without him. The door on the driver's side of the truck was still open, and through the opening his brother watched him as he climbed out of the rental.

"I'd about given you up," Mac said. He was a big man, bigger than Chase, taller and broader. He had the clear blue McCullar eyes, but his hair was darker than his younger brother's, and the bold sweep of his mustache hid the sensitive curve of his upper lip.

Chase had always thought Mac looked exactly like a Texas sheriff ought to look, from the crown of his Stetson to the soles of his well-worn boots. If Chase had grown cynical in the pursuit of justice, Mac had seemingly been unaffected. But of course, the stakes here were not the same, the dealings not as dirty. At least not yet.

"I had a visitor," Chase said, closing the door of his car.

"What kind of visitor?" Mac's voice was slightly amused, anticipating, perhaps, some creative excuse for his brother's tardiness.

"Rio said to tell you pesos or bullets." Chase let his bitterness color the message, watching the slow impact of the words appear on his brother's face.

"Rio?"

"You *do* understand what it means?"

"Drug dealers. You take their bribes and you look the other way, or..." Mac shrugged. "But I don't—"

"Somebody offer you money, Mac?"

"Hell, somebody's always offering. You know that."

"Rio mixed up in what's going on?"

"Not to my knowledge," Mac said decisively. He turned in the seat, putting his foot on the gas pedal, but still he didn't close the door. Apparently thinking instead about what he'd been told, he looked down a second at the key he'd inserted into the ignition when he'd gotten into the truck to wait for Chase. ''Now, why in hell—'' Mac began to question, his fingers automatically turning the key.

The truck exploded, becoming nothing more than a brilliant fireball that shot flames and pieces of burning glass and metal into the star-studded darkness of the winter sky.

Chapter One

Almost five years later

Samantha Berkley set the last of the brown paper sacks into the back of the Jeep and pulled down the door. Heat rose around her in waves from the asphalt parking lot. It had hit her with almost-physical force from the moment she'd come out of the grocery store. Although she had grown up in this climate, the contrast between the frigid air-conditioning of the stores and the sweltering reality of August in south Texas was always a shock.

"Ready to head home, Cupcake?" Samantha said to the little girl who was sitting, eyes squinted against the glare, patiently waiting in the seat of the grocery cart she'd just unloaded.

It was the end of their Wednesday-in-town outing. Buying groceries was the last stop on the familiar itinerary that usually began with a trip to the library, included some shopping, lunch, and maybe even a movie if anything suitable for Mandy to see was playing. Samantha lifted the child out of the buggy, giving her time to untangle legs that were getting a little too long for the toddler seat.

"You're getting too big to ride in one of these, kiddo," Samantha said. "All grown up." She couldn't resist dropping a quick kiss on the sun-warmed top of her daughter's head, right where the pink scalp showed through the precise part that separated two curling blond ponytails.

She set the little girl on her feet, holding her hand as she pushed the shopping cart over the bumper lines of the return chute, which was conveniently next to their parking space. Samantha then turned back to use the remote on her key ring to unlock the Jeep, opening the back passenger door for her daughter.

"You'll just have to get another baby," Amanda suggested as she clambered into the high seat.

"As if I didn't have enough to look after already," Samantha said, smiling. She pulled the shoulder harness of the seat belt across her daughter's small chest and began to secure the lock.

"Granddaddy Sam says we need us a daddy," Amanda offered.

Samantha's eyes flicked up from the seat-belt mechanism in surprise. Her daughter's sky-blue gaze was guileless. Mandy was only repeating what she'd been told, Samantha knew. Except she also knew that Sam had counted on that repetition, his message being delivered by a messenger she wouldn't be rude to.

"What we really *need*," Samantha said, her voice only the slightest bit clipped, "is for Granddaddy Sam to mind his own business."

She closed the back door, a little harder than was absolutely necessary, and climbed into the driver's seat. It would take her about fifty minutes to get back to the house, and she knew that Sam's remark would needle her all the way home.

She took a deep breath, trying to block her automatic resentment. It didn't seem that her father would ever learn to stay out of her life, and because of Mandy, she could never totally break the ties that bound them all together, no matter how angry she got at his interference. Neither of them deserved that.

She started the engine, and then turned the air condi-

tioner up full blast. Glancing in the rearview mirror in preparation for backing out of the parking space, she met
Mandy's eyes. For a moment it was as if time had been
suspended. Or had flashed back a few years. The sensation
happened only infrequently, but when it did, it was still
enough to take her breath.

Maybe this time it had been precipitated by Sam's comment. Or maybe it was simply a trick of the afternoon light.
She had long ago stopped trying to explain what happened
at those moments. She had just learned to endure them and
then get on with her life.

She smiled at the child, and raised a trembling hand to
adjust a mirror that needed no adjustment. No one else ever
drove her Jeep. She knew she was just trying to erase that
momentary reflection of the past. And she also knew that
was an impossibility.

SHE HAD CHOSEN THE shortest route home, using the maze
of unpaved ranch roads that the Jeep had no trouble negotiating. Mandy had dozed off, despite the roughness of
the ride, and occasionally Samantha would glance in the
mirror to check on the sleeping child, whose long lashes
rested peacefully against rose-tinged cheeks. Despite the
fact that she slathered sunscreen on them both every morning, by this time of the summer, their fair skin had begun
to take on a tan. With its exposure to the sun, Mandy's
small nose, a carbon copy of her own, had acquired a
matching dusting of freckles.

At least she didn't inherit my hair, Samantha thought,
enjoying the sight of the blond head nodding slightly with
the motion of the car.

It was at that moment she became aware of another car
on the narrow road, rapidly approaching behind them. Too
rapidly, she decided, given the condition of the caliche one-
lane. She thought about pulling off to the side and letting
whoever was in such a hurry go around her, but before she
could make that decision, the black car slowed, its speed

now sedately matching her own. She watched it for a few minutes, green eyes flicking back and forth between the road ahead and the following sedan. Men. Four of them. Two in the front seat and two in the rear.

There were very few houses on this road—a couple of turnoffs that led to small, isolated ranches before she reached the one that would take her home. She knew the families who lived on those spreads, and for some reason these men didn't look as if they might be the kind of visitors that would be welcomed there. She wondered briefly if she should call Sheriff Elkins's office, and then realized she had nothing to tell them. Nothing except there were some people on the road that she didn't recognize. *Pretty small-town,* she thought, smiling at her own xenophobia.

She had topped a rise, eyes still on the car behind her, before she realized there was a panel truck parked across the road directly ahead of her. She slammed on the brakes, hard, and the Jeep slewed sideways for several yards before it crashed into the side of the parked vehicle, and then bounced away, coming to rest almost aligned again in the direction she'd been traveling.

Despite the shock of the collision, her first thought was, of course, for Mandy. She turned to examine her daughter, who was apparently unharmed, her small body safely held in place by the shoulder harness. The child's eyes, still dazed by sleep, met hers and then moved past her mother's face to focus on something outside the window.

"You okay, Cupcake?" Samantha asked. Mandy nodded, her gaze still fastened on whatever had attracted her attention outside.

The driver's-side door opened, and when Samantha turned around in response, she understood the child's fascinated silence. In the seconds since the car had stopped moving, it had been surrounded by men holding guns—all of them pointing at the occupants of the damaged Jeep.

Even as her mind was beginning to register what was happening, the dark, mustached man who had opened the door reached across her to yank out the car phone. He stepped back, pushing the phone into the pocket of his pants, and then he motioned her out of the car with a silent, but unmistakable command, expressed with the long barrel of what appeared to be an old army-issue Colt.

A million thoughts flashed through Samantha's head. Things she should have done. Bitter regret that she hadn't recognized what was happening sooner. Scenarios involving her taking some action to get them safely away. But at the back of them all, blocking all the panicked urgings that she ought to be doing something, loomed that one word. *Safely. Keep Mandy safe.* At least two of the guns were focused on her four-year-old daughter. *Just don't do anything stupid that might get Mandy hurt.*

"What do you want?" she asked. The question sounded remarkably normal, considering the fact that she couldn't seem to get enough air into her lungs. Considering the fact that her heart was going like a jackhammer in her chest. Considering.

"Get out of the car, please," the man who had opened the door said politely. Despite the gun, there was nothing frightening about his demeanor. He was a good-looking man. His calm eyes, set in the darkly handsome face, were somehow as reassuring as his politeness. Until he added, "We don't want to have to hurt anyone."

Her Spanish was certainly good enough to understand that. To fasten her mind on it. To hope it was the truth.

"I have to unbuckle my seat belt," she said in the language he'd used. She couldn't afford to do anything that might set them off. No sudden moves. No surprises and nothing they might misinterpret. She couldn't afford any bullets flying around inside the Jeep with its precious cargo.

He nodded permission, and with trembling fingers Samantha released the lock of the belt and stepped outside. The man had moved back only enough to allow her room to get out of the car.

"Hold out your hands, please," he ordered.

"What do you want?" she asked again. She had maybe twenty dollars on her. And her watch, which she knew was valuable because Sam had given it to her last Christmas. A gold wedding band. Not much, it seemed, to exchange for her daughter's safety, but maybe it would be enough. *Please, God,* she prayed, *let it be enough.*

Even as she was taking a silent inventory of her valuables, the realization was also beginning to grow in the back of her mind that this robbery had been carefully orchestrated. The truck had been parked behind the rise in anticipation of her approach. The car following her had timed its arrival perfectly. Pretty elaborate for a holdup.

"Your hands," he said again, gesturing with the gun. "Palms together."

"I don't think—"

"Now," he said. "Do it now before I lose patience, Miss Kincaid. Before I am forced to do something we will both regret."

Kincaid. Her mind registered the name even as she obeyed him, holding out her shaking hands. The sight of the silver duct tape was somehow more terrifying than anything that had happened so far. The other man who had been standing on the driver's side with them laid his shotgun on top of the Jeep and then proficiently wrapped the tape around her wrists. He cut it off the roll with a pocketknife, which he handled as casually as he had the gun. Only her hands. He taped nothing else, and for some reason she was immensely relieved that he hadn't covered her eyes or her mouth.

The one who had done all the talking nodded again, but not, this time, to her or to the man who had wrapped her wrists. His eyes had moved to the men standing on the other side of the wrecked Jeep. She heard the car door open and couldn't keep from whirling around to see what they were doing.

"No," she begged, watching one of those men crawl into the back seat and begin to unfasten Mandy's seat belt.

"It's all right," the leader said. "No one will be hurt, I promise you. Everything will be fine if you do exactly what you're told."

"What are you going to do?"

"You'll be sent information about what to do. Instructions will be sent to your father."

"My father?" Samantha repeated unbelievingly. By this time, the man was lifting an unprotesting Mandy out of the back seat. "What kind of information? What are you talking about?"

"For the ransom," he said simply. "Information on how it should be paid. On how to recover your daughter."

For the first time she realized what was going on, and sickeningly, how foolish she had been. Kidnapping was a threat she had lived under most of her childhood, a threat her father had taken very seriously.

"Please don't do this," she begged. "Anything you want. I'll give you anything you want, but don't take her. Please, don't take my daughter." She had already begun to move toward the man carrying the sleepy child when the muzzle of the leader's revolver was placed against her throat.

"Don't do something foolish and make us have to hurt you or your daughter. Your father will pay the ransom whether you are dead or alive. If you make us kill you," he said reasonably, "all it will mean is that your daughter, when she's safely returned in a few days, will be forced to grow up without her mother. However, if you do exactly what you're told, I promise you that no one will be injured. Neither you nor your daughter. Then, in only a few days you'll be reunited."

Mandy was watching her over the man's shoulder, her blue eyes beginning to widen as the distance grew between them. Or maybe widening at the sight of the gun pressed against Samantha's neck. Another of the men had moved to walk beside the one carrying Amanda, his shotgun pointing casually at one of the bobbing blond ponytails.

"Mama," Mandy called, hoping, Samantha knew, for reassurance.

"It's okay, Mandy. Everything's okay," she said aloud, and then softly, urgently, to the mustached man beside her, "Please. I'll do anything you say. Just don't take her away from me."

"We'll contact your father about the arrangements. No police. Do you understand? It's very important that there are no police involved. If you call in the authorities, I make no promises about the child's safety."

"Please don't do—" Samantha began again only to be cut off by a minute increase in the pressure of the gun that rested against her throat.

"I have a daughter myself, Miss Kincaid. I will see that no harm comes to the child. You have my personal guarantee. My word. I shall care for her as if she were my own daughter. We have no desire to hurt a child. All we are interested in is your father's money. In the ransom. It is very much in our best interests, as in yours, that everything should go smoothly and that no one should be hurt. But there must be no interference from the authorities. Do you understand?"

Samantha nodded, watching a crying Mandy being loaded into the car that had followed her down the narrow twisting road.

"I am sorry that I must leave you out here alone. Do you know your way back to civilization?" His politeness was almost bizarre, given the situation.

"Yes," she whispered.

She wondered if she should tell him that she was no longer Samantha Kincaid. She could tell him that Sam wouldn't pay what they asked, but she couldn't be sure what effect that might have, and she also knew it wasn't true. Sam would pay any amount to recover his granddaughter. While she stood there, hands taped and the kidnapper's gun pointed at her, the door of the black car that had followed her closed, shutting off the sound of Mandy's terrified sobs.

The big car began to back down the narrow road to a small turnaround, only a few hundred yards behind. All meticulously planned. In her stupid arrogance, she had walked right into the trap. Sam had tried to warn her when Mandy was born. A warning she'd ignored because she had believed that it was simply a ploy to exercise further control over their lives. And now...

The man with the mustache walked to the front of her Jeep and, releasing the latch, held the hood open as he pumped a single bullet into the engine. Startled, she flinched away from the noise. Steam flared briefly into the dry air and then he dropped the hood.

He turned to look at her again, his dark face softening at the tears tracking unchecked down the pale, shocked translucence of her cheeks. "As if she were my own," he said again. "I promise you that on my mother's grave." And then, casually shifting the gun to his left hand, he crossed himself.

Samantha made no reply, her breath catching in a small sob.

"Don't worry," he said almost kindly. "You'll be told exactly what you should do. Everything will be fine if you obey the instructions."

She watched him climb into the cab of the panel truck that had been parked across the road and start the engine. She stood motionless until it had pulled around the wrecked Jeep and headed back in the direction the car had taken, the dust rising in an acrid cloud around her. Then she was alone.

The entire encounter had taken perhaps three minutes. Three minutes to destroy her life. Three minutes to change everything about her existence.

She put her bound hands down on the hood of the Jeep, trying to think. Her sick fear felt like a fog in her mind. Maybe she should at least try to start the engine, she thought, but she could see the liquid pouring out from the bottom of the car, pooling in an oil-sheened puddle on the white roadway.

Finally, she just began to run. Not the way she had come, not following the two vehicles that had disappeared in the cloud of dust. Instead, she ran in the direction she and Mandy had been heading when they'd been stopped. Toward home. Toward the nearest telephone.

"CHASE MCCULLAR?" a voice called, the words echoing as hollowly across the deserted concrete of the San Diego parking deck as Chase's footsteps had been. Late-night deserted, but he hadn't even thought about the emptiness of the place until the man spoke to him. "We'd like to talk to you, Mr. McCullar."

Despite the fact that it was almost ten o'clock and he hadn't stopped for dinner, or for lunch for that matter, Chase hesitated and then, curiosity overcoming his better judgment, he turned around. The man who had called to him was standing directly across the parking deck from where Chase's vintage Jag was parked, standing just beyond the deepest shadows, barely visible. He wasn't alone. There were three of them, all wearing suits, but Chase had been around too long to believe they were businessmen.

"It's been a long day, gentlemen," he said pleasantly. "Maybe tomorrow."

"Tonight," the one who had called to him said. He took a step out of the shadows, and his companions moved to stand behind him.

Just like a well-rehearsed dance routine, Chase thought, resigned amusement tugging at the corners of his mouth. A lot of his clients had entourages like this, serving to insulate them, they had hoped, from having to deal with the brutal realities of today's world.

"People who want to talk to me generally come to my office," Chase said, his voice still patient, still polite, but he was having to work at keeping it that way. "I'll be in again in the morning at nine. You can make an appointment with my secretary.''

''I'm afraid this can't wait, Mr. McCullar. It would really be better if you come with us now.''

The gun in his hand was deliberately revealed, held so Chase couldn't possibly miss it. Not that he hadn't been expecting something like that. It had been in the man's voice from the first—that certain arrogance created by the knowledge that whatever he said could be backed up by a bullet.

Chase watched, unmoving, as they walked toward him across the painted lines of the exit ramp. They stopped too close to him, giving him an opportunity to act if he chose. They were big men, all three of them, chosen for muscle power, Chase thought with amusement, rather than intellect.

He could feel the adrenaline flooding his body. Despite the ever-present potential for something to go seriously wrong—potently represented by the big gun—Chase found he was almost anticipating what was going to happen. It had been a long time since he'd had a chance to relieve stress in such a physically satisfying way.

''Turn around, please,'' the one who had done all the talking ordered, ''and put your hands on the top of the car. Spread-eagle.''

''I'm not planning to shoot you,'' Chase said, again fighting an urge to smile.

''I'd like to make sure of that, if you don't mind.''

Chase hesitated for a second longer, looking into gray eyes that seemed totally emotionless. ''Have it your way,'' he said easily.

He bent his knees slightly as if preparing to set his briefcase down, but the motion he began swung the heavy leather satchel upward instead, accurately catching the .44 in its rising arc. The gun fired, probably simply a reaction to the case striking the gunman's fingers, but he heard the bullet ping harmlessly against one of the metal girders over their heads.

Before Chase heard the gun itself hit the concrete somewhere behind the men, he had let go of the satchel and then caught it again. He repositioned his hands, one on either side of the case, using it now like a battering ram, slamming the hard, skin-covered metal edge into the first man's forehead. With the force of the unexpected blow, the leader fell backward, briefly disrupting whatever action the other two had been attempting.

By the time Chase had thrown the heavy case into the midst of the three of them and had taken his own gun from its holster that nestled at the base of his spine, it was all over. The leader was sitting on the concrete, holding his fingers against the reddening mark the briefcase had made. The others looked as if they had just witnessed some sort of performance. Sleight of hand. And maybe they had. Chase's only regret was that the encounter had been too brief to be satisfying, not even as stress reduction.

"If you could get away with taking me down, I doubt whoever sent you here would still want to talk to me," Chase said reasonably, no trace of anger in his voice. It was the simple truth. In his business, there was a certain reputation that had to be maintained.

"We weren't going to kidnap you, Mr. McCullar," the fallen man said. "We were warned that you carried, and that…" He hesitated, and Chase had time to wonder just what he'd been told and by whom before he finished. "That you might not come willingly."

"I guess you should have listened to whoever warned you," Chase said. "Now, why don't you all just back up. Get away from my car. I told you it's been a long day."

"Look," the speaker said, getting to his feet, his tone subtly altered now that the balance of power had shifted. "I'm sorry if—"

"I asked you to get the hell away from my car."

"Maybe we made a mistake, but—"

"I don't talk to people who pull guns on me. I don't talk in parking garages. If you want to see me, make an appointment. Tomorrow." The adrenaline was beginning to fade, to be replaced again by hunger and fatigue.

"Mr. Kincaid ain't gonna like this," one of the others said under his breath.

Chase wasn't sure if the remark was directed at him or at the man who had botched the errand they had been sent on, but whichever of them he intended to warn, the name was enough to cause a reactive tightening of Chase's gut. Mr. Kincaid. When you had grown up in south Texas, there was only one Mr. Kincaid.

"Sam?" he asked, trying to figure out why Sam Kincaid would want to talk to him. He might have expected something like this heavy-handed summons five years ago, but not now. Not after all this time. And especially not when you considered the present circumstances.

"Yes, sir," affirmed the one who had just issued that probably highly accurate opinion.

"Sam Kincaid is the one who wants to see me?"

"Yes, sir," he said.

"Why didn't you just say that to begin with?" Chase asked.

Chapter Two

Chase had never been on the huge Kincaid ranch, whose southern boundary lay almost thirty-five miles from the modest McCullar spread. Despite the social standing of the people he associated with these days, he couldn't help but be impressed. He hadn't been able to see much of the acres they'd driven across on the short trip from the private strip where Kincaid's pilot had set the jet down. This was still a working ranch, he knew, although it was more noted nowadays for the horses it bred than for anything else it produced.

The house he was taken to was a big, white pseudo-Colonial that Sam had built for his second wife, Samantha's mother, when they'd married. The old adobe ranch house, built by Sam's great-grandfather, was still standing, several miles away from the new. Sam was too sentimental to tear it down, of course, but Texas gossip said Betsy Kincaid had made it clear she didn't intend to live in a dwelling that held so many memories, especially memories of the first Mrs. Sam Kincaid.

Betsy had died of cancer more than twenty years ago. Sam Kincaid had buried two well-beloved wives before he had turned fifty. He had never married again, saying that he didn't intend to take a chance on having to do something that painful a third time.

Chase expected to be made to wait, given his reception

of Kincaid's messengers, and he was surprised to find himself taken from the front door straight into an office where Sam Kincaid himself sat behind an antique rosewood desk, apparently just waiting for his arrival.

The old man had changed in the nine years since Chase had last seen him. He'd aged, of course. The thick mane that had still been salt-and-red-pepper then was now almost pure white, and the lines cut into the weathered skin were etched more deeply. The hazel eyes, hard and unflinching as adamant, were still the same as the night he'd ordered Chase McCullar to stay the hell away from his daughter.

Pinned by that unwavering stare, Chase felt remarkably the same as he had then. Despite the distance between that night and this, despite the changes in his own life, he felt as if he had been judged and found wanting. Just not good enough. Still not good enough. Not by a long shot.

He'd be damned if he'd speak first, Chase decided, fighting those now unfamiliar feelings of inadequacy. Sam Kincaid had sent for him, and he could make the first move. He worked on keeping his features incurious, but despite his best efforts, in the back of his mind were forbidden images that involved no one now in this room. Images of the one person who connected him to Sam Kincaid.

"They say you're the best," the old man said finally. "Is that true?"

Chase hesitated, wondering about the source of Sam's information. And then, realizing that the comment could be taken in a couple of ways, he found himself fighting an unbecoming urge to laugh.

"I guess that depends on what I'm supposed to be the best at," he said. He hadn't been invited to sit down, but he walked to the maroon leather chair placed before the desk and sat in it anyway.

"Negotiating," Sam said.

For a moment the quick spurt of fear in his belly almost overcame Chase's control. Samantha had been his first thought, of course, but that didn't have to be what this was all about. Kincaid had lots of friends. Maybe he was simply inquiring for one of them. Dealing secondhand wasn't all that unusual in his business.

Chase swallowed the sick bile that had risen in his throat before he answered. He was pleased to think that nothing had changed about his expression or about the disinterested quality of his voice, but then he had had a lot of experience the last few years at hiding what he felt.

"I'm the best," he acknowledged, almost without arrogance.

It was true. His was a relatively new profession, and one that Chase McCullar, given his heritage and experience, had been eminently suited for. The first time had happened by accident. He had been in the right place at the right time to do a favor for a rich Mexican friend whose wife had been kidnapped, and he'd been successful. No one had been hurt. The money had been delivered and the exchange made—all in a matter of days, and without the authorities being involved in any of it.

The next time it had been a request from a company that had, with the signing of the NAFTA agreement, moved part of its operations into Mexico. The CEO had ended up held hostage by a guerrilla group who had asked for twenty million dollars and settled for six. Again the exchange had been flawless, and Chase McCullar, who had been referred by the friend he'd originally helped, had been in business.

He hadn't known much about the financial aspects to begin with, but he knew the country on both sides of the border, and he was smart. The other he had learned.

Now he had a set commission. For companies it was fifteen percent of whatever the payoff was. Most corporations below the border carried insurance against the possibility of an employee being kidnapped. For negotiating the release of private individuals Chase charged only ten percent. Given the wealth of his clients, he could probably just as easily have gotten his normal fifteen, but he sometimes felt that what he asked was too much for what he did.

Sometimes he had to fight his own guilt over requiring those so anguished by the kidnapping of a loved one for any fee at all. Sometimes he felt as if that aligned him on the other side—with the kidnappers, with the bad guys.

Only to Jenny had he ever expressed those doubts. She had reminded him that he was providing a valuable service to people who could well afford to pay for it, and that he was the one taking all the risks. Transporting enormous amounts of money in a country that was rapidly becoming as lawless as its South American drug-cultured counterparts was incredibly dangerous.

Most companies and families were more than willing to pay his fee in order to have someone else take care of all the details and to assure them that nothing would go wrong. Ten percent wasn't enough to cause resentment among the wealthy; it was enough for his needs; and it was small enough to get him a lot of quiet referrals in the elite circle that was usually targeted. The kidnappers were becoming bolder with every success, even on rare occasions venturing across the border for their high-profile victims.

A couple of jobs he had done for free, because amateurs had made a mistake and the families targeted weren't really wealthy enough to raise the ransom. Despite their lack of resources, those families had still needed his expertise—maybe needed it even more so—to negotiate the safe release of their loved one.

"Then I've got a job for you," Sam Kincaid said, bringing his attention back to the present.

"I pick my own jobs, Mr. Kincaid," Chase said. He wondered if that was the old feeling of inferiority speaking. Or if, like Samantha, he just wanted to resist doing what Sam Kincaid told him to do because no one else ever did. "*I* decide what jobs I do."

"You ever turn one down?" the old man asked. The question was subtlely mocking, and echoes of their last interview again intruded into the room.

"A couple."

"Why would you do that? I understand you make good money doing what you do."

"Because they didn't feel right."

"Not on the up and up?" Sam asked, still shrewd, despite his seventy-plus years.

"Because I believed they were home-cooking," Chase agreed. "Somebody was out to make a quick buck from the insurance company."

"That ain't what this is," Sam said. His eyes dropped for the first time, locking on the gnarled, arthritic fingers of the big hands that were laced before him on the gleaming surface of the desk.

"Why don't you tell me about it, and then I can make a decision," Chase suggested.

Sam nodded, hooded eyes still focused downward. Chase could see the depth of the breath he took. His lips tightened, almost pursing, before they opened again.

"Some Mex bastards took my grandbaby," he said.

The hazel gaze cut up to Chase's face, deliberately raised to catch whatever reaction he'd had to that statement. Chase didn't think there had been one—at least not outwardly. And now that he knew for sure it wasn't Samantha who was being held, the band around his chest loosened minutely. Until he realized what Sam's statement meant.

"Samantha's baby?" he asked. He hadn't known there was a baby. He had heard about her marriage, of course. Jenny had told him. He had always figured she had so he wouldn't have to find out from someone else. Samantha had married one of those men Sam would consider ideal to be her husband. Somebody rich and powerful. Old money. Position. Somebody she'd met on a trip to Europe, he thought Jenny had said. He hadn't listened too closely to anything but the first.

He had long ago recognized it was his fault that he'd lost her. In the first few weeks while he'd been trying to deal with what had happened to Mac, he honest-to-God hadn't even thought about contacting Samantha or worried about what she might be feeling. Not while he'd taken care of Jenny and made all the arrangements. Not even while he had been consumed by making sure that Rio paid for what he had done. He had simply trusted that Samantha would be waiting for him. Just as she had before.

It had been like a kick in the heart when Jenny told him the truth. One more agony at a time when he had thought he couldn't bear any more. It had seemed then to be just another treachery. It had taken him a few months of endless grief and fury over Samantha's betrayal before he remembered what he'd said to her that night. The crap about just doing it and getting on with their lives. One-night stand.

He had thought, then, that she'd understood that had only been an attempt to drive her away. He had thought she had called his bluff. Gradually the realization had come that she might not have understood, not unless she was a mind reader. And finally the bitter understanding that no matter the reasons, with her marriage it was too late to do anything to change what had happened.

But Jenny hadn't told him anything about a baby. Of course, he hadn't talked to his sister-in-law in almost six months. It was too hard. Too painful. She always wanted to talk about Mac. That was something he still couldn't bear.

"I don't have but one child," Sam acknowledged, the hazel eyes still focused on Chase's face.

"Have the kidnappers communicated with you yet?" he forced himself to ask, pushing the old griefs and regrets to the back of his mind.

"Just happened this afternoon. They said they'd be in touch."

"They will. That's one thing you can count on. You want to tell me what happened?"

The old man's lips pursed again, and Chase thought he was considering how much to share. Instead, he reached for the buzzer on his intercom as he answered. "I'll let her tell you. Samantha. I wasn't there." Then he spoke into the machine. "You can come in now," he said to the soft feminine voice that had responded.

A voice that still had that slight Texas accent. A voice Chase would still have known anywhere. While he was waiting, the soundless vacuum built around him again. And when the door opened, he felt his heart jump and then begin pounding in his chest as if it might explode.

She hadn't changed. That was ridiculous, Chase thought, amending his first reaction. Of course, she had changed. They all had. That was the kind of thing your emotions said that your logic knew was crazy. Except, he thought, studying the slender figure standing in the doorway, she *hadn't* really changed.

Her red-gold hair was still long, its natural curl allowed. She wore less makeup than she used to, and she still didn't need any. She was wearing an emerald-green dress, its lines elegantly simple. Silk, he guessed from the way the fabric followed the curves of her body.

Samantha's eyes had automatically sought her father's when she entered the room, holding for a second before her gaze shifted to include Chase. Her face had already been pale, reflecting that terrible anxiety all his clients expressed, but seeing him, all color drained from the lightly tanned skin, leaving her features as blanched as parchment, the small scattering of freckles stark across the bridge of her nose.

It felt like an eternity to Chase that her shocked eyes held his, their dark pupils slowly widening until they almost eclipsed the rim of green that surrounded them. In reality he knew it was only seconds before her gaze swung back to her father.

"What do you think you're doing?" she said. Whatever was in her voice was beyond anger. "Why did you bring him here, Sam? What the hell are you trying to do?"

"You said you wanted the best," the old man said calmly. "No chance anything could go wrong. *He's* the best."

"But…"

Chase could see her trying to think, trying to decide what to do. Weighing her father's claim against all that lay between them. He found himself wondering how much the old man knew about what had happened that night. The same night…

"No," she said, interrupting those memories, the perfection of the one always colored by the horror of the other. She hadn't looked at him again. Her furious eyes were locked on her father's, their hardness almost matching his. "You'll use *anything* to get your way. And anybody. Even Mandy."

"I don't know what you're talking about," Sam said.

"You know *damn* well what I'm talking about. But this isn't going to work. Not even now. Get somebody else, Sam. Somebody besides him. Or I will."

The two men watched as she turned and left the room, pulling the door sharply closed behind her. Kincaid's lips pursed again, but he didn't say anything for a moment, his gaze still directed toward the doorway where Samantha had stood. There were splotches of color over his cheekbones. Finally he turned back to face Chase.

"You got any recommendations on who I should call?"

"I can give you a couple of names, people who are reliable," Chase said, still working at his own control. Working at sounding undisturbed by what had just happened.

"But they're not as good as you," Sam said.

Chase didn't bother to answer. There didn't seem to be anything left to say. Samantha didn't want him to have any part in what was going on. Despite the fact it was Sam's money that would pay the ransom, she had the right to make that decision. The people he would mention to Sam were competent. That seemed to be all he could do.

"She's too much like me," Sam said into the silence. "Always has been. We struck sparks off each other from the get-go."

"I'd like to get back, Mr. Kincaid. It's been a long day."

"I let my pilot head on home. I didn't think she'd turn down the best man for the job, in spite of..." The old man's voice trailed away, but he looked at Chase from under the thick white brows.

He hadn't thought Samantha would go against his judgment, given the situation. Maybe he *didn't* know anything about that night, Chase thought, if he had believed Samantha would welcome Chase McCullar's help.

"It's late. Spend the night," Sam suggested. "I got plenty of beds. I'll pay you for your trouble coming out here, enough to make it worth your while, I promise, and I'll have you flown home in the morning."

Chase wondered briefly what Samantha would think about that arrangement. Probably as little as she'd thought about him in the role of negotiator. He stood, preparing to suggest that Sam make the phone call and wake up his pilot. None of this had been his fault. He just needed to get this entire episode over with and get on with his life. Get back to work at forgetting Samantha Kincaid all over again.

Even as he thought it, memory intruded. That was exactly what he had said to Samantha. That night. The night he'd taken her virginity. *Let's just get it over with and get on with our lives.* And so what he said to Sam Kincaid was nothing like what he had intended to say when he stood.

"Throw in a sandwich and a glass of milk, Mr. Kincaid, and you've got yourself a deal," Chase offered.

"She ain't gonna change her mind," Samantha's father said. "Stubborn as a mule."

"I know. I never thought she would. I can give you those names in the morning. There's no rush to do anything, no matter how bad doing nothing feels, until you get some instructions from the kidnappers."

The uncomfortable silence stretched between them for a moment. He and Sam Kincaid didn't have anything in common to make polite conversation about. For that matter, neither of them was the kind of man who made small talk.

"How's your sister-in-law?" Sam asked.

The question surprised him. Maybe because he didn't expect the old man to remember. Maybe because there seemed to be some genuine interest in his voice. Genuine concern.

"She's fine," Chase said. The muscles in his face felt stiff and cold, just as they always did when someone brought up anything connected to Mac.

"I been there," Sam said reflectively. "No matter what she tells you, she ain't fine. Not even after all this time."

Chase looked into the old man's eyes, slightly clouded with age and red-rimmed from the lateness of the hour or from the events of the day. He wondered if Sam was right. Then he cleared that guilt from his mind also.

"You mentioned a bed," he said.

"And some chow. I remember."

Kincaid punched the intercom button again, and for a second Chase wondered if he were resummoning Samantha. Instead, when the door opened, it was to reveal a tall, dark-haired man with a distinct pattern of discoloration across his high forehead. The man from the parking lot. They had ridden back together in Sam's Citation, but they sure hadn't exchanged any conversation.

"McCullar, this is Jason Drake, my right-hand man. Drake, Mr. McCullar is spending the night. He needs some supper and a bed. You treat him good now, you hear. He's my guest."

Chase knew then that the old man had been told about what had happened in the parking garage. The story probably wouldn't change Sam's opinion of him, maybe even up it a notch or two, and that wouldn't endear him any to Jason Drake.

"Yes, sir, Mr. Kincaid," Drake said. His voice was carefully emotionless, but something in his eyes said that Chase McCullar could sleep in hell tonight if it were left up to him.

Chase forgot the feeling of enmity that had emanated from the man as he followed Sam's assistant upstairs. He found himself wondering instead where in this maze of rooms Samantha was. He didn't have to wonder what she was feeling. He knew. He'd dealt with too many people in this same situation to doubt that he knew exactly what she was feeling tonight, what she was thinking. Remembering. Regretting.

It was not until some time between finishing the two thick roast-beef sandwiches that had been brought up to his suite and taking a hot shower to help ease the long day's tensions, that he also thought to wonder where the hell Samantha Kincaid's husband was.

SAMANTHA HAD TURNED the shower up full force, knowing that nothing that happened in this house went unreported to the old man. She had held such a tight rein on her emotions that she was surprised at how easy it was to finally let go, to let it all pour out. The strong spray that pounded against the white tile walls didn't quite hide the harsh, gasping noises her crying made, despite the fact that she pressed both hands hard over her mouth to stifle the sound.

When she had finally cried it all out, she found herself huddled on the floor at the back of the shower enclosure, curled almost in a fetal position, emotionally and physically drained. She had promised herself all day that she'd find a time to cry it out, to scream against the circling guilt. She just wanted to hold Mandy. To keep her safe. That had been her job, to keep Mandy safe. It was the only important job she had ever had in her entire life, and she had failed.

I'll get her back, she had kept telling herself as she ran this afternoon. Her father was rich and very powerful. He loved Mandy as much as she did. But when she arrived here tonight, she realized that the kidnapping had hit him hard. For the first time in her life she had seen Sam vulnerable and scared. That had been one of the most frightening things in this terrifying episode—the realization that Sam Kincaid was afraid.

The shock of finding Chase McCullar in her father's

study had been almost more than she could stand. Despite everything, for one split second she'd had an almost-unbearable urge to throw herself into Chase's arms and let him handle it. *"He's the best,"* her father had said, and she knew Sam would have used all his many resources to find that out. If he said it, it was certainly true. She had asked him to find someone who could get Mandy back to them safely, but she had never dreamed it would be Chase McCullar.

Trembling from reaction and exhaustion, she pulled herself up, using the bar on the side of the shower stall. She felt like an old woman—naked, drenched and trembling. For the first time in her life, she felt powerless. Afraid. Just like Sam had looked when she'd arrived at the ranch. Only Chase had seemed in control. *Why shouldn't he be?* she thought bitterly. He had nothing to lose. He didn't know Mandy. He didn't give a damn that someone had taken her.

She couldn't get the image of his calm features out of her mind. Cool and strong and competent. He always had been. *The best man for the job,* echoed again in her head. But not this job. Not this situation. There was too much to lose.

And what else do I have to lose? she thought, mocking her fear. What else did she have besides Mandy? She had already lost her daughter. She had let a bunch of strangers take her baby away from her at gunpoint. She knew that nothing worse than that loss could ever happen to her. Not even having to deal with Chase McCullar.

Chapter Three

Chase was awakened at nine the next morning by a discreet knock immediately followed by a maid who entered his room carrying a silver-and-glass carafe of coffee, very good coffee. He finished it before he answered the summons that had been delivered along with the tray—an invitation to join Sam Kincaid for breakfast. Chase found that he felt far better today than he had last night. More capable of dealing with the old man and even with his own emotions. More in control of them.

Jason Drake was waiting outside his room when he finally stepped out into the wide hallway. Chase was sorry that he had made the man wait. He had no animosity toward Sam's assistant. They were both just trying to do a job, trying to make a living.

"Sorry. I didn't know you were waiting for me," he said.

"Mr. Kincaid asked me to show you to the breakfast room."

The gray eyes weren't nearly as cold this morning. Chase figured that might have as much to do with the fact that the discoloration across his forehead was beginning to fade as with Sam's admonition to treat him like a guest.

"You worked for Mr. Kincaid a long time?" Chase asked as they descended the stairs.

"Almost two years."

Chase shook his head, wondering what that would be like, being at Sam Kincaid's beck and call every day. "Then you're a better man than I am," he said.

"It's not as bad as you'd think, if you're judging from what people say about him. Mr. Kincaid's fair, and he's honest. I guess you can't ask much more than that these days."

"And the pay's good," Chase suggested, smiling.

"The pay's good," Drake agreed, the words almost without inflection.

He supposed that he ought to admire the man for not talking about Sam behind his back, and besides, by that time they'd reached their destination—a bright breakfast room with a small round table. It had been set in a windowed bay that looked out on some of the primest real estate in the state.

The monochromatic beauty of south Texas didn't appeal to a lot of people, but love of this land was in his blood as strongly as it was in Sam Kincaid's.

When Drake excused himself, explaining that Mr. Kincaid would be joining him shortly, Chase walked to the windows and pushed one of the sheer curtains aside, looking out on early-morning sunshine that had probably already driven the temperature past ninety.

"It was all supposed to be hers one day," Sam Kincaid said.

Chase dropped the curtain and turned around.

"Mandy's," the old man explained. "There ain't nobody else to leave it to. I'd hoped for a grandson, but I guess that ain't gonna happen." He shrugged and then moved to one of the two places set at the table, sparkling in the morning light with fine china and crystal and sterling-silver flatware. "You might as well eat before you go," he said, gesturing to the setting at the other side of the table. "You probably got things to do this morning."

"A few," Chase said, trying to remember what he was supposed to do today, back in San Diego. In addition to the more exotic aspects of his job, he taught seminars on the precautions foreign nationals should take to lessen their chances of being taken hostage in Mexico. He was also under contract as a private security consultant to several of the companies now operating there. But he thought his first appointment today wasn't until afternoon, and so, curious as to what the old man wanted from him, he sat down across the table. And he acknowledged the irony that he was sitting at Sam Kincaid's breakfast table.

The service was flawless, handled by a pleasantly rounded Latino woman named Rosita who kept the coffee hot and her efficiency unobtrusive. Sam treated her with casual friendliness and for some reason, Chase was surprised that she truly seemed to like the old man, to enjoy taking care of him.

They were almost through when the swing door of the small room was pushed open. Samantha was dressed today in a black cotton sundress. She had put her hair up, but she wasn't wearing any makeup and the bruise-like shadows under her eyes were pronounced.

"Is he really the best?" she asked her father.

She hadn't looked at Chase. On purpose, he thought, so he stood, holding his linen napkin in his left hand. Her eyes tracked to him, just as he'd intended. Maybe she was surprised by his manners. Maybe her own were too deeply ingrained to allow her to ignore him standing there, his unfinished breakfast in front of him.

"Please don't get up," she said. "This isn't a social occasion."

"I never thought it was. And yes, I'm the best."

"I didn't ask you," she said. Her eyes went back to her father's face.

"That's what they say," Sam confirmed into the small silence that fell after her deliberate rudeness. "His was the only name I got. The best. That's what they all told me. Everybody I asked."

"Are you sure?" she asked finally. "You're not just trying to…"

To control everything, Chase finished for her when she hesitated. Trying to make all the puppets jump on his strings. He wondered again what the old man knew, and then he wondered if Sam was that cold-blooded. But the emotion in his voice when he had talked about his grandbaby had been real. Undeniably real.

"He's the one," Sam said. "But you got to tell him everything that happened yesterday. He's still trying to make up his mind if he wants the job."

Again the mockery from last night was evident, less subtle this time. Chase supposed he deserved it. Once, he would have cut out his heart with a butter knife if Samantha Kincaid had asked for it, and last night he had pretended that he might not be willing to help her get her baby back.

Samantha's eyes met his again. Chase didn't know what his own face revealed, but she swallowed, the movement hard enough to be visible, before she nodded. She walked around Sam to take the chair in front of the windows, and Chase sat down again in his.

She was near enough that he could smell her. The same fragrance that had invaded his bedroom that night. The same one that had seemed to linger in the small house even the last time he'd gone there. Just before he'd put up the For Sale sign.

"We'd been in to town," she said, her eyes on her fingers that were twisting a narrow fold of the linen tablecloth. "We always go in on Wednesdays. Everything's less crowded."

She paused, controlling emotion, he knew. Fighting the pain of remembering those last hours.

"Town?" he repeated, because he needed to know the exact location.

"Eagle Pass," she said.

Although it surprised him that she had been shopping

there, he pushed the question to the back of his mind so he could concentrate on what she was saying.

"Mandy was asleep. In the rearview mirror I noticed a car following me. I thought about calling the sheriff's office, but they weren't…doing anything, so I decided I was just being silly. And then, all of a sudden I looked up and there was a truck across the road ahead of me. I couldn't stop in time and we hit it. Mandy wasn't hurt. That's the first thing I checked, and by the time I had, they had already surrounded the Jeep. They were all around us. They had guns. Shotguns. Rifles. They took the phone away and made me get out of the car. Then they taped my hands together…and they took Mandy."

"I need to know what they said. *Exactly* what they said."

"They…the leader…he kept telling me that if I did what they told me, no one would be hurt. That I'd get Mandy back in a few days. That if I cooperated, I'd be around to watch her grow up. Otherwise…" She paused, swallowing again before she went on. "He said all they wanted was the money. And that we'd be contacted about how to pay it. So…I didn't do anything. I just watched while they put her in the car and drove away. I didn't do anything to stop them."

The halting words had grown softer and finally the pained narrative faded. Her shadowed eyes looked up at him, begging for absolution, he understood, for relief from the guilt that she had let strangers take her baby.

"You did the right thing. The only thing you could have done. Otherwise, you could have gotten your baby killed."

He had said the words before, had said them to assuage this same guilt. And they were true. He had just never said them with as much conviction as he did now.

"You never know how nervous the kidnappers are. How inexperienced. They were probably just as scared as you were," he assured her. "In situations like that, if someone does something stupid, all hell can break loose." He had fought the urge to touch the twisting fingers. Her eyes continued to search his, trying to read if he were telling her the truth. "All they want is the money," he finished. "Just like they told you."

"Who are they?" she asked, eyes still on his, still needing the reassurance that he really knew all about these kinds of incidents, that he was really as good as they had told her father he was.

That was the pertinent question. One Chase couldn't answer. At least not yet. "We won't have any idea until we get their demands. And we may not know even then. It literally could be anybody."

"Hell," Sam said, "there can't be *that* many of the bastards around. Why don't somebody do something to stop them?"

"There were over two thousand kidnappings in Mexico last year. Maybe that many different groups involved in them. It's the newest cottage industry down there. It could be anybody," he said again.

"They were very concerned that the authorities not be called in," Samantha said. "He kept saying, 'No police.'"

"They don't want the police involved for a lot of reasons. If it's antigovernment guerrillas, the Mexican authorities don't want them to get their hands on the ransom and use it in their fight against the government, so sometimes the police interfere to prevent the exchange. Occasionally there's been corruption. The ransom ends up in the hands of the officials rather than the kidnappers, and then the victims are…"

"Not released?" she questioned, her eyes again reflecting that fear.

"It's in everyone's best interests to see that the ransom is paid, as quickly as possible, and the hostage released. Their continued success at this very profitable business depends on that."

"And yours," Sam said.

"I offer a service for people who prefer to have someone

experienced deal with the kidnappers. You came to me, Mr. Kincaid, I *thought,* because you wanted my services.''

"It just seems a hell of a way to make a living," the old man said, disgust in his voice. "What happened to being a lawman like your brother? Not enough money in it?"

The force of the fury that surged through his body surprised Chase. It shouldn't have. The old man had always been able to rattle his cage. Sam Kincaid might care that much about money, but he should know that a McCullar wouldn't.

Besides, the old man knew damn well what had driven him from law enforcement. They both knew. Sometimes Chase still woke up at night, sweating and trembling from watching again as that truck exploded. From seeing his brother's burning body thrown out of it. From reliving all that had come after that.

Despite his determination not to let the old man goad him, Chase found he was on his feet. To hell with Kincaid. To hell with whatever he thought about what he did for a living. To hell with being a puppet again, his strings pulled by that manipulative old—

"Chase," Samantha said quietly, looking up at him. "It doesn't matter what he says. If you're really the best, I need you to get her back. To get Mandy. Please."

He looked down, straight into her eyes, and he knew that it really *didn't* matter what the old man said. Nothing had changed, despite the years. He would still cut out his living, beating heart if she asked him to. Considering that she was married to someone else and that he would have to have contact with her until this was over, that felt like a remarkably accurate description of what he imagined lay ahead.

Suddenly the swing door opened again. Jason Drake came in, holding a plain white business-size envelope in his hand.

"This was in the post-office box in town, Mr. Kincaid," he said, walking across the room to offer the letter to Sam. "I think maybe it's the one you were expecting."

''I sent Drake into town to see if anything…personal had come in the mail,'' Sam explained.

Automatically Sam reached for the letter, and Chase said, ''It might be better if you let me look at it first.''

Sam's hand paused in midair. The old man was unused to relinquishing authority to anyone, but finally he nodded to his assistant. There was a minute hesitation before Drake walked around the table to hand the envelope to Chase.

''And it might be better if we look at this somewhere more private,'' Chase added.

''My people are trustworthy, Mr. McCullar,'' Sam said. ''Rosita's been with me since before Samantha was born, and Drake handles most of the ranch's business now. I got nothing to hide from them.''

Rosita's hands had hesitated over the dishes she'd been clearing away, but nothing about Jason Drake's expression had changed. It was professional and disinterested.

''It's okay, Mr. Kincaid,'' he said easily. ''I've got some work outside.''

''Thanks for getting the mail,'' Sam said.

''Of course. I'll see you all later. Mrs. Berkley,'' he said, nodding and smiling at Samantha. He walked out the swinging door, and there was a brief silence.

''You want me to come back later, Miss Samantha?'' Rosita said softly.

''No, Rosita. You go ahead and get the dishes. I know you have a lot to do. We don't want to hold you up.''

They waited through another silence, punctuated by the occasional ping of glassware, until Rosita had finished clearing the table and disappeared back into the kitchen.

''That was uncalled for,'' Sam said as soon as she was gone. ''I'd trust my people with my life.''

''That's your business. I won't trust them with mine. Ask Mrs. Berkley if she'd trust them with her baby's,'' Chase suggested. ''You hired me to make decisions, Mr. Kincaid. This is one of them. Only the three of us will know about the arrangements to pay the ransom.''

"Those are my people," Sam said. "My friends."

"But I'm the one who's going to be carrying a whole lot of your money across the border. The fewer people who know anything at all about that, the better."

"He's right," Samantha said.

"About not trusting Rosita?" Sam asked sarcastically.

"About paying him to make the decisions. It's what we hired him for, Sam. Let him earn his money."

Sam led the way back to his office, automatically taking his place behind the massive desk. Samantha sat in the maroon leather chair, and Chase found himself moving as far away from her as he could manage without being obvious about it. He declined Sam's offer of another chair, leaning instead on the edge of a big library table that stood against the wall between the room's long windows.

He examined the envelope he held, noting that it had been addressed to Sam Kincaid, at the Kincaid Ranch, and sent to the post-office box the ranch maintained in nearby Crystal Springs. There was no return address. He didn't worry about fingerprints or any physical evidence the letter might contain. Nobody involved in this had prints in any computer in the States. The only reason the envelope and its contents were important was for the information they would provide about paying the ransom. They weren't interested in catching the people who had taken the baby, just in getting her back.

He used his thumbnail to tear open the flap and then pulled out the single sheet of paper it had held, laying the envelope on the table beside him. The very short instructions were handwritten and in Spanish. He read them carefully, once and then again, just to make sure he hadn't missed anything.

He didn't like what he read.

"How much?" Sam asked.

"A million dollars," Chase answered, glancing up over the paper he held.

No one said anything in response.

"Which means they're amateurs," Chase added, just in case they hadn't understood. He didn't like dealing with amateurs. He liked people who knew what they were doing, who understood exactly how the game was played.

"Why?" Samantha asked.

"Because your father could afford a lot more. A hell of a lot more. Everybody along the border knows that. Except apparently these guys don't, which means they didn't do their homework. Amateurs. And they want us to go into Mexico before they'll give us directions on where they'll meet us to make the exchange."

"That's not the way it's usually done?" Sam asked.

"Not for me. In and out. That's what's supposed to happen. As close to the border as possible. We'll try to negotiate when we meet them. We can probably get by with half a million, convince them that—"

"No," Samantha said.

Both men looked at her.

"You just do whatever they say. No negotiations. No delays. You just do whatever they ask and get Mandy back."

"That's not the way that I—"

"It is now," she said, holding his eyes. "Whatever they say, you do it. That's what I'm paying you for."

It angered him. It sounded too much like her father. Like somebody talking to the hired help.

"I thought your father was paying," he said. "Or your husband. Maybe *he* might be interested in trying to save half a million dollars. I know that's not much to the Kincaids, but most people would be interested in that kind of deal."

So far there had been no mention of Samantha's husband from either of them. He wasn't sure, now that he thought about it, exactly who was hiring him. *Mrs. Berkley,* Drake had called her. It seemed to Chase that *Mr.* Berkley might like to have some say-so in what was going on.

"Maybe we should wait until your husband gets here to

settle the financial details of our arrangement," he suggested.

There was a silence that lasted for a few heartbeats before Samantha said, "My husband has nothing to say about this."

"That seems pretty arrogant," Chase said, "even for a Kincaid."

"Divorced," Sam added, his eyes on his daughter's face.

Chase felt his heart rate accelerate, but he ignored the emotions thudding around in his chest. Concentrated on trying to say something in response that made some kind of sense. *Divorced*. The word beat at his consciousness.

"Still, this is his baby we're talking about," Chase said. "I don't think—"

"Believe me, Amanda's father isn't interested," Samantha averred. She made no effort this time to hide the bitterness.

Divorced, he thought again. Then the significance of that hit him, and his brain started working again. "You have custody?" Chase asked.

"Yes," Samantha said.

There was a hint of defiance in the single syllable, and it, too, was tinged with bitterness. Which probably meant that what he'd begun to suspect was true.

"Full custody?"

"Yes," she said again, this time without the defiance.

There was instead a question growing in her eyes. She didn't understand what he was getting at. He found himself wondering how it had all gone so wrong between the two of them. Not with Berkley. He didn't give a damn about that. Between him and Samantha. How they had managed to screw up what they once had had to this extent.

He held her eyes for a moment, for the first time in his life feeling pity for Samantha Kincaid. Berkley, he corrected himself, and then he turned to Sam. "I don't think I'm the man for this job, Mr. Kincaid." He straightened, putting the letter down beside the envelope on the table.

"You can't just walk out on us," Sam blustered.

"I told you. I choose my own jobs."

"I thought we had a deal."

"Things change. I'm not the man you need. I suggest you contact the FBI. Maybe they can help you."

He had already started toward the door when she stopped him.

"Because I'm divorced?" Samantha asked. "Is that it? I promise you, Mr. McCullar, that I'm no longer interested in you. Your virtue is safe from me. The only thing I need you for is to get my daughter back. I assure you I'm no longer interested in anything else you may think you have."

Stung by the contempt in her voice, he turned around. There was a lot of the old, volatile Chase McCullar beneath the veneer he'd put on in the last few years, and he suspected that everyone in this room knew that the polish he'd been trying for was just a veneer. So he let himself express his anger.

"Whether or not you have a husband has nothing to do with my decision not to take this job, Mrs. Berkley. I just happen to know the statistics. Better than ninety-five percent of the child abductions in this country are carried out by the noncustodial parent. Given the fact that Amanda is your father's only grandchild, the stakes here are very high. I suggest you contact your husband's lawyers. Tell them you aren't fooled by the games he's playing."

"You think my *husband* had something to do with the kidnapping?"

It was clear she was furious about the suggestion he'd just made, but he knew that there were unresolved issues here. He had felt the tension whenever Berkley was mentioned. From Sam and from his daughter. They must have had their own suspicions from the beginning, but for some reason they had chosen to hide the facts from him. They had chosen, in essence, to lie to him.

"I don't know your husband. But I'm willing to bet on

one thing. Your daughter wasn't taken for the money. You may need a negotiator, but this isn't the kind of job I work."

"Do you think I didn't know what was going on yesterday?" she said. "The men who took Amanda were Mexicans. The tags on both vehicles they used were Mexican." She paused, fighting her anger in order to continue more calmly, more convincingly. "This has *nothing* to do with my husband."

"I heard he was rich and important enough to get even Sam's seal of approval. It wouldn't take much to arrange something like what happened yesterday. It even makes sense. It sends you and your father on a wild-goose chase looking for phantom kidnappers in Mexico while he has time to hide the baby. Maybe even get her out of the country. Take her to Europe. And given that possibility, I suggest you move as quickly as possible to stop him. *If* you want to see your baby again."

"It ain't him," Sam said. His voice sounded remarkably flat after the emotionally charged exchange that had been going on between the two of them. "She's right about that."

"How sure are you?" Chase asked.

"Sure enough not to call the feds. And sure enough to give you a million dollars of my money to take across the border. You remember that I don't back losing hands. He ain't involved in this. You can take my word on that, McCullar."

The surety in the old man's voice made Chase hesitate. Sam Kincaid was no fool. He hadn't gotten where he was without being a pretty accurate judge of character. He'd read Chase's like a book. Years ago. Even now, it appeared.

Considering Sam's conviction that the father wasn't involved, Chase knew they would hire someone else to do this if he turned them down. Someone else would take the money across and get the baby back. It might as well be him. Because, just as he had told them, he really was the best.

"How soon can you have the money ready?" he found himself asking. He didn't look at Samantha again. It would be Sam's money. At least that was clear.

"When do they want it?"

"Immediately. They don't give you much time to make the arrangements, which also shows they're new at this. They want someone to be in Melchor Múzquiz on Saturday. Whoever shows up will be met and given instructions for the exchange."

"*Whoever* shows up?" Sam said.

"My fee is ten percent." He still didn't know why he had made the decision, but *divorced* kept echoing in the back of his mind.

"Deal," Sam said, holding out his hand.

Chase eased in a breath before he took the three steps that brought him close enough to the desk to accept it. He was surprised at the strength in that knotted, liver-spotted hand.

"I'll need pictures. The most current you have. A good close-up. And a description of any identifying marks. Scars. Birthmarks. With a baby it's hard to—"

"No," Samantha said. "No pictures."

"Samantha," Sam said.

"There are no pictures," she said again. Her eyes lifted to Chase's, and despite the olive-toned darkness of the skin that surrounded them, they were very clear and very calm. "I haven't had time to get any made."

"A snapshot. A Polaroid. It doesn't have to be a studio shot."

"I told you there are no pictures."

She was lying, and it made no sense under the circumstances. The dynamics of this situation were getting stranger, and despite the old man's assurance, Chase wasn't sure that he hadn't been right about the husband.

But did it really matter? he thought. He had been hired

to do a job. To take Sam's million to Melchor Múzquiz on
Saturday and see what happened. If nothing did, then he
might be able to convince them to reevaluate what was
going on.

"Look," he said, trying to be patient, trying to remember
that people in this situation sometimes said or did weird
things. He was used to that. Samantha's baby had been
taken, he had no doubt about that, and she was entitled to
act a little peculiar. "I have to have some way to identify
the baby."

"Why?" she asked.

"So I'll know we're getting the right one back," he said.
It was getting more bizarre by the minute. Apparently whatever had happened between Samantha and the baby's father
had had some pretty far-reaching effects—a lack of trust,
for one. Or maybe his own actions five years ago had had
something to do with that, his conscience reminded him.

Samantha looked at her father, but the old man's face
was unrevealing. Sam's reputation as a good poker player
was apparently well-deserved. His lips pursed, but he didn't
say anything, and finally she turned back to Chase.

"Why would they try to give you the wrong child?" she
asked. "You said that it was to their advantage—"

"If they figure out that I can't identify your baby, Mrs.
Berkley, they can give me any child. They could keep
Amanda and ask for another million. Maybe two. Or maybe
we just won't hear from them again." He said that deliberately, trying to remind her that things could go wrong if
he wasn't allowed to do his job. "I don't know what they'll
do if we do something stupid. I thought you wanted her
back," he said. "If not, then we're wasting our time."

"I'll go," she said.

"You're going to handle the exchange?" he said, allowing his sarcasm to show.

"No," she said softly. "You are. That's what Sam's

paying you for. *I'm* going along to make sure you bring back the right child. To make sure that the baby you get in exchange for Sam's million dollars is really my daughter.''

Chapter Four

"What's the point?" Sam had asked her later that night.

They were standing on the balcony of Samantha's bedroom, looking out on the darkness. It didn't seem that anything terrible should happen in a world that was heavened with such a sky, she had been thinking. Sleeping somewhere under it, safe and warm, she prayed, was Amanda.

"As if she were my own daughter," the leader had promised her, and she had held on to his vow like a talisman. To it and to the fact that he had crossed himself as he'd made it. *Please, God,* she prayed again, *keep her safe.*

"I don't know," she said. "I honestly don't know. It just seemed that…it was better to do it this way."

"Whatever Chase McCullar may be, he ain't no fool."

"I know, but I needed some time, Sam. Maybe if you hadn't just sprung him on me. Maybe if I'd known that your expert—"

"It's dangerous, baby. Going down there with him. There ain't any reason for it. There's nothing you can do."

"I thought there was nothing to it. To dealing with the kidnappers." Her mockery was obvious. "That's what you both told me. Just hand over the money and get Mandy back. I thought it was in everyone's *best* interests that it should go smoothly."

She certainly wasn't gullible enough to believe that nothing could go wrong, and she knew Sam understood that, even if Chase might not. Of course, there were dangers involved, most of them revolving around carrying that much money in cash—ripe for the taking. But since even she didn't entirely understand what had prompted her to decide to go along with Chase, she certainly couldn't explain it to her father.

"You know better than that," Sam said. "Nothing in this life is without risk. Nothing that's worth doing."

"Or worth having," she whispered.

"What?" Sam asked, turning to face her. He had been looking out over the land, hidden now by darkness, which had been in his family's keeping for five generations.

"Nothing's without risk," she said, smiling at him. "I was just agreeing with you. Mandy's worth any risk. At least we agree on that."

"Is it because you think…" He paused, searching for the right word. "Because you're hoping—"

"I'm hoping to get my daughter back, Sam. That's all I'm hoping for. Don't let your imagination run away with you. Nothing's changed. Nothing's going to change."

She turned and went inside, closing the French doors behind her. Sam Kincaid put his big hands on top of the railing, the knotted fingers closing hard around the wood.

Stubborn as a mule, he thought again. But then so was he. Muleheaded, his daddy used to say. And once a mule made up his mind to something, right or wrong, it usually took a two-by-four between his eyes to change it. You might not like the two-by-four, or like using it, but results were what mattered. Especially with a mule.

"SING IT AGAIN," MANDY begged, blue eyes pleading.

"But then you must go to sleep," the man said. "It's very late and past the time when all good little girls should be asleep."

She watched his mustache move as he talked. She had never known anyone who had a mustache. She liked the way he sang, too. The way the words all sounded different, even the Spanish ones. Different from how Rosita had taught her. Thinking of Rosita made her miss her Mama again, but he had said that she could go home soon. Very soon, he'd promised.

So she had settled down on the bed he had carried her to and listened again to the song about the cat. She was trying to remember all the words so she could sing it to Mama when she got home.

"I have a cat," she said when he had finished.

"You told me. I'm sure that he misses you. Soon you'll be home to take care of him."

He pulled the sheet up over her shoulders and tucked it in as he talked. He wasn't as good at putting her to bed as her mama was, but still, he was nice.

"I miss my mama, too," she whispered. She didn't know she was going to cry when she said that. She didn't mean to, but he didn't seem to mind. He smiled at her and wiped the tears away and that made her feel better.

"Very soon," he promised. He had already turned to leave when she remembered.

"You forgot to listen to my prayers," she called to him.

He turned back, the silver chains on his boot heels making a noise as he crossed the room.

"Say your prayers, little one. God and I are listening."

She folded her hands right in front of her face and closed her eyes tight as she said them, very fast, the familiar words coming out almost in one breath: "Now I lay me down to sleep, I pray the Lord my soul to keep. If I should die before I wake, I pray the Lord my soul to take. God bless Mama and Granddaddy Sam. And God bless my new friend. Amen."

"Amen," her friend said softly, and moved his hand up to his face and then across his body. "Now go to sleep, and soon, sooner than you can believe, you'll be back with your mama, I promise you."

"Good night," she called softly as he was leaving.

After she was sure he was gone, she slipped her thumb

into her mouth. She knew she was too big for that, but she was just a little lonely lying here in the dark. And in spite of what he had promised about going home, she still missed her mama.

CHASE HAD BEEN surprised by his reaction to Samantha's announcement that she was going with him across the border. If any of his other clients had made such a suggestion, he knew what his response would have been. He would have walked out without looking back, no matter how much they needed his help. There was enough to watch out for in his profession without having to baby-sit a member of the family.

He hadn't walked out, of course, maybe because the very thought of traveling with Samantha had taken away his breath. Maybe because his imagination had begun working overtime. Or maybe because he had suddenly been remembering a hell of a lot of the things he'd spent the last five years trying to forget.

Like how Samantha Kincaid's body felt under his. How soft her skin was, how smooth. How her perfume clung to the dampness on her neck and in the small, scented hollow of her throat. How it had clung to him.

And so for the first few minutes he hadn't been able to formulate an argument, and the idea had become set, hardened like concrete. Suddenly it had been decided and was not open to discussion. Nothing he said later had made any difference. Once Samantha had made that decision, she hadn't even listened to him. Maybe she'd listened, he amended, polite and distant, but she sure as hell hadn't heard. Stubborn as a mule, her father had called her. Apparently Sam was right.

Chase hadn't said the one thing that he knew might have made a difference. He hadn't threatened to leave. He lost sleep during the next two nights trying to decide exactly why he hadn't.

It had taken Sam only one day to arrange for the money.

The kidnappers hadn't specified any denominations. Apparently the amateurs knew that even the larger U.S. bills could be passed without question almost anywhere below the border and certainly along it. As a result, they were able to keep the bulk of the ransom as small as possible. Small enough to be carried in two suitcases. Small enough to be unobtrusive, Chase hoped. They still had far more empty and lawless territory to cross than he was comfortable with.

He had guessed that somewhere on the ranch Sam would have a car they could use, but he couldn't have picked a better one than the Land Rover he was offered. It looked unremarkable, painted desert tan, was several years old, and as dependable an all-terrain vehicle as it was possible to own. In Mexico, with its miles of unpaved roads and sparsely scattered service stations, that was very important. Best of all, the paperwork for taking it into the interior was complete and up-to-date.

He had called his office and explained that he'd be away for a few days. His secretary was used to dealing with unexpected absences, and the few firms for whom he handled security—former clients for the other services he offered—understood the nature of them.

He and Sam had made all the arrangements for the trip into Mexico. He hadn't talked to Samantha since the day they had received the ransom note. Although he'd protested vehemently to the old man about the sheer stupidity of allowing Samantha to accompany him, he was unnerved to find that on some level he was still anticipating their journey. *Divorced* kept repeating with regularity in his brain, and he dreamed about her again—about making love to her.

Nothing would go wrong, he kept telling himself. There was no reason not to take her with him. If Sam was right and the ex-husband had nothing to do with all this, they'd simply hand over the money to the kidnappers and get the baby. He'd done it more times than he cared to remember. Or, if what he still suspected was true, they'd probably not be contacted at all when they reached the small Coahuilan town the ransom note had directed them to, and all this would turn out to be a wild-goose chase. They'd wait a day or so to be sure—waiting together, he realized with another frisson of anticipation—and then head back.

Sam would then have to start legal action in the States against the baby's father. The authorities wouldn't like the delay in being notified or Chase's part in what had gone on, but there really wasn't much they could do about what he did for a living below the border. Either way, he reassured himself, there was no reason to think things wouldn't go as smoothly as they had on the other missions he'd undertaken.

He had decided to make the crossing at Eagle Pass. Entering Mexico at Piedras Negras would give him a straight shot down Mexican Highway 57, a well-maintained, smooth-surfaced road that would lead straight to the turnoff for Melchor Múzquiz.

He had asked Sam to tell Samantha to be ready to leave the ranch at six on Saturday morning, but unable to sleep, he himself been awake long before his alarm went off. He wondered if he were as big a fool as he was beginning to think he was. He wondered also just what he was expecting to happen on this trip. Nothing had changed. Sam Kincaid still found him inferior, even if the reasons seemed to have shifted. Samantha had made it clear she had agreed to his staying for only one reason. He was the best man for the job.

His lips curved into a small, bitter smile at that, a self-mocking grimace. That was all he was to both of them. The hired help. He might wear a suit now and work out of an office in California, but nothing had changed as far as the Kincaids were concerned. Except now it seemed that Samantha agreed with what her father had always thought about him.

When he was dressed—jeans, a cotton shirt, and a battered leather vest long enough to hide the gun and holster he wore in the small of his back—Chase walked out onto the balcony of his bedroom. The sun was beginning to line the rim of the horizon with gold. The air still held the cool, nighttime breath of the desert, touched by the almost-forgotten savor of salt cedar and creosote bush.

It had been too long since he'd been back home. Too long since he'd *had* a home, he amended. A real home. Something besides an apartment and microwave dinners. Despite the vast wealth of his hosts, he had recognized from the time he'd walked in the front door that this house was a home and always had been. The Kincaids were still a family. Still living on family land.

Chase pushed the memories away. And the regrets. Maybe that was why he was good at dealing with the families of the victims. He knew a lot about loss and guilt. He took one last breath of the morning, and then he turned away from the sweep of low, grass-covered hills that stretched away into the dawn-shrouded distance.

CHASE HAD OFFERED no advice on how she should dress, but he was pleased to see that Samantha had been sensible enough to also wear jeans, a long sleeved shirt with the cuffs turned up a couple of times, and hiking boots. The boots were probably the fashionable kind, he thought, but at least she wasn't wearing silk and high heels.

"Ready?" he asked. He couldn't stop himself from watching her walk across the stone patio that backed the big house. The Land Rover was waiting in the driveway that circled it, serviced and holding a full tank of gas.

She nodded, opening the back passenger-side door to throw a small canvas carryall she'd brought out of the house into the back seat. The bags that contained the ransom were in the trunk, the cash hidden in their false bottoms and covered by a couple of layers of clothing. Just for insurance. He hadn't asked where Sam had found the suitcases, but they had been just what he'd requested—inexpensive and well-worn. Only someone who knew what he was looking for—someone who knew there was something to find—might uncover the money's simple hiding place. Chase knew they wouldn't be searched at the border, not going in the direction they were headed and not at that particular crossing.

"Goodbye, Sam," Samantha said. She had closed the back door, and was looking over the top of the Land Rover at her father who was standing by Chase on the driver's side.

"You call me," Sam ordered. "Soon as you know something. You hear?"

"As soon as it's safe," Chase agreed, preventing Samantha from making any promises that might be impossible to keep.

"You take care, now," the old man said, seeming to address them both. "Take care of my baby."

Chase wasn't sure if he meant Samantha or his grandbaby, but since he intended to do both, he nodded and stepped into the waiting car. Samantha got in on the other side, pulling her door closed. The noise it made disturbed the quiet peace of the morning.

"Go with God," Sam said softly, and then he closed Chase's door and they were inside the close confines of the car—together and alone—after almost five years.

The soundless vacuum built again, surrounding him with the scent of her body. That wasn't a distraction he could afford. Not something he could even think about until this was over and they'd recovered the baby. Maybe then...

He turned the key, something he never did without a knot in his stomach. Such a simple act. You did it a thousand times in your life and then once—

"Where to?" Samantha asked, thankfully interrupting that memory.

"North," Chase said. "Through Eagle Pass."

She nodded, the movement caught out of the corner of his eye. Deliberately, he hadn't looked at her. *Later,* he thought again. *Maybe later, when this is all over.*

THE CROSSING HAD BEEN as smooth as he'd anticipated, Chase thought, as he finally drove across the narrow stretch of river that marked the international boundary between the two countries. As far as the topography was concerned, it was really no boundary at all, of course. Especially when they had cleared the dozen or so blocks of the downtown area of Piedras Negras and had driven out on Avenida Lázaro Cárdenas, which very shortly became Highway 57. The scenery that surrounded them was a familiar reflection of the south Texas landscape they had just left—semidesert terrain covered with yucca, mesquite, and a variety of grasses.

Samantha had said almost nothing since they'd left the ranch, not even the polite commonplaces that you'd exchange with a stranger you were forced to share a car with. He wondered what he'd been hoping for. That she would somehow become the girl who had once made her fascination with him apparent to everyone, even to her father? The same girl who had given herself to him that night? Too much had happened since then, he knew. To them and between them.

It was after nine when they stopped in Nueva Rosita. Chase wanted to top up the tank and check out the traffic behind them. He hadn't seen anything suspicious, no one following or seeming to be interested in the Land Rover at all. But a tail would have had to make the same turn off the main highway as they had, and any interest in their progress would be much more obvious now on the smaller, less-traveled state highway.

Seemingly there was no one behind them, but even as he got back into the car, Chase couldn't dismiss the nagging sense that something was going on that he should know about. Something that he should have picked up on. The Kincaids hadn't told him everything, he knew, but he also was certain that they were both anxious to get the baby back and that they, at least, were convinced the ransom note was on the up and up.

Chase didn't understand why he was so antsy. It wasn't like him. Maybe it was just being this close to Samantha. Maybe the fact that he couldn't take a breath without being reminded that she was sitting beside him. But somehow, as disturbing as that was, he didn't think that was it. All the old lawman's instincts he and Mac used to joke about were awake. And that was something you never wanted to happen, not when you were carrying a million dollars—money that someone else's life depended on your delivering.

WHEN THEY DROVE INTO the square at Melchor Múzquiz, it was far busier than he'd anticipated. There were too many people who didn't belong. Tourists, maybe, but this wasn't the normal tourist territory. It took him a few minutes to realize what was happening. When he had, he began to wonder if this could be why they'd been sent to this particular location.

Anyone who lived along the section of the border where he and Samantha had grown up knew about the Kikapu. The tribe had lived in the area since the late 1700s, splitting the year seasonally between their village near here and one south of the town of Eagle Pass. During August they displayed their leather work in Melchor Múzquiz, the town nearest their Mexican settlement.

At his quiet suggestion, he and Samantha wandered through the display of goods the Indians had brought into town to sell. Playing her part, Samantha fingered the suede garments, asking questions and giving compliments in Spanish, which the Indians understood very easily.

As Chase walked beside her, his eyes searched the small crowd for anyone who looked as if he might be their contact. He had parked the car on one side of the square so he could keep an eye on it as they shopped. Neither they nor the Land Rover seemed to be attracting anyone's interest.

His mind continued to worry at the connection between this isolated location and the stretch of border where the baby had been taken. The link of the two Indian settlements seemed too obvious to be coincidental. He'd heard that some of the Mennonites had been caught running drugs, but he couldn't believe the Kikapu had suddenly gotten mixed up in the ransom racket.

Hell, he thought, mocking that rare naiveté. *Why not? Everybody else seemed to be.*

But if it meant nothing else, he finally decided, the increased activity in the normally quiet town provided a cover for their presence. They would have seemed far more out of place without the other *norteamericanos* who were wandering around. Maybe that was the only reason they had been sent here.

At lunchtime, which by Texas standards was closer to midafternoon, the small shops began to close and the square started to empty of pedestrians. Still nobody had made contact. Nobody had tried to make arrangements to pick up the million dollars. That wasn't normal and it didn't make sense. Why take the child and then not pick up the ransom? Because, Chase was beginning to believe, just as he'd suspected, what was going on wasn't about the ransom at all.

His anger built as the crowd, locals and tourists, melted slowly away from the public area of the town. Chase and Samantha stayed in the square, their isolation providing an opportunity for the kidnappers to approach without witnesses if that was what they had been waiting for. Still nothing happened. *And nothing's going to happen,* Chase thought.

He took Samantha's elbow, almost pulling her with him, and began walking toward the eighteenth-century Baroque-style church that stood at one corner of the plaza. Its darkened interior would at least offer sanctuary from the heat and a place for the private confrontation that was overdue.

Using a quick pressure of the hand with which he was grasping her arm, he stopped Samantha before the wooden doors, standing for a moment in the shadows of the church's portico to glance back across the nearly deserted square. No one was looking in their direction. No one had paid any attention to them during the hours they had been here. *Wild-goose chase,* he thought. He had felt that all along.

Angry that he'd allowed himself to be manipulated again by the Kincaids, that his own emotions had made him agree to what he'd known was a wasted trip, he pulled Samantha into the church and up the narrow aisle. He directed her into the last of the wooden pews. He sat down beside her and then took a quick look around. It seemed they had the building to themselves. There were lighted candles, but apparently the worshipers had taken the same lunch break as the merchants.

"Why weren't we met?" Samantha asked. She was looking toward the altar, not at him, and her voice was very hushed. Maybe that wasn't a conscious decision. Maybe it just seemed appropriate to whisper in the dimness of the church.

"You tell me. Tell me why we weren't met. Why we weren't contacted. Why don't you tell me what's really going on here?" he countered. He'd been had, had by somebody. He knew it, and it made him feel like a fool.

"What's *really* going on?" she repeated. "I don't know any more than you about—" She stopped, realizing what he was thinking. "You still think this is a hoax. A trick to get custody of Amanda. Well, you're wrong, Chase. This has *nothing* to do with my husband." The anger was clear despite the fact that she was still whispering, still facing the altar.

"Then I guess the people who took Amanda don't really want Sam's money after all. I wonder what they do want."

She turned to face him at that, and even in the darkness, Chase could see the color drain from her cheeks and her eyes widen.

"What does that mean?" she asked. "What the hell does that mean?"

"It means that nobody's real eager to collect their

hard-earned loot. And believe me, that hasn't been my experience.''

"They didn't give us a time," she argued. "Maybe we're just early. Maybe after lunch. When things are less crowded. Maybe they're just waiting—''

"Why don't you level with me, Mrs. Berkley? Tell me what's really going on.''

"I don't know what's happened. Don't you think if I knew anything that would help us get Mandy back, I'd tell you? Why would I lie to you when my daughter's life is at stake? What the hell do you think I am? Do you think I don't care about her? Do you really think I'd do anything to jeopardize our chances of getting Mandy?''

Her voice had risen with her growing agitation. Chase put his hand down hard on the top of hers, and the angry questions cut off abruptly. He looked around to see if anyone had heard what she'd said, but they still seemed to be the only occupants of the sanctuary.

Satisfied that they were alone, he looked at her again. The fear of the first day was back in her face. She hadn't said much during the long morning, but he had been aware of the hope that had radiated from her tense body. The hope that he would be able to put her baby back into her arms. Whatever had gone wrong, Samantha wasn't to blame, and he felt like an SOB for making her more afraid than she already had been.

"Look," he began again, keeping his own voice only slightly above a whisper. "Maybe you don't know anything about what's gone wrong, but you and Sam haven't leveled with me. Not from the start. You haven't told me everything I need to know to get Mandy back for you, and I want to know why. What *didn't* you tell me, Samantha? I need to know what you and Sam are hiding.''

Her eyes were on his, and they didn't flinch before the accusation. But they didn't give in, either. They sat in silence, his demand between them. He saw her take a breath, and her lips parted, but before she could say anything, the door of the church was pulled open from the outside.

The sudden shaft of sunlight flashed like a spotlight into the dark interior. They both looked toward the door, but the dazzle of light after the shadowed dimness was blinding. Chase had time to see the silhouette of a man, starkly outlined against the open doorway. Then the light was gone, the heavy door closing with a small thud that echoed off the plaster walls.

Unconsciously, he allowed his gaze to come back to find Samantha's face. Wordlessly, in response to the question in his eyes, she shook her head. She apparently had seen no more than he. He wasn't even sure whether the man had come in or had stepped quickly back outside before the door closed.

"Wait here," he ordered.

He slipped out of the pew and walked toward the door. The shadows were deeper here, farther from the filtered light that spilled from the stained-glass window above the altar at the other end of the nave. When he reached the door, there was no one there. He pushed it open and looked out into the brightness of the now empty square. His eyes squinted against the sudden change, but he could see well enough to verify there was no movement across the sun-baked plaza. He looked at the Land Rover, sitting undisturbed under the shade of the single tree on that side of the square.

"Do you think that might have been—" Samantha spoke from directly behind him.

"Shh," he cautioned, still listening in the afternoon's quiet lethargy for footsteps or for a motor starting somewhere. Listening for any disturbance of the sleeping stillness. There was nothing. Whoever had opened the door of the church had disappeared.

Samantha moved forward to stand beside him.

"A man?" he asked.

She hesitated for a moment before she answered. "I

thought so. It happened so quickly, but...my impression was a man.''

"Yeah, mine, too," Chase said, still looking out on the plaza.

"Could it have been whoever was supposed to contact us?"

"It could have been anybody," he said.

He wondered suddenly if whoever had opened the door had had time to identify them, given the extremes of light and dark. He walked across the portico and pulled opened the church's wooden door. He tried to duplicate the figure's stance in the doorway, peering into the sanctuary. His eyes barely had time to adjust to the interior darkness before the door swung closed behind him. He had been able to find the spot on the last pew where they had been sitting. That was about all.

He stood in the dark church, trying to put it together, trying to think about what to do next. This wasn't the way it was supposed to be. Nothing like this had ever happened before. It had always been as straightforward as he'd promised Samantha, the kidnappers more than eager to make the arrangements and to pick up their money. This time somebody appeared to be playing games.

His eyes lifted to the stained-glass window at the other end of the narrow aisle. He recognized the scene portrayed easily enough, although it had been a long time since Chase McCullar had been inside a church.

Even the phrase from the story was still in his memory, one of the countless instilled in his childhood. "*Suffer the little children...*" Sunday school at the Mount Ebenezer Baptist Church in Crystal Springs. Ears scrubbed and face shining, dressed in clothing that he donned only on that occasion, Chase had listened, fascinated, to all the stories Mrs. Wexman had told. There wasn't much time at home for storytelling. There was always too much that had to be done, and even before his mother's death, she was too exhausted after the long day's work to entertain her boys with stories.

The outside door opened, and Samantha was there before he had time to get it all straight in his head. Exactly what he thought was going on here. Exactly what they should do next.

"What are you doing?" she asked. Her gaze followed his to the window above the altar. "Chase? What's wrong?"

Amateurs, he thought again. Maybe the guy *had* been trying to give them the message. Maybe he had seen them come in, but hadn't been able to find them in the dark. Maybe something had scared him off. Or maybe he had nothing at all to do with the kidnapping.

"Come on," he said finally, still no closer to figuring out why they hadn't gotten the word they had waited for most of the day. "Let's get out of here. We need to be out where we can be seen." He put his hand against the small of Samantha's back to direct her out the door.

"Are you sure there wasn't a note?" she asked. "Maybe he put the note where we were sitting after we went out."

And maybe he's a magician, Chase thought. *Maybe he can disappear into thin air and then reappear somewhere else.* But maybe, just maybe, she was right. He didn't have a better suggestion.

He walked to the pew they'd occupied, his footsteps echoing off the stone floor, the sound floating upward toward the high, arched ceiling to be lost in the shadows there.

There was nothing, of course. Just as he knew there would be. He looked on the floor and even on the nearby pews to be certain he wasn't missing anything—anything beyond the central question that seemed to be escaping him.

"Did you find anything?" she asked.

"There's nothing, Samantha. He didn't leave a note." He walked back toward her, seeing the loss of hope reflected in her strained features.

"I just hope he's doing what he promised," she said softly.

"Who?"

"The leader. The one who did all the talking."

"What did he promise?" Chase asked.

"To take care of Mandy. To care for her as if she were his own daughter. He has a daughter."

She hadn't told him that. It didn't seem to have any bearing on what he'd been hired to do, but he liked to know everything that had been said and done during the abduction. Neither Samantha nor Sam had mentioned that part of the conversation.

"Samantha…" he began, and then he hesitated because he knew that what he was about to say was sheer cruelty. If she was finding comfort in the kidnapper's promise, he should just leave it alone. Let her think whatever made it easier, but things were not going as they should, and maybe she needed to be prepared for the possibility—

"You think I'm putting too much store in that, don't you?" she asked.

"Maybe," he agreed. "I don't know what's going on, but I have to tell you—"

"You're *supposed* to know," she interrupted angrily. "You're the one who's supposed to have all the experience at this. All the damn expertise."

"Yeah," he agreed. "That *is* what you hired me for, isn't it?"

She could probably hear the bitterness. Despite it, he wasn't angry at her any longer. He was just frustrated because he didn't understand what was going on. Felt inadequate.

"Where are we going?" she asked, forced to move again in response to the sudden pressure of his hand against her back.

"We're going to have lunch. Somewhere public. Very visible."

"To give them another chance to contact us?"

He didn't answer the obvious, and so she asked the question he didn't have an answer for. The one he'd been dreading.

"You still think they will, don't you?"

He didn't know what he thought anymore. He didn't know much of anything except whoever was doing this didn't give a damn about the effect it was having on Amanda's mother. The trouble was, Chase was finding out how much he did. Five years, her marriage, the fact that she had given birth to another man's child—none of those things, he was finding, had changed any aspect of the way he had always felt about Samantha Kincaid.

Chapter Five

They ate at a small *lonchería* near the square, Chase choosing a table from which he could watch the Land Rover. There wasn't much conversation. Samantha picked at her meal, pushing the food around rather than eating it, but stoically Chase made himself eat. He worked at appearing as confident as possible, given the fact that nothing was going the way it was supposed to.

It was not until after four that the town began to exhibit signs of renewed life. They wandered out into the plaza, again mingling, again allowing the kidnappers the opportunity to make contact.

But it was a long time later, after the shadows had begun to lengthen across the square at twilight, when Chase felt that instinctive tightening of the muscles along the back of his neck. This time it was a feeling that they were being watched. With Samantha's growing tension and unspoken distress as the slow hours of their vigil passed, he sure as hell hoped that what he was feeling was valid and not just wishful thinking.

They finally wandered into a cramped little shop that sold painted animals, about the only place they hadn't visited during the day. The carved wooden shapes on display were fantastical, portraying creatures of myth rather than reality, and the multihued, handpainted designs that covered their soaring wings and abstract bodies were incredibly beautiful, intricately detailed.

Chase watched as Samantha ran her fingers over the smooth surface of one of them, a stylized rendering of a cat. He knew she was thinking about her daughter. About how much any child would love such a toy. In a couple of years, the baby would be old enough to enjoy the carving for its bold, childlike exuberance. Old enough if...

Someone pushed aside the curtain that separated the shop from the heat of the street, and Chase's gaze swung away from Samantha's fingers to focus on the doorway. The newcomer was simply dressed, wearing what most of the men they had seen here today had worn—jeans and a cotton shirt. The eyes of the man who had entered met Chase's and then widened in surprise. Their gazes locked for a second before the man nodded slightly, almost a greeting, and then moved quickly back out the doorway through which he'd entered.

It took Chase maybe ten seconds to remember where he had seen that face. It wasn't remarkable. A southern face, more *mestizos,* perhaps, darker and flatter than the faces of most of the *norteños* they'd encountered today. But he remembered it, all right. Someone he had dealt with before. Another kidnapping. Another negotiation. Maybe two years ago. In Monterrey, Chase thought.

The man hadn't expected to see him here. That had been obvious by his reaction, by the shock in his eyes. And then he had disappeared. There was no one else in the shop, and if the man had been sent here by Amanda's kidnappers, it seemed to Chase that it would have been more natural for him to have stayed. To have spoken to the proprietor. To have spoken to them. The three of them together in the small shop should have provided the perfect opportunity, and yet again, nothing had happened as it should have.

Chase walked to the doorway, trying not to appear to hurry. Like at the church, however, when he looked out across the darkening square, there was no sign of the man.

It was dark enough and there were enough people around that he spent a couple of minutes making sure of that.

Chase stepped out onto the sidewalk and walked a few feet down the street. He stopped, allowing his eyes to scan the darkening square again. Then he leaned back against the adobe wall of the building, trying to present the picture of a patient husband who has seen the inside of one too many shops, but who is willing to wait for his wife, who apparently wasn't yet through with her shopping.

Samantha came out less than two minutes later carrying a package. When she saw him leaning against the wall, she walked over to him, her eyes questioning.

"What happened?" she asked. "I looked up and you were gone. Did something happen?"

"I saw someone I recognized."

"Who?"

"We didn't exchange names. When we met down here before, it wasn't a social occasion." He looked back across the square, still hoping for another glimpse of the man.

"You mean…you saw someone who was involved in _another_ kidnapping?"

He nodded, his eyes still on the street before him.

"He seemed surprised to see me," he added.

"Would our kidnappers be?"

"I don't know. It may have nothing to do with Amanda."

"Just a coincidence?" she asked, but her voice expressed her doubt.

"Maybe. There have been a hell of a lot of coincidences, it seems to me, since the beginning of all this."

"I don't understand."

He turned toward her then, studying her face. That had sounded sincere, and he couldn't read any deception in the green eyes. "Maybe I'm just being paranoid," he acknowledged. "I don't like it when things don't go according to plan."

"So what's the plan now?"

Good question, he thought. Another one he didn't have a very good answer for.

"If we aren't contacted in the next couple of hours, I think we ought to think about finding a place to stay for the night. The shops will begin to close around nine."

"I was afraid…" she began, her voice very soft, but when she went on, she had forced it to be stronger. "I thought you'd probably want to head back."

"Maybe they had car trouble," he said. He allowed himself to smile at her, hoping the lame joke would be reassurance. As much as he hated the uncertainty of this, he could imagine what she was feeling.

"I need to call Sam, I guess," she said.

"Do that from the hotel. It'll be safer."

She nodded.

"Let's walk some more," he suggested, automatically putting his hand against her back. They had taken a few steps before he noticed the package she was carrying. "You got the cat?" he asked.

"I thought she'd like it. We have a calico at home. Not as colorful as this one, but nearly."

For the first time today, her lips tilted upward. She was remembering, he knew. Remembering life before all this had happened to change it forever. He could empathize with that. He understood how much one event could change everything, could change what you had always thought your life would turn out to be.

"We'll get her back," he said. He had made these same easy assurances to her before, and all of them had turned out to be far from true. He didn't know why she should believe anything he had to say anymore.

"Thank you for telling me that," she said softly.

At her tone, he turned to look down into her eyes.

"I thought you'd given up," she explained. "I've been afraid all afternoon that you'd want to get in the car and just leave. I'm glad you don't."

"I'll get her back, Samantha. That's my job."

Something changed in the depths of those remarkable green eyes even as he watched.

"Of course," she said, "a screwup like that probably wouldn't look too good on your résumé, would it? Bad for business, I guess."

She moved past him, increasing her pace until they were no longer walking side by side. For a moment she had seemed like the old Samantha, the one who had liked him, who had admired the man he was. Chase fought the sharp sense of regret that he'd destroyed that moment.

The best man for the job. The hired help. But that was all he needed to remember in his dealings with the Kincaids, he reminded himself. He just needed to remember his place.

"NO," SAMANTHA SAID, working at keeping her voice as normal as possible. She could see the surprise in Chase's eyes. She was making a fool of herself. What he'd proposed was for her own safety. She understood all the reasons, but she still didn't think it was necessary. Or a good idea. "I'm a big girl now, Mr. McCullar, and I'm not afraid of the dark, thank you very much."

"There's no way—"

"I *said,* get another room," she ordered sharply.

It had come out wrong. Demanding. Rich bitch. That wasn't a tone she normally used. She didn't talk to people that way. But she wasn't about to spend the night in the same hotel room with Chase McCullar. She didn't stop to analyze why she was so opposed to that. She just acknowledged, to herself at least, that she was. Very opposed.

"I thought you weren't ready to go back," he said.

"Go back? Across the border? What does that have—"

"Because you're going to be where I can keep an eye on you, or you're going back to being Sam's responsibility. There's not an option here, Mrs. Berkley. Not about that."

He wasn't bluffing. She could read it in his eyes. Ice blue and cold, far colder than she'd ever seen them.

"And I'll be glad to return your assurance," he added.

She shook her head slightly, not understanding the comment.

"Your virtue's certainly safe with me. Even the first time, if you'll remember…"

At least he had the grace not to finish it. He just let the brutal reminder trail away. She had been the one who had come on to him that night—undressing like she thought she was some exotic dancer, a stripper or something. A two-dollar whore was more like it, she thought bitterly. She could feel the heat of that memory flooding into her cheeks. That was the worst part of being a redhead—the damn blushing. She still hadn't learned how to do anything about that.

"I've got a million dollars *and* Sam Kincaid's daughter to look after," he continued when she couldn't get past the embarrassment to come up with a rejoinder. "I'm a hundred miles from nowhere, in a place where you make your own law. I'm trying to carry out kidnap negotiations that for some reason seem to have fallen apart. I signed on for all that, I guess, but I don't intend to spend the night wondering what's going on in your room. Wondering whether I'm going to have to be negotiating next for your release. I've got about all I can handle already, Mrs. Berkley, so we share this room or we go back to Texas."

"*You* go back," she said.

She didn't know why she had said it. She couldn't do this without him. She had known that from the beginning. She was just making a bigger fool of herself by arguing. Stubborn as a mule, Sam had always called her, but she didn't have to be as stupid as one. For some reason, however, she didn't take it back. She couldn't seem to back down.

"Fine," he agreed, "but just remember that the money goes with me."

Along with any chance of getting Mandy back, she realized. "That's not your money, Mr. McCullar."

"And it's not yours. It belongs to a man named Sam Kincaid, and my deal's with him, not with you. I leave, I take Sam's money with me. I stay, you, me and the money all stay together. In one room," he added.

His eyes hadn't softened. He wasn't backing down either, she realized.

"All right," she said. She didn't know what she was afraid of. He had made his disinterest obvious, starting about a decade ago. And she was certainly no longer the person she had been then.

"Good choice," he said.

He fitted the key into the lock and opened the door of the room she had just agreed to share with him. She didn't know what she had expected, and she guessed she should have been better prepared for the room after the fading, turn-of-the-century tackiness of the lobby downstairs. They had chosen the hotel nearest the heart of the small town, nearest the plaza where they had spent the day.

She spent a second wondering regretfully what the two on the outskirts of town looked like before she walked into the room and laid the canvas bag on the foot of the iron bed. There was a threadbare rug on the floor and an ironstone washbasin and matching pitcher on a stand. A small night table beside the bed held a shaded Victorian lamp and a decanter of murky water on a tray with two small glasses. There was nothing else. Not even a chair.

She turned around to find Chase still standing in the open doorway. His mouth moved slightly, only the smallest twitch at one corner, but she could have sworn he was fighting an inclination to laugh.

"Nice," she said.

"It's a place to sleep. That's all we need."

She put her hand down on the mattress and pushed, hard enough to provoke a rusty squeak. "Not much of a place. And probably not much sleep. You can have the bed," she said. "I'll take the floor."

"Suit yourself," Chase agreed. He closed the door, carried the two bags containing the money over to the bed and bent down to slide them underneath it. "You'll probably have some company."

"Company?"

"The crawling kind."

Despite herself, she swallowed. Cockroaches? She wasn't afraid of roaches. She might not like them. Who did? But she wasn't scared of them. Or maybe that wasn't what Chase had meant. The place was a little more primitive than she'd expected. Maybe...scorpions? she thought, and then she realized that she was doing exactly what he'd intended.

"I told you I wasn't afraid of the dark, Mr. McCullar. I'll take my chances with the vermin down there."

Chase's mouth moved again, but not in amusement. The muscles in his jaw tightened, but he didn't respond in kind, and suddenly she wished she could take it back. No matter her bitterness over what had happened between them almost five years ago, her chance of getting Mandy returned depended on Chase McCullar's skills. It wouldn't help her cause to make an enemy of him because of what must be just a little bit of ancient history to him.

She walked across the room, a matter of maybe three steps, and opened the door of what she had supposed was the bathroom. It wasn't. It was a closet that, despite the climate, smelled of mildew.

"Down the hall and to the right," Chase advised.

"Thank you," she said.

When she stepped out into the hall, she realized he was following her. She turned around, abruptly enough that he almost bumped into her. She looked up. His eyes weren't cold anymore. They were almost luminous in the shadowed hallway. Almost the way they had looked that night in the darkness of his small ranch house.

"I don't need an escort," she said, fighting that memory. "And besides, aren't you forgetting that you left…something in the room. Something that you're supposed to be guarding for Sam.''

''I'll wait out here. Just don't be long.''

He was still waiting, leaning against the wall halfway between their room and the bathroom, when she came out. She brushed past him, concentrating on the stained maroon-and-gold carpeting of the hall as she walked by him and then on to open the door of the room, which was just as depressing as it had been when she'd left it five minutes before.

She went over to the bed and sat down on the edge and began to remove her boots. There wasn't much else she could do in preparation for the night. She hadn't brought a change of clothes, and although she had thrown a night-gown into her carryall, she certainly didn't intend to put it on. She heard Chase open the door and come back into the room after a long enough delay that she knew he'd made his own visit to the facilities. She didn't look up even as he closed and locked the door.

She pushed one of the pillows into a wad in front of the headboard and put her feet up on the bed, leaning back against the thin iron railings. The limp pillow didn't do much to protect her from their discomfort.

Another iron bed, she thought. Chase McCullar and another iron bed. Five years. Considering the changes in both their situations, what had happened between them then seemed almost to have occurred during another lifetime. Somebody else's lifetime.

''I was sorry about Mac,'' she said, thinking about that awful time. It was the simple truth. In spite of everything else, she had always understood how Mac's death would have affected Chase. ''I never had a chance to tell you how sorry I was. He was a good man.''

Chase nodded and walked to the single window that looked out on one of the narrow streets below them. She wondered if that had sounded as if she were asking for an explanation of why he'd never contacted her. She hadn't meant it that way. All of that was over a long time ago. Except, of course...

She raised her eyes. Chase's profile was outlined against the rose-tinted glow that came through the thin curtains. A neon sign was shining into the darkness, touching the room with the tawdry splendor of the town's cantina.

"I heard that you made sure Rio—"

"I don't want to talk about any of that. It's over and done with."

She couldn't blame him. She understood the need to put it all behind him. All the pain and betrayal. The silence grew, expanded, pushing them further apart.

"You ever see Jenny?" he asked finally.

She almost smiled, but even if she had, the darkness would have hidden it. "Occasionally," she said.

"Sam said that she wouldn't be...over Mac, no matter what she says. You think that could be true?"

Five years, she thought. How much do you forget about a man you were crazy in love with in five years? How many details do you manage to wipe out of your head? The way he looked? The way his body smelled? The way he touched you in the darkness? How his callused hands felt moving over your skin, evoking sensations you had never imagined your body could feel? Do you ever forget those things?

"She's dating somebody," she said instead of expressing any of that. The music had started in the club below, *norteña* from a jukebox, drifting upward like a memory. "That's what I heard, anyway," she amended.

Chase turned his head, looking toward the bed. She couldn't read his features, despite the pink glow from the street that backlighted the strong line of his brow and nose and chin.

"Yeah?" he asked. And then he laughed. "I guess that shouldn't really come as a surprise."

"But it did."

"Yeah, I guess it did. Somehow, I just thought that with

Jenny…'' He didn't finish the sentence, although again she waited for a long time in the dark silence.

"You thought that she'd never stop loving Mac," she suggested. "Never stop grieving for him."

"Maybe."

"It doesn't work that way, Chase," she said. "Not for most people."

"Mac and Jenny weren't most people."

"Mac's dead. He's been dead a long time."

He turned back to face the street, but he nodded. She could see the movement.

"Things change," she said. "And people…just go on with their lives. They don't have a choice."

He nodded again. She wondered who she thought she was to try to explain that to him. What did she think she knew about moving on?

"What went wrong?" he asked softly.

"With Jenny?"

"Between you and Amanda's daddy."

Her eyes burned suddenly, sharply and so painfully that she had to fight the tears. Maybe it was the expression he'd used. *Amanda's daddy. What went wrong between you and Amanda's daddy?* Maybe it was hearing him ask it, with something like sympathy in his voice. Or maybe it was because she didn't have an answer. Not a good one, anyway. She had always wondered how she was going to explain it to Amanda when her daughter was old enough to need to understand.

"I don't know. A lot of things, I guess. What goes wrong for most people?"

He didn't say anything for a few minutes, and the music filled up the silence between them, made it less threatening. A little less painful.

"I'll sleep on the floor," he said finally.

"Thank you," she said. She watched him for a long time, but he was still standing by the window, still looking out into the rose-tinged darkness, when she fell asleep.

THE KNOCK ON THE DOOR startled her, echoing out of the near dawn like a nightmare. She opened her eyes to find Chase's blue ones directly in front of her, his head resting on the other pillow of the bed. She hadn't even been aware of when he'd lain down beside her, and she couldn't believe she had slept that soundly.

She had thought when Mandy was taken that she would never sleep again until she was holding her baby. And she hadn't. Not really. Maybe three or four hours of exhausted, restless tossing over the course of the last three days. Then tonight, despite the fears and disappointments of the long day, she had fallen into an apparently dreamless sleep as if there were nothing frightening to keep her awake.

She wondered if finally being able to sleep might have had anything to do with the man who had stood vigil by the window. She had time to wonder about that before Chase spoke into the darkness in answer to the unexpected knock.

He had rolled onto his back, pulling a gun from beneath the pillow he'd been using and pointing it at the door, almost all of this done, it seemed to her, in one fluid motion.

"Who is it?" he asked in Spanish.

"There's a message for you, *señor*."

"Slide it under the door," Chase ordered.

"It's the telephone. Someone on the telephone for you. You must take it in the lobby."

"Sam," Samantha whispered. "I forgot to call Sam."

"I'll be down," Chase called to the messenger. "Ask them to hold on."

He got out of bed and walked over to the window. He spent a second studying the street below in the thin light of dawn. Then he recrossed the small room and held out the gun to her.

"Keep it pointed at the door while I'm gone and shoot anybody who comes through it."

"Even you?" she couldn't resist asking.

"Not if you can possibly help it," Chase suggested, a subtle hint of amusement in his tone.

Maybe that's why he's good at this, she thought. *It's all a game to him. Dangerous and exciting.*

"I'll identify myself before I open the door," he conceded. "Think you can recognize my voice?"

"Yes," she said. Anywhere. In any lifetime.

"I'll be back as soon as I can. Don't let anything happen to Sam's money."

"Okay," she promised, sounding a lot more confident than she felt. This was not a game to her. Mandy's life was riding on it. Maybe that was why Chase could do this time after time. After all, it wasn't anything to him. It wasn't his— Except this time, she thought, before he interrupted that chain of thinking.

"Be careful," he warned. "Don't let anybody else in, no matter what they tell you."

He slipped the chain off the door and looked out into the dark hallway before he disappeared. She raised her knees and, holding the gun in both hands to keep it steady, she propped her wrists on top of her bent knees, lining the muzzle up with the center of the closed door. It was just Sam, she told herself again. Nothing to get excited about. He'd probably called the three hotels in town until he'd located them. Just Sam.

But despite her efforts, the hope that had taken a beating yesterday came back so strongly it filled her chest, making it hard to breathe. *Please, God,* she prayed. The same endless litany of hope she had prayed since Wednesday afternoon.

IT WAS MAYBE FIVE minutes before she heard Chase's voice.

"It's me. I'm going to open the door."

"Okay," she called. She kept the muzzle of the gun centered, but when the door opened, he was alone. She waited until he'd closed and relocked it before she relaxed.

"Was it Sam?"

"We've got a location," he said, his eyes meeting hers.

"A location. You mean…for the exchange? To get Mandy?"

Chase nodded.

"How far away?"

"It's pretty isolated. Dirt or gravel roads part of the way. Maybe three hours."

She felt like shouting. Screaming. Hugging him. But she didn't. She nodded instead, fighting to contain her elation.

"We'll need to get gas and buy some water," he added.

"Water?"

"Just in case," he assured her. He walked over to the bed and squatted down to pull the suitcases that contained the ransom out from under it. "And I think we'll keep these with us up front."

"You think it was the guy you saw yesterday? The man you recognized?"

"I don't know. It's hard to say. The voice didn't sound familiar, but the connection was pretty bad."

"But whoever called asked for you by name?"

"Apparently he described me. It wasn't hard for the manager to narrow it down," Chase said. With his coloring and the scarcity of other guests at the small hotel, that would be true.

"I should call Sam," she suggested. "Let him know what's going on."

Still balancing on his toes beside the bed, Chase looked up at her. "Why don't you wait until we've made the exchange. It might be safer that way."

"Safer?"

"The same rules still apply. The fewer people who know anything about this, the better. There's always the chance someone could overhear if you call from downstairs."

"What are the odds of that?" she said dismissingly. She knew her father would be worried. She should have called him last night. It had been cruel not to.

"Whatever they are, we're not going to take the chance."

"Your decision?"

"That's what you're paying me for. To make the decisions." He stood. "Get your things together. This time we have a deadline."

"They gave you a time to meet them?"

"Eleven o'clock."

She glanced at her watch. It was already six-thirty. The kidnappers hadn't allowed them much slack, especially if Chase was right about the condition of the roads. Still, it took her far longer than she wanted to manage her boots. Her hands were shaking, but she worked at not letting that be obvious, at not letting him see how nervous she was.

"Where are we going?" she asked when she'd finished. She stood and slung the carryall over her shoulder.

"A little mining camp called San Miguel del Norte."

She shook her head. "Do you know it?"

"Only from the map. It looks like the end of civilization, the jumping-off place for the civilized world. Somewhere in Las Maderas."

"Las Maderas?" she repeated, trying to place the name.

"Sierra del Carmen. The Mexican half of the Dead Horse Mountains."

"Then… That's almost back into the States, Chase. Why there and not down here?"

"Because we won't be disturbed, maybe," Chase guessed, shrugging away the question he couldn't be expected to have an answer for. In the desolate Sierra del Carmen they wouldn't run into anybody else, that was for sure.

"Did you ask them about Mandy?"

"She's fine. He said that a couple of times. Sorry I didn't tell you."

"Did you ask to—" She stopped the question just before she blurted it out, gave it all away. She had almost asked Chase if he'd spoken to Mandy, almost given away that she wasn't a baby. Of course, in a matter of a few hours whatever she said wouldn't matter anyway. As Sam had reminded her, Chase McCullar was no fool. He'd figure it out soon enough. She'd deal with that when the time came, she had decided. One crisis at a time.

"Did I what?" Chase asked, picking the gun up off the bed and pushing it into the concealed holster in the small of his back.

"Nothing," she said. "It wasn't important. I'm ready whenever you are."

HE HAD CERTAINLY BEEN right about the condition of the roads, Chase thought. The highway leading north out of town had been paved and fairly well-maintained. There was the occasional rough spot, but nothing too bad. They had traveled less than half of the distance indicated by the map to their destination, however, when the road seemed to run out. It didn't happen all at once. First there were patches where the runoff from the heavy rains had washed potholes in the pavement. Then there were areas where the paving had disappeared altogether to be replaced by gravel, and finally there was no longer any blacktop at all.

After they made the turn to the west that the map seemed to indicate would lead to their destination, they entered the foothills of the rugged, almost-pristine range known as Sierra del Carmen—Las Maderas. As they had climbed, the vegetation had begun to change. There was still plenty of mesquite and yucca, but there was also shrub live oak and manzanita and desert olive.

Dead Horse Mountains. Chase wondered where that more colorful English name had originated. He hoped the terrain where they'd been sent wasn't as ominous as that made it sound.

The road, which had climbed steadily for some time, had narrowed even more. It was deeply rutted from the summer rains. The jolting grew so bad at times that Samantha put her hand against the roof of the Land Rover to brace herself. To accommodate the worsening conditions, Chase slowed until Samantha was glancing at her watch every few minutes.

"Relax," Chase said. "We've got plenty of time."

"How much farther?" she asked.

"I'm not sure. Maybe ten miles. The maps are a little vague about distances up here."

Chase had been hoping that the trail didn't run out before they got to wherever they were supposed to go. That was always a possibility, and he didn't relish hiking across any of this country. Not without provisions and a guide who knew exactly where he was going. And not with Samantha, he thought, glancing over to see that she was still braced against the roughness of the ride.

The narrow road churned upward now between rugged rock faces and increasingly sheer drops. Given the number of blind curves and places where the natural cut they were following rimmed precariously near one of those drop-offs, Chase knew he was driving far faster than conditions warranted. He had just thought that it might be smart to slow down, that it would be better that they be a few minutes late than that they not arrive at all, when it happened.

He realized, when he had time to relive it later, that he had subconsciously been aware of the sound of the rifle shot that blew out the rear tire. At the time he hadn't known what it was, but he knew something was wrong as he wrestled with the steering wheel, which suddenly seemed to come alive in his hands.

He might have known something was seriously wrong, but still, given the carefully chosen location where it happened, he couldn't do a damn thing about. The Land Rover swerved and the outside wheels slipped off the edge of the roadway and over the drop-off, which was, of course, exactly the effect the single shot had been intended to produce. They never had a chance.

Chapter Six

The Land Rover rolled at least twice, bouncing down the side of the incline almost, it seemed, in slow motion before the front end came to rest with stunning force against the side of a massive boulder.

After the banging jolts of their descent, the silence that surrounded them when the Land Rover had finally been brought to a stop was eerie. It encouraged the lethargy that had stolen over Chase, almost an inability to move, an inability to think, to make any further effort. Or maybe it was simply gratitude to find he was alive or a need to savor that surprising discovery for a moment.

"Samantha?" he asked, as soon as his mind began to gear back up to face what had happened. He knew he would manage to deal with anything else as long as Samantha was all right.

"I'm okay," she answered reassuringly.

He turned his head carefully, and he could see her. The car was tilted upward, the bottom of the front end wedged against the rock that had stopped them. The roof had been pushed into the interior during the rolls, and it was crowding their heads, but the supports hadn't buckled. That was the only reason they were still alive. Sometime in the descent, part of the car or one of the suitcases, which had probably become flying projectiles, had struck his neck and left shoulder with numbing force. But at least they were both still alive.

Samantha's upper body was secured to the seat by her shoulder harness, but her legs had slipped toward him, following the downward slope of the car, so that her knees were resting on his right thigh.

"We have to get out of here," he said.

It would have to be through the passenger door, crawling out her side of the Land Rover, which had become the top. But in the process of doing that, he also was aware, they would be making themselves targets for whoever was out there.

There had been a lot of places above the roadbed where someone could conceal himself to take the shot that had caused the wreck. But they might be slightly protected now by the sloping sides of the shallow ravine they'd landed in. Their best chance to get out of the car, to get the ransom away, was to do it before the shooter had time to reposition himself at another vantage point where he could get a better look down into the small canyon.

Chase released his seat belt and reached back blindly for the handle of the smaller of the two suitcases, the feminine one, which was lying on top of the shattered back window of the driver's side. He managed to pull it into the front seat with him, but there wouldn't be enough room to get the other one up here because, he realized, Samantha was in the way.

"Go on," he ordered again. "We have to get out of the car."

She released her belt and immediately slid out of the slanting seat and into the suitcase that was now between them. The force of her fall banged his shoulder into the side of the Land Rover. He carefully eased his body around so his back was against the twisted metal of the door, not only in an effort to protect his injury, but to give him some leverage to support the suitcase.

"Get up on top of the bag and then climb out. Keep as

low as you can. Whatever you do, keep your head down and stay behind the car. Use it as a shield.''

"What about you?" she asked, trying to obey. She had clambered to her knees and was trying to maintain her balance on top of the shifting suitcase. He grabbed the bottom edge of the bag with his right hand to steady it, to provide a more stable platform.

"I'm right behind you. Just go. Get the hell out."

It wasn't graceful. She struggled to open the door for endless seconds. There was nothing Chase could do to help her, but finally she pushed it upward and climbed out. His vision blocked by the suitcase he was holding, he couldn't tell if Samantha had followed his advice about keeping her head down, but at least he hadn't heard another shot. And if they were very lucky...

He pushed the smaller case up and powered it out the door she'd left open, stifling a gasp as the resultant pain in his shoulder sliced through him like a bolt of lightning. But he heard the case bump to the ground. As he reached into the back seat, trying to find the handle of the other bag, he could hear Samantha pulling the first suitcase across the ground to get it nearer to her. She'd have to carry it if they got a chance to make a run for it. He couldn't carry both of them and the water.

He finally located the second suitcase and shoved it through the open door, the movement even more painful this time. He wasn't feeling too optimistic about the condition of his left arm and shoulder. The initial numbness was wearing off and what had replaced it wasn't comforting. Or comfortable. That was all he needed, he thought bitterly. A busted arm.

It was taking too long to do what he had to do, he knew. He seemed to be moving in slow motion. Too much time, allowing the shooter to reposition, to line up his sights on another target.

Forcing that thought into the back of his mind, he reached for the water he'd bought, which was in a plastic gallon jug. That was not nearly enough, he knew, not for this country, not even in late summer when the rains had been the heaviest and there might still be pools formed by their runoff. But then the gallon was only supposed to be for an emergency. And their present situation might just qualify, he thought with a touch of macabre humor.

"Samantha," he called, praying she was right there on the other side of the upturned vehicle. Hoping she was the only one out there.

"I'm here."

"The water. I'm going to hold the jug up in the opening. Reach up and grab the handle. Keep your head down."

"Okay," she agreed.

He could see her hand meet his over the handle, and he let the jug go. Everything out but him, he thought. Everything—

There was no doubt about the sound this time. The jug exploded first, spraying them both with the precious water, and then the bullet that had gone through the thin plastic ricocheted off a rock somewhere, a distinctive whine that cut into the echoing report of the shot itself.

"Keep down," he ordered.

Sound played tricks in rock canyons, so that he couldn't tell exactly where that one had come from. Maybe it was just a lucky shot. Maybe they hadn't been aiming for the jug at all. Maybe whoever was shooting at them hadn't seen Samantha crawl out, wouldn't know there was anyone alive down here. He knew he was making up positive scenarios because otherwise the deadly accuracy of those two shots was pretty scary. First the tire and then the water. Two shots and two targets taken out.

Whoever was shooting might decide just to wait them out. Pick them off if they moved. Maybe he and Samantha should play dead until night and then try to get out. Even as he thought that, he realized it wouldn't work. Whoever was shooting at the car wouldn't give them that chance. Whoever it was would eventually come down here—before night. It was the money they were after, and even if they believed the occupants of the Land Rover were dead, they'd still make the descent.

He struggled to turn his aching body in the cramped space of the damaged car, trying to get his legs under him. Finally he managed. He braced his boots against the crushed driver's-side door and, reaching up, put his hands on the outside of what had been the passenger seat. He surged up and over the bottom of the opened passenger door, ignoring the pain, and fell awkwardly on top of Samantha and the two cases.

There were at least four shots this time, maybe more, ringing out in quick succession, the exact number disguised by the echoes and by the whining ricochets. He crawled up over Samantha, pressing his body down over the entire length of hers. Covering her. Protecting.

A sliver of rock stung his forehead, and he put his left cheek down against hers and at the same time, held his right hand, fingers spread, beside their faces, trying to shield them both. He could feel her heart racing beneath his. Too fast. Terrified. He didn't blame her. He was pretty damn terrified himself.

Finally the noise of the ricochets stopped. Waiting in the silence that followed was worse. He still believed the up-turned Land Rover was between them and the shooter because every bullet had seemed to strike it first.

He turned his head very slowly, looking to his right, trying to find cover somewhere on the slope of the far side of the ravine, the one opposite the roadway they'd plunged off. There wasn't much. Some scattered boulders, far smaller than the one that had caught the car. Plenty of yucca. Clumps of needlegrass and prickly pear. He angled his chin down slightly, looking toward the back of the car, and found something, the best cover he probably could hope for in this country.

There was small pile of tumbled rocks, probably dislodged in the same slide that had sent the boulder down the slope. Piled on top of one another, they were just big enough to offer shelter for one person.

When he turned back to explain what he wanted her to do, he found himself looking down into Samantha's eyes. He was still lying on top of her, and all at once he became aware of her body beneath his. Aware of the fact that this was *Samantha's* body. Unbelievably, he reacted. His sudden arousal was uncontrollable. So damn hard. Just like five years ago. Just like forever.

He knew she would have to feel what was happening. With their positions, it would be impossible for her not to. Her eyes held his, widening slightly as she felt the change, the knowledge of his reaction in her eyes.

And there wasn't a damn thing he could do about it, he realized. Unless he had a death wish, there was no way to separate his body from hers. No way to keep her from understanding that nothing was different about the way he felt or about the effect she had on him. Another veneer he'd worked hard at creating was stripped away in an instant.

Something was changing in her eyes. Some emotion moved behind them. A question, maybe. Or disbelief. Revulsion. He couldn't identify it, couldn't think of anything to say in explanation. There *was* no explanation for what was going on except the obvious one—he wanted her, desired her. Still loved her, he had already admitted to himself, just as much as he always had.

"I've heard danger is an aphrodisiac for some people," she said. "You got an itch, Chase?" Her voice was very soft, but he remembered, and he understood that what she had asked wasn't meant to be an invitation.

It was what he'd said to her the night she had come to the ranch. *"You just got an itch, and you picked me out to scratch it."* That comment had been prompted by desperation, an attempt to get her out of his house before he broke his word, destroyed whatever honor he thought he still had. She hadn't understood why he had said it, of course, and she couldn't know that he had never gotten over how he felt about her. Or know that sometime in the last five years he had even stopped trying. Stopped substituting. Stopped hoping.

I've got an itch, he acknowledged. *The same one I've always had. Only now...*

He arched his back, easing his hips upward, trying to lessen the contact between his aching need and the slender body that lay just beneath his. "There's cover," he said instead of answering. "Behind us. A pile of rocks. Not much, but it's our only chance."

She held his eyes for a moment longer, maybe trying to reconcile his body's unexpected reaction to the lack of emotion he had forced into those instructions. But finally she gave in, forced to ignore what had happened because he was. Denying the reality of it.

"Why are they shooting at us? They're the ones who sent us here. We're trying to follow their instructions. Do you think that means something has happened to Amanda? Why wouldn't they just—"

"This isn't the kidnappers. Not the people who have the baby. They wouldn't want to play games. They'd just want to deal and then get out as quick as they can."

"You think... You think it's somebody else?"

He could see the relief of that thought reflected in her strained features. "That's the *only* thing that makes sense. Which means we have to get out of here. Take the money with us."

"Why can't we stay here," she argued. "Stay behind the car. We're more protected here than—"

"Because he'll come down."

"You've got a gun. Shoot him."

"He's got a rifle. And we don't know where he is. He can wait us out. A couple of days if he has to. And we can't lose any more time."

Chase didn't even realize he'd slipped into the singular. One shooter, he'd already decided—the man who had rec-

ognized him in the shop. "In the meantime he can keep us
pinned down until he can work himself into a position
where he *can* see us. Maybe get behind us. Then the car's
no protection."

"But…"

"He wants the money, Samantha, and he'll kill us with
as little emotion as you'd kill a roach to get to it. That's a
hell of a lot of money for down here. I know it doesn't
seem like much to you, but to most people in this country
it's a fortune. Worth a couple of murders, at least."

"Okay," she said, nodding agreement. He could see the
realization of their situation finally reflected in her eyes,
but she had guts, he would give her that. Once she understood what they faced, the agreement to do what he'd suggested had been unflinching.

"You'll have to take the smaller of the cases. I'll get the
other. I'm going to create a diversion at the front of the
Land Rover, try to focus his attention up there. If it works,
you should have time to make a run for the rocks. Keep
your body down, as low as you can, keep the suitcase between you and him, and keep moving."

"Okay," she said again.

"And Samantha."

"Yes."

"If anything happens to me, give him the money. Tell
him who you are and convince him to call Sam. Tell him
Sam will be glad to pay another million if he'll just make
contact with him. Make it worth his while to deal."

"What about Amanda? If I give *him* the ransom, what
happens to Mandy?"

He didn't know what to tell her because he still didn't
know anything about the kidnappers. She believed the
leader's promise that he would take care of the baby, but
there was no way to really know how a delay would affect
them. Amateurs, he thought again. That one fact screwed
up any surety he might have had about how they would
react.

"Chase?" she questioned his silence.

"Sam can send someone else in after you get back. Get the word out that somebody interfered with the exchange, that we were trying to deal in good faith. Make them an offer. Make it in Melchor Múzquiz. Make it up here. Spread the word. Somebody will respond."

"They won't...hurt her if we don't show up?"

"They want the money. They'll wait." *I hope,* he added silently. *For your sake, sweetheart, I hope to hell they'll wait.* "The important thing is that if you have to go it alone, you let him know who you are. Who Sam is. Do you understand me?"

"Yes," she said.

"Now I'm going to move around the boulder and toward the front of the Land Rover. Get the bag and get ready. You'll see the clump of rocks partway up the slope well behind the car. When I give you the signal, sweetheart, make the run. Low and fast."

"Chase," she said, and unable to resist, he looked back into her eyes.

"Just one more thing," she said softly. He waited, wondering what else she wanted to say to him. Maybe the last thing they would ever say to each other. Was she finally going to ask him for an explanation of what had happened five years ago?

"I'm *not* your sweetheart," she said instead. "I'd appreciate it if you'd remember that."

More of his stupid dreams, he thought, thinking she wanted to say something to him about the past. More of his fantasies about his importance in Samantha Kincaid's life. She didn't want anything from him, not even an explanation. Just someone to get her baby back.

"Yes, ma'am, Mrs. Berkley," he said, unable to prevent the edge in his voice. He couldn't seem to reconcile the woman she'd become with the girl he remembered. The girl he had loved. Who had been in love with him. The girl whose memory he'd lived with a long time. Fantasy, he mocked himself. Nothing but fantasy.

He eased his body away from hers, careful to stay in the shadow of the overturned Land Rover as he crawled around the boulder on his hands and knees. Once at the front of the car, he could see part of the ridge the road ran along and the rock face behind it. He could even see the disturbance where the wheels had gone off, sending them down into the arroyo.

He reached behind to get his gun out of the back holster. The movement was a mistake because it pushed his left shoulder against the car. The pain blindsided him, blurring his vision until he was afraid he was going to pass out. He waited for a moment for his head to clear and for the agony to ease before he tried to complete the movement he'd begun. Nauseated, covered in a cold sweat despite the heat, he finally managed to wrap his right hand around the grip.

Ignoring the pain that was gradually easing to a sickening throb, he raised his eyes to scan the ledges and outcroppings on the side of the hill above the road. Nothing moved. He hadn't seen anything to shoot at, but he knew he had to try something. Somebody was up there. Waiting. Just waiting.

He pushed up onto his knees, exposing as little of his head as possible, but making sure the shooter would at least see some movement at the front of the Land Rover, so his attention would be focused there.

"Now," he said to Samantha. He moved when she did, raising his body from behind the protective barrier of the car and squeezing off a shot that echoed in the rocks just as the others had. The tone of the revolver was different from the high-powered rifle and under its sound, he could hear Samantha moving. He didn't turn to watch. His eyes continued to search the rock face, ready to shoot if someone popped up to draw a bead.

Nothing happened, and when he finally turned for a quick look toward Samantha, he could see her crouched safely behind the pile of rocks, the suitcase on the ground beside her.

"I'm coming there," he said, keeping his voice low. He knew she could hear him because she nodded, although her eyes were on the face above where the road ran, so he went on. "As soon as I clear the back of the Land Rover, you start up the rise behind you. Don't look back, just climb as fast as you can and then dive over. Got it?"

Again she nodded, but her eyes were on his now. Despite the distance, he could feel the intensity of her gaze. He smiled at her, trying to be reassuring. "Remember what I told you."

"Chase."

"Don't be scared. He's going to be paying attention to me rather than to you. I'm the one he needs to take out."

"That's not exactly comforting," she said.

"I'm going to be right behind you. Just get over the top of that hill. Don't look back."

She nodded again, her eyes still on his face.

"It's okay," he said. "Nothing's going to go wrong."

"Promise me something," she said.

He laughed, trying to make it sound reassuring, dismissing. "Come on, Samantha. We don't have time for this. I'll promise you anything you want once we're on the other side."

"Now, Chase. I need you to promise me something now. If anything…happens to me—"

"Nothing's going to happen to you," he interrupted. She had repeated the euphemism he'd used. *If I end up dead* was what she meant. Only he wasn't going to let that happen. And he sure didn't want to talk about the possibility.

"Shut up, Chase, and just listen to me," she said sharply. "We both know that's a possibility. If you get out of this…and I don't, I want your promise. Get Amanda. No matter what happens, you have to get Mandy. And you take care of her. Promise me."

He should be the logical one the shooter would go for,

but there was no guarantee, of course, that it would play out that way. She understood that as well as he did. *Take care of Mandy.* It seemed to him that should be Sam's place, or her husband's, but they weren't here to make that promise. Just him. *Take care of Mandy.*

"I don't know a damn thing about babies, Samantha," he said instead.

"You can learn. Anybody can learn. Promise me, Chase."

"Sam and her daddy might—"

"No. *You* promise it. I don't go over until I have your word that you'll get her back and then…if I'm not here, that you'll look after her."

A rock fell from somewhere high on the ridge above the road, and they turned to watch it bounce downward. Somebody was moving up there. Repositioning, maybe. They were running out of time, Chase thought again.

"You got it. You got my word," he said softly. Anything to get her out of here.

She smiled at him, her relief obvious, and then she nodded.

"You ready?" he asked, fighting the need to tell her how much he loved her. The need to tell her something that would make what had happened almost five years ago make some sense. She might not need an explanation, but he needed to make one. But there wasn't time. Not here. Not now. So instead he began to move, and so did she.

He held the suitcase in his right hand, held it as high as he could manage, hoping that it might provide protection against a body shot. He had the gun in his left hand and kept his back bent so low that the run was awkward. He could hear Samantha struggling up the slope to his left. He saw the bullet hit the ground at his feet an eternity before he heard the shot. The shooter was leading him, like a good hunter, and he was only a little off.

The boulders had seemed a lot closer from the shelter of the overturned car. He realized suddenly how brave Samantha had been to make this journey, and then to trust him enough to attempt the climb out of the ravine that he'd demanded of her.

He had time to wonder if she was over the top yet when the bullet slammed into the case. It knocked him to the ground, maybe because of the awkward position he was in, maybe because it was that powerful. The case went spinning out of his hand as he fell to his left, driven sideways by the impact. He was crawling almost before he hit the ground, but another shot kicked dirt in his face before he was finally behind the rocks.

He turned, leaning back against them, trying to catch his breath. He became aware again of the pain in his shoulder. It was amazing how much a rush of adrenaline could make you forget, he thought. He raised his eyes, and then said a prayer of thanks when he found that the side of the rise that led out of the ravine was empty. Samantha had made it over the top. At least she was safe. For the time being, anyway.

So was he, as long as he stayed put. The problem was, however, that staying put was a luxury they couldn't afford. He had dropped the suitcase, and he needed to recover it and then follow the route Samantha had taken up the slope. There would be no one to provide a distraction for his climb.

He turned, edging carefully to look around the rocks without exposing himself to the shooter on the hill. He could see the suitcase. It had slid maybe ten feet down the slope, and it might as well have been ten miles. He couldn't reach it without leaving the shelter of the pile of rocks.

Half a million dollars. Half of the ransom needed for Amanda's release.

"Chase?"

Samantha's voice came from above him, and he looked up and was thankful when he couldn't see her.

"You okay?" she asked.

"I'm all right."

"I thought… When I heard the noise, I thought you'd been hit."

"They got the bag. I dropped it. I think it's too far out to try to reach."

"But…" she began, and he could guess what she was thinking. Amanda's ransom. He had to reach it. But she didn't say that. "What now?" she asked instead.

Damned if I know, Chase thought. "You need to go. Just take that bag and run. Find a place to—"

"Not without you."

He didn't know how to respond to that. He wished he could believe it meant what he wanted it to, but logically he knew it was just a demand for his assistance in getting the money to San Miguel. *The best man for the job. The hired help.* She just wanted him to do what he'd contracted for.

"I'm going to try for the bag," he said.

"Chase," she called again. "It isn't important. You said they'd take less. You said they were amateurs."

It was a possibility. He moved again to where he could see the suitcase. Too far. Way too far. If he was going to be a target, he wanted to be moving up and over. Trying for the top of the rise behind him instead of back in the direction he'd come from. And then they could see just how good a negotiator he really was, he thought, with half a ransom to work with.

"Throw me the gun," she suggested. "I'll cover you while you come up."

He wondered if she could hit the broadside of a barn and then realized it wouldn't matter. There was no visible target. If she could just get off a couple of rounds in the general direction of anybody moving on the opposite ridge, he might have a chance. Probably about the same chance as he had now, he thought. Somewhere between null and zero.

"It's coming up," he agreed.

Here goes nothing, he thought, hefting the weight of the

gun in his right hand. If he didn't get it over the top, he could try to pick it up on the way over. It really didn't make a hell of a lot of difference, not considering the accuracy of the shots that had been fired at them. If the shooter could hit a tire and a jug of water, he wasn't going to miss a target the size of Chase McCullar.

This wasn't the way he would have picked to die, but then not many people got their wish when it came to that. At least he'd seen Samantha again. Had talked to her. Spent a few hours with her. Somehow thinking about that didn't help. He remembered what he'd been thinking on the way down here. The idea that after this was all over, he'd try to make it right with her. Only now it seemed there wouldn't be a chance of doing that. So many chances wasted.

He threw the gun as hard as he could. It wasn't his best throw because he was sitting down, but the revolver sailed upward in an arc and beyond his line of sight. Behind the top, he prayed. Just get over the top.

He heard it hit and thought he could even hear Samantha moving to it.

"Got it," she called. "I'm ready when you are."

"Just keep scanning above the road. Fire at anything that moves, but keep your head down."

"I thought you were the one they wanted," she said, and unbelieving, he heard the hint of amusement in her voice. "They wouldn't bother with me. That's what you told me when *I* had to climb."

"I lied," he said and heard her laugh.

"The money's what they want," she said. "Maybe they'll let you go since we're leaving the suitcase behind."

"Are you trying to psych me up, Samantha?"

"I'm trying to get you up the damn slope. What are you waiting for? An invitation?"

Yeah, he thought. That would be real nice. Not the kind he knew she meant. The kind she had made before. That night. The night he'd made love to her. Another fantasy.

He looked up the slope to where her voice was coming from. That was the reality. Making that climb and all the while expecting a bullet to slam into his spine or the back of his head. And then it would all be over. No more chances. No more dreams. Just bleeding to death in a nameless ravine somewhere on the backside of Mexico.

He thought briefly about telling her. Telling her how he felt. Just laying it all out there. And then if he got blown away... Then there would be nothing left but more regrets. More pain, maybe. Telling her he loved her wouldn't make anything about their situation better.

"Okay, sweetheart," he said instead. "When I count to three."

"You sure you can count that high, McCullar?" she teased, her voice sounding relaxed, amused at the kids' game he was playing.

"One," he said, easing his body upward a little, trying to get his legs under him for the push without exposing his head.

"Two."

I love you, Samantha Kincaid. I've always loved you, and I guess I always will. For as long as I live.

"Three," he said, too softly, trying to speak around the lump in his throat. It wouldn't matter, of course. She would hear the sound of his scramble. The shifting of the rocks he dislodged. She would know he was on the way.

He pushed off, using all his strength, the muscles of his legs seeming to explode with power, propelling him upward under the influence of the adrenaline that surged through him.

Samantha, he thought again, even as he heard the first bullet impacting into the earth beside him.

Chapter Seven

He could hear the cough of the revolver Samantha was firing above him echoing intermittently with the higher-pitched sound of the rifle behind him, that noise reaching him a fraction of a second after each hit. Zigzagging up the incline, the toes of his boots and his fingers digging hard into the shifting earth, he lost count of those impacts. He expected at any moment to feel a bullet slam into his body instead of hearing it strike nearby.

It didn't happen. Not from any lack of effort on the part of the shooter, he acknowledged, as the spurts of dust kicked up by the shots kept pace with his progress. Maybe it was because Samantha's fire distracted the rifleman just enough to put his eye off. Or maybe because Chase was giving it all he had, scaling the rock-strewn rise like a terrified cat going up a tree.

He felt something tug sharply at his vest as he dived over the top. He slid down the other side on his stomach for a couple of feet before he could stop his momentum, his hands clawing at the dirt and stones. Last shot, he realized. The last shot had come close enough to touch the leather vest he wore.

He lay against the unpleasant roughness of the down-slope, panting, willing his heart to slow before it burst out of his chest. He wasn't dead, he gradually began to realize with a sense of awe. Reaching the top alive wasn't something he had had any right to expect when he'd started that climb. He shouldn't have made it, and he had no explanation for why he had. No logical explanation.

Except maybe some unfinished business, he thought, as he listened to Samantha edging carefully across the loose rocks to where he lay.

"Chase?" she whispered, leaning close enough that he could smell her. The same sweetly seductive scent of her body that night, the fragrance released in response now to the heat and excitement. *Unfinished business.*

"I'm okay," he said. He raised his head just off the ground, turning his face so he could see her. There was a smudge of dirt across her chin and a film of moisture on her upper lip and under the small curls that feathered around her temples and forehead. She had never been more beautiful. He thought about telling her, but he knew that that, too, would have to wait.

"We need to go," he said, but like after the wreck, the effort to move seemed beyond him. He had expended every last ounce of strength to make it over the top, and his shoulder was a burning agony. His success was just a reprieve, he knew, a few minutes of safety; but still he couldn't seem to work up the energy to do anything but lie here.

"I know," she said. Almost tentatively, she put her palm on his right shoulder and then moved it gently over the shoulder blade, a small comforting circle. "Do you know you've got a bullet hole in your vest?" she asked, still making that caressing movement with her hand.

"Last shot," he said. He put his head back down on his forearm, fighting the fear he hadn't had time to think about on the way up. Not after he'd started, at least. Close. He'd come so damn close to dying before he'd had a chance to make anything right.

"Come on," she said. "We have to get out of here."

"The suitcase?"

"I'll get it."

He listened as she crawled across the short space, the

sound of her jeans-covered knees slithering upward against the roughness. He listened to the noises made by the small rocks that tumbled down the slope toward him. Maybe by the time she got back, he'd be able to move.

"Okay," she said.

He rolled over, feeling whatever was wrong with his shoulder burn again, like somebody had pointed a blowtorch at his body and again, ignoring it. He sat up and pushed down the slope a few more feet, sliding on his butt until he thought he was far enough down to be hidden if he stood.

Which was a lot harder to accomplish, as weak as his knees suddenly seemed to be, than he had expected. By the time he'd managed it, Samantha was beside him, his gun in one hand and the suitcase in the other.

"You sure you're all right?" she asked, real concern in her voice.

"I banged up my shoulder in the wreck. It's okay. Just sore."

She nodded, eyes still searching his face.

"I can carry that," he said, reaching to take the suitcase from her.

"What about the gun?"

"We might as well put it up. Hopefully there won't be anybody close enough to shoot at for a while." He took the .38 out of her hand and slipped it back into the holster.

His eyes scanned the terrain in front of them and he realized perhaps for the first time what they faced. The mountains of the Sierra del Carmen stretched before them. Somewhere within those high canyons and rock faces were the kidnappers who were holding Amanda. And behind them was someone who knew they were carrying the rest of the ransom. Someone who was very willing to kill them to get his hands on it.

"Which way?" Samantha asked, her gaze focused on the same hostile and forbidding territory he was surveying.

He turned to look at her and realized that she really expected him to know. He sure hated to have to disillusion her.

"Damned if I know," he said, allowing himself to smile at her. "I'm just making this up as we go along."

Her eyes widened involuntarily, but she didn't show any other reaction. "I guess maybe Sam should have taken bids," she said after a moment, surprisingly returning the smile.

The best man for the job, he thought, but for some reason it didn't hurt this time. It didn't make him feel inadequate. He knew that hadn't been her intent.

"If we get out of this," he said, "I'll give Sam a discount."

She laughed. "Don't even offer, because I promise you he'll take you up on it. Even if you manage to get us all home safe and sound, he'll probably take it. He didn't get to be Sam Kincaid for nothing."

He could feel the warmth of her laughter curling deep inside, down where the icy fear of death was beginning to thaw. All the way down to his gut. That eyetooth was still just a touch crooked. Her mouth spread a little too wide when she laughed. The dusting of freckles was still visible beneath the layer of real dust.

"That way," he said, nodding toward what he thought was northwest, the direction the rough little trail they'd been following had taken on the map. He didn't wait for her, but instead began the half-sliding descent down the back of the ridge that was the only thing between them and the guy with the rifle.

CHASE FOUND THE *TINAJA* in the floor of a narrow rock arroyo at midafternoon. They had moved more slowly as the day progressed, resting frequently in whatever shade the outcroppings provided, but the need to replenish the fluid their bodies were losing was becoming urgent.

The pothole wasn't deep, but the water trapped in it from the runoff of the last rain was sweet and cool. He watched

Samantha drink, her movements still feminine and graceful somehow, despite the long hours of thirst and exertion, and then he forced his eyes away, back to the direction from which they'd come. Trying to see if there was anyone following. Trying to decide what he'd done wrong. He must have done something wrong because they hadn't come across anything that looked like civilization. No camp, no village, and no kidnappers.

His sigh must have been audible because Samantha looked up. There was moisture from the water hole dewed around her lips and chin. She wiped it away with the back of her hand and then used the same hand to push back the curls that had escaped from the braid she'd bound her hair into this morning, but she didn't say anything. She hadn't questioned him during the long hours they'd struggled on the course he'd chosen.

They both knew that the time the kidnappers had given them for the exchange had long since past, and they were no closer to getting the baby than they'd been when they set out from the Kincaid ranch. He was grateful for Samantha's restraint in not blaming him. He'd done enough of that himself.

"We need to drink all of this," he said. "It may be the last fresh water we find for a while."

"There's always the cactus," she said. "What do we do after we leave here?"

"We keep looking. There's got to be someone in this godforsaken wilderness."

"You said we might be as much as ten miles away."

They hadn't been that far, he thought, not when they'd wrecked, but apparently they'd been far enough. They would never make it ten miles, not in these conditions and not given the ruggedness of the country they were crossing. And they both knew it.

"Maybe less," he said. "Drink some more," he ordered, cutting off that useless speculation.

When they had finished off the water, they headed out

again. He was trying to follow the mental image he had of
the map he'd studied this morning. Asking directions back
in Melchor Múzquiz would have been risky, but he wished
now that he had. At least he should have verified that the
map he'd been following was correct. Hindsight was always twenty-twenty.

They had seen or heard nothing of the rifleman since
they'd left the ravine, and as they trudged upward through
the long afternoon hours, other considerations took precedence over the danger he represented. They needed water
and a relatively safe place to spend the approaching night.
His job, he thought. His responsibility.

When he spotted the cave, which from below appeared
like a dark slit high on one of the rock faces, he knew it
was better luck than he could have hoped for. The mountains that stretched down northern Mexico were honey-
combed with caves cut into the limestone by the action of
the runoffs. Some of them were majestic, multiroom cav-
erns. The one they had stumbled upon was small, but
roomy enough for the two of them. There was water left
in a shallow depression in the floor at the back of the cave
to rehydrate them and even enough to save for tomorrow
morning. The cave itself would offer some shelter from the
cooling temperatures of the mountain night and from whatever predators were out.

He debated about building a fire and then decided that
they had come far enough that they should have lost any
pursuit. The fire would offer protection from the night
roamers, and if the light attracted human interest, the odds
weren't great that the person who came to investigate
would be the rifleman. It would be better to take the chance
than to do without the warmth and protection of the fire.

There was enough dried plant material and deadfall on
the ridge around the cave to provide a small but steady
flame. As night fell around them, full of both familiar and
unfamiliar noises, the small glow was more than worth-

while in terms of morale, despite the slight danger it might represent.

He hadn't seen any game although he knew there was a wide variety of wildlife in these mountains. Chase wasn't sure he would have fired his gun even if he had seen anything that might provide them with a meal. Hunger wouldn't be a problem for a while, and there was always the ubiquitous prickly pear, which with the spines removed could be grilled over the fire. That wasn't a task he relished, and besides, they could live a long time without food as long as they could find water. So far, they had been lucky—mostly the luck of being in these mountains so soon after the rains.

Through the narrow opening of the cave Chase watched the stars pop out against the indigo backdrop of sky, their brilliance undiminished by any competing glow from the artificial lights of human habitation. As darkness fell, it was as if the two of them were the only people on earth, surrounded by the whispering night sounds.

He looked back into the interior of the cave. Samantha was sitting cross-legged before the fire, her hands lifted and working by feel, replaiting the long braid that had loosened in the course of the day. The firelight touched her face with mystery, subtly highlighting the contours of its perfect bone structure.

She must have felt his gaze. She turned to face him, her eyes lifted in question. This was still not the time to tell her, he thought. Not before he had completed the job Sam Kincaid had hired him to do. Not before he had found her baby. But the words he wanted to say crowded his throat until it ached with the need to make it all right. To try to explain to her why he had done what he'd done nearly five years ago.

"Chase?" she questioned softly. "What is it?"

"We probably need to take turns," he said, choosing to articulate those words instead of the ones that had echoed in his head since he'd faced the realization of his own mortality this morning. "Sleep in shifts."

"Okay," she agreed, but her eyes were still searching his face. "You want me to take the first watch?"

"I'll go first. I'll wake you."

Her hands had stilled. "You think we'll be able to find them tomorrow?" she asked.

He had expected that kind of question all day, and been grateful that he hadn't had to answer it. He tried to decide exactly what he wanted to tell her about their chances. Finally, he took the coward's way.

"Probably," he said. "Find them or the river. Eventually, if we keep traveling north, we'll hit the river."

She nodded, and then her hands resumed the task she had started. He watched them moving through the curling strands and wanted to replace them with his own. He could picture his fingers, callused and dirty, touching the porcelain satin of her skin, brushing over the small curve of her cheekbone as his thumb skimmed the arch of her brow. He swallowed against the force of that image and deliberately looked down into the heart of the fire, burning the picture off his inner eye with the heat of its flame.

"The man who shot out the tire, the man with the rifle," she said, and he looked back up. "I've been thinking. It must have been the man you recognized. The man in the shop. If he recognized you, he'd know you were carrying money. He'd guess what you were down here to do."

"That's what I figure."

"It probably had nothing to do with Mandy. Just somebody who thought…" She hesitated.

"Who thought if he could get rid of me, he'd collect on a ransom that he hadn't worked for."

"The one thing that bothers me is how he could have known where we were heading."

"Maybe he followed us until the turnoff and then took another trail to get ahead of us. Maybe someone listened in on my conversation with the kidnappers. Or maybe they talked too much and word leaked out."

"It seems to me that the more often you come down here, the more likely something like that is—running into someone who knows what you do."

"It's something I've considered," he agreed. "The danger of too many people learning my face. A professional hazard," he added dismissively.

"Then…each trip becomes more of a risk."

"Probably." He wasn't blind to the possibility of that happening. In the beginning the money had been so important it had overridden any other consideration. But now, things seemed to be changing, needing to be reevaluated.

"Have you thought about giving this up?" she asked. "About doing something else with your life?"

The silence stretched. He couldn't tell her the things he had been thinking about during the last five days. Most of them involved her, and he knew she wouldn't want to hear them. More of his dreams. His fantasies.

"I sold my half of the ranch," he said. "I don't think I can go back to law enforcement, and that has nothing to do with Sam's suggestion that it doesn't pay worth a damn. If I eliminate those two things, I guess I don't know how to do much else." Although his voice was self-mocking, he knew that what he had said was true. And a little frightening. Where did he go from here?

"Why did you sell out, Chase? I know how much that ranch meant to you. Owning McCullar land. If anybody can understand what that meant," she said softly, "I guess Sam Kincaid's daughter can."

He thought about what to tell her, and while she waited for an explanation, the night sounds and the soft crackling of the fire enfolded them.

"I couldn't go back," he finally confessed. "Not after what happened. I tried to convince Jenny to let Mac's half go, too, to move away, go on with her life, but she was determined to stay. She seemed to feel that she had to hold on to the McCullar legacy.''

His laughter was softly ironic, and he knew Samantha would understand. The McCullar land wasn't like Sam's. Despite its proximity to the Rio Grande, it was rocky and desolate, too arid for farming, and a struggle even to ranch successfully.

"Maybe staying there was Jenny's way of holding to what she and Mac had.''

"Maybe.'' He pushed another branch of shrub-oak deadfall into the fire, and again it was quiet for a long time except for the small noises the flames made as they caught in the dry wood.

"Do you ever go home anymore?'' she asked. She had finished the braid, and her hands were resting in her lap. He knew she was watching him. He could sense her gaze on his downturned face.

He shook his head, and when he looked up, it was into her eyes. They were filled with something that looked like compassion. Compassion that he knew he didn't deserve and couldn't deal with.

"Jenny told me that the people who bought my place have made a go of it.'' He offered the change of subject to move away from things that were too hard to talk about, to move on to something safer, less painful. "That's probably more than I would have done.''

"That's good. That they've succeeded.''

"Neither Mac or I had kids. I guess it's good that somebody has the land who'll be able to pass it on to their own blood.''

He realized only belatedly how strange that would sound coming from a man his age. Too final. Denying the possibility of ever having children. But Samantha didn't question what he'd said, and the fire-touched stillness of the night drifted back into the cave.

"You'd better get some sleep,'' he suggested after a long time, looking up at her again. She was still watching him, but she nodded and obediently lay down on her side, using her arm as a pillow. He looked out at the sky and allowed himself an indulgence he usually fought. He allowed himself to remember. And to savor the memories.

HE HADN'T HAD THE HEART to wake her even when it was time to change shifts. He had watched the fire burn down to a small glowing mound of embers, and the air in the cave had gradually chilled. He knew he had drifted off a couple of times as he leaned, eyes closed, against the wall. He hadn't slept much the night before, sharing a bed with Samantha Kincaid after all these years, and the long day they had spent had been exhausting for him as well as for her.

Although he was aware of them, he didn't worry too much about his brief catnaps. The discomfort of his shoulder, painfully stiffening in the night air, woke him pretty regularly. He had decided the injury was no more serious than maybe a cracked collarbone and some bruising. The climb up the ravine hadn't exactly been what it needed, and it hurt like hell when he moved, but everything was still functional, and that was all that mattered. Besides, the pain was proving to be a pretty good alarm clock.

Not that he thought standing guard was all that important. He was fairly certain they had lost their pursuit. In the areas between the ridges they had struggled up, they had crossed too much open space during the afternoon where they would have been easy targets. Nothing had happened, and he wouldn't have stopped for the night, wouldn't have chanced the fire, had he not been pretty confident that no one had been able to follow them.

He glanced over at Samantha, still asleep by the dying fire. She was huddled into a ball, knees drawn up, seeking warmth from her own body. He thought about venturing outside to find something else to add to the low fire. That was one option, one that he wasn't too eager to undertake. It was dangerous terrain to be wandering around in the dark. He had resisted the thought of the other option for a long time, but watching Samantha huddled in the predawn chill was a pretty strong incentive to do something.

Finally he eased over to kneel beside her. He put his hand down on her arm and rubbed slowly up and down, trying to create some heat through the friction. Her eyes opened, the long lashes sweeping upward suddenly.

"It's so cold," she said, shivering slightly. Her eyelids fell back down, hiding the beseeching emerald eyes. He knew she hadn't really been awake. It hadn't been intentional because she couldn't know what he'd been thinking. But still, it was all the invitation he needed.

He eased his body down behind hers, lying close against her back and resting his injured arm over her. She reacted to his warmth by curling into him like a cat, and gradually he felt her breathing settle back into the smooth, relaxed rhythm of deep sleep. Reacting naturally to that peaceful rhythm, despite the temptation of her body next to his, it didn't take long for him to join her.

SAMANTHA SUPPOSED SHE had been aware of the noise on some level for a while. It had just drifted into her dreams without bringing with it any sense of danger, any sense that it didn't belong. She opened her eyes. She was looking directly toward the fissure in the rock that led to the outside. It was daylight. Just barely, she decided, judging by the milky quality of the light.

There was a man's arm across her body, she realized gradually. Chase's arm. Then she became aware of his body fitted against the back of hers. That was why she was so warm, why she had felt so secure. Only…given the condition of his body, she probably shouldn't be feeling that secure.

Just a healthy adult male's biological response to morning, she told herself. Even as she thought it, she acknowledged that that had not been, however, what had happened yesterday.

That had been something entirely different. Something she still didn't understand. Because what she had seen in Chase McCullar's eyes yesterday, in the middle of somebody doing his best to kill him, was the same thing that had been there the night she had come to his ranch.

Considering the five years between those two events, the long years in which she had heard nothing from him, what had been in his eyes hadn't made much sense. *Healthy adult male,* she reminded herself. *One-night stand.* Maybe that was all that had ever been there. Maybe the rest she had just read in so long ago because she had wanted those emotions to be there so badly.

Even as she made that humiliating admission, which was not exactly a new one, she realized that awareness of Chase's body behind hers hadn't been what had awakened her. It had not even been the growing awareness of his arousal. Not even the memories. That hadn't been what she had been dreaming about—one of the few times when she'd managed some sleep that she *hadn't* dreamed about him since he'd reentered her life.

What had awakened her, she was gradually remembering, was the singing. Someone was singing. She could still hear it. The voice was clear and young. A child or...a woman? She lay in the pleasant lethargy of just waking, listening, still feeling no sense of alarm.

"Chase," she whispered finally when she was forced to acknowledge that the singing was growing louder. Whoever was singing was coming nearer, and Chase needed to know that. He came awake with a start, instantly responding to her whisper.

"What's wrong?" he asked.

His mouth was against her ear, the question loud enough only for her to hear, his lips near enough that she could feel his breath moving through her hair.

"Listen," she whispered.

They listened together, neither daring to breathe. The

singing was definitely louder than when she had first heard it.

Almost silently, Chase disentangled himself from her body and tiptoed across the width of the cave. She watched him take the revolver out of its holster and position himself to one side of the narrow opening.

Suddenly the thin light that had been filtering into the cave was blocked. A boy stood in the opening. He was perhaps ten or twelve years old, judging by his stature. She couldn't see his face, only his silhouette backlighted by the morning sun.

"Buenos días, señorita," he said politely.

"Buenos días," she answered, beginning to breathe again. A child. But perhaps one who knew the region. Someone who could give them directions.

"Are you lost?" he asked, still in Spanish.

Bright kid, she thought, a little amused. Astute enough to know she was certainly out of place out here.

"My friend and I," she said, gesturing toward Chase who had already slipped the gun back into its hiding place, "have lost our way."

In response to her gesture, Chase stepped forward into the light and the boy's eyes focused on him.

"You came across the river? From the north?" the child asked. It was a logical question, considering the remoteness of the region.

"We came from the south. We had an accident and our vehicle was damaged," Chase explained. There were no details included in his account, of course. As he had urged all along, the fewer people who knew anything about their movements, the better. "Do you know San Miguel del Norte? We need someone who can take us there."

"Perhaps my father can help you. He knows many places in the mountains. I will take you to him."

"Thank you," Chase said. "We would like very much to speak to your father."

Chapter Eight

It had taken them almost three hours to reach the boy's home, although most of that had been due to their difficulty with the terrain rather than to the distance. The child, who had clambered over the rocks with the agility of a monkey, told them he had been looking for a lost goat when he had approached the cave.

The *ranchería* the boy guided them to was obviously another victim of the grinding poverty that afflicted so many below the border. The settlement was small and agricultural. There was some anemic-looking livestock, both cattle and goats, and corn and beans were cultivated on the small hillside plots. The houses seemed to be little more than huts. Brown-skinned women and children gathered in the curtained doorways to watch their progress. The boy led them to one of the larger houses. A woman, who Samantha assumed was the child's mother, swept up a naked baby that had been playing in the sunshine on the threshold and quickly disappeared inside.

"If you would please wait here," the boy said politely and stepped into the dark interior.

They had waited for perhaps a minute before the child reappeared, followed by a man who seemed much too old to be his father. His seamed features marked him as almost certainly *indígenas,* Indian, as did his black eyes, ageless and unfathomable. He listened to Chase's explanation of

the accident without any change of expression. Nor did he
question their need to reach San Miguel del Norte, but still,
the whole time Chase talked, the dark eyes assessed them.
However, when Chase had finished his abbreviated version
of their mission, he made the offer they were hoping for.

"I can take you to San Miguel, but there is nothing there,
señor. There are no longer any inhabitants."

"A ghost town?" Samantha asked. She had had trouble
following some of what the man had said because of his
dialect.

"Apparently," Chase confirmed.

She guessed that made sense from the kidnappers' point
of view. There was less danger for them if there were no
witnesses to the exchange. And more dangerous for her and
Chase, of course.

"But you can take us there?" she asked. "Would you
take us today?"

The man's eyes shifted to hers and held for a moment
before he nodded. He gestured to the boy to come closer
and then bent down to speak to him. The words were very
low. Chase's eyes flicked to her, questioning if she were
able to make out what was being said. She shook her head,
keeping the movement tiny and she hoped unobtrusive.
When the man turned back to them, the boy slipped into
the doorway of the hut and disappeared.

"If you will follow me, *señor*," the man invited.

Chase's eyes met hers again, but like their guide, he hid
whatever he was feeling. She didn't trust the old man any
more than Chase did, but she had to believe that they would
find Amanda more quickly with some local help. And if
this man didn't intend to take them to the kidnappers, if he
had other, more sinister intentions, at least she knew that
Chase was alert to that possibility.

THEY TRAVELED MOST OF the afternoon, climbing higher
into the mountains and through the endless maze of canyons. At least it was cooler, but the altitude made their

work just as hard as it had been in crossing the lower, hotter, semidesert terrain. Their guide explained that the place where they were heading had once been a mining camp, small even when it was worked, and when the mercury had played out, there was nothing there. He shrugged as he said it, perhaps wondering why they were so insistent on reaching such a destination.

They arrived in the late afternoon. The trail they were following suddenly snaked around the side of the ridge to reveal a narrow arroyo where a small collection of buildings stood. Samantha wasn't sure what she had expected, but the sight of the deserted adobe shacks wasn't encouraging.

"There," their guide said. He had gestured downward, stepping back from the vantage point to allow them a better view. A disappointing view.

"Are you sure this is San Miguel del Norte?" Chase asked.

"San Miguel," he affirmed, nodding, his eyes on the buildings below.

"Will you show us the way down?"

"Of course, *señor*," the old man said, and set off, picking out an invisible trail in the rocky decline.

"Do you think this could be right?" Samantha asked softly.

Chase shook his head. "We don't have much choice except to go down and see what happens."

It didn't look any more promising when they'd reached the bottom of the canyon. It was as desolate and deserted as it had appeared from the top. Chase had stopped at one end of the single street that ran between the line of buildings. Samantha moved up to stand beside him. There was no sign of life. No sign that anyone had been here in a long time. This was where they had been sent, and they'd finally arrived. Thirty-six hours too late.

"Are you sure there's no one living here now?" Chase asked.

There was no answer, and they turned to find the man
who had brought them had already begun the climb back
up the side of the ridge they'd just descended. He moved
as agilely as the boy, and it was only a few minutes before
he'd disappeared into the lengthening shadows between the
rocks.

"I guess he wasn't expecting a tip," Chase said.

"I don't like this, Chase. It doesn't feel right."

"Don't you start," he said.

"Start what?"

"Getting premonitions. Lawman's instincts," he added
softly, and thinking of Mac, he smiled at her. Then his eyes
returned to the narrow street before them.

"You feel it too."

"I didn't like him sending the kid off somewhere. Any
more than I like the idea of him disappearing as soon as
we arrive. It doesn't take much intuition to figure there's
something strange about that."

"But we're still going to…check it out," she finished
awkwardly. There didn't seem much to check. Had they
been sent on a wild-goose chase? And if so, why?

"It's what we came here to do. To find San Miguel del
Norte. To find the kidnappers. And if this *is* San Miguel,
Samantha, then I guess we're a lot closer to doing what we
came to do than we were this morning."

They systematically worked their way to the end of the
street, peering into windows and doors. It was obvious the
old man had been right. There was no longer anyone living
here. It was a ghost town and had been left for dead a long
time ago.

Samantha didn't ask, not even when they had reached
the last of the buildings, because she had sensed Chase's
frustration. It wouldn't do any good to ask him what they
would do next. It seemed they had come to the end. All
along, someone had been playing with them. They had
spent the last two days chasing shadows. She fought the
memory of Mandy looking over the shoulder of the man

who had carried her away, crying for her mother to help her.

"Damn it," Chase said. The words were almost under his breath, too quietly despairing to be profane.

"*He* sent us here," she said. "Just to set up the ambush. There never was any message from the kidnappers."

"We don't know that. We were late. It's possible that they just—"

"But isn't it also possible that this place has nothing to do with Amanda?" she demanded, interrupting him. "Isn't it possible that he just gave you the name of some place at the back of nowhere, and all the time we've spent getting here has been wasted?"

"A wild-goose chase," Chase said softly. He had thought that from the beginning. He briefly considered asking her again about her husband, but then decided it wouldn't do any good to bring that up now. She was right. If anyone had sent them in the wrong direction, it had been the guy with the rifle, the guy who had never expected them to succeed in reaching the place where he'd sent them. They hadn't been supposed to leave that ambush alive.

"Come on," he said. "We need to pick out one of the buildings to sleep in before it gets too dark to see what we're doing."

"And in the morning? Can you get us out of here?"

"I can get us back to the old man, to the *ranchería*. Someone from there can take us to the border."

She nodded. There didn't seem to be that many options left, so she started back up the street.

"Samantha?" Chase said softly, stopping her by cupping his hand around her elbow. "I can't tell you how sorry I am. Sorry for everything."

She looked up at him. He looked almost as bad as she felt. Almost as defeated, as exhausted. Belatedly she remembered his shoulder. He hadn't mentioned the injury since they'd left the ravine, and concerned about getting to Mandy, she had forgotten about it.

"I know, Chase," she said. "It's not your fault. I'm not blaming you. I know you've done the best you could."

"Not quite good enough," he said. The muscles around his mouth tightened so that his lips firmed into a thin line before he repeated it. "*Still* not good enough."

She didn't understand what he meant, but she truly didn't blame him for what had happened.

"This isn't anybody's fault," she said. "Except maybe mine for making Mandy such an easy target, for never dreaming that something like this could happen. You *never* think any of the bad stuff can happen to you. Not really. Not to my child. Not ever to my child. And when it does…"

"Something just went a little wrong with the arrangements," Chase comforted softly, squeezing her elbow. He could probably hear the unraveling of control in her strained voice. "They'll still want to deal," he reassured her. "We just have to find them."

She nodded, not believing a word he was saying. She was to blame for what had happened. She had known that since the day she'd let them take her baby.

"We'll get her back," Chase said. "I swear to you, sweetheart, I'll find her. You just have to trust me."

A soft sob of reaction to his kindness caught at her throat, and embarrassed to cry in front of him, knowing that crying wouldn't change anything, she tried to turn it into a laugh. It wasn't a very effective laugh, a little strangled, and at the same time she had to wipe at the welling tears. She hadn't even been aware that she was crying until she had looked up to explain and realized Chase's face was only a blur.

"I guess I don't have a good enough track record to make you believe you *can* trust me," he said. His hand lifted to touch a spot beside her mouth where an escaping tear had begun to streak through the dirt, and then his thumb moved slowly across her cheekbone, brushing away another.

So gentle, she thought. She had never forgotten how he had touched her that night, those big, strong hands moving with slow, sensuous intent over her body. The thought must have been reflected in her eyes because, despite the situation, despite the fact that she knew he hadn't been trying to seduce her when he had touched her, his hand hesitated.

His eyes changed, probably reacting to what was clearly in hers. And then his palms were framing her face, lifting it to his. His mouth began to lower and she felt her own open. Inviting. Welcoming. This was right. It didn't feel wrong in any way. Not even out of place. Even with Mandy in danger, it was right that Chase was holding her. That they were holding one another.

He was close enough that she could feel the warmth of his breath, could almost taste the sweetness of his mouth. Never forgotten. The memories had never been lost in spite of the years, the bitterness, the regret. Once more she was in Chase McCullar's arms, exactly where she wanted to be, watching his mouth lower to fasten over hers.

"Forgive me, Miss Kincaid. I seem to be interrupting something very…private, but I had *thought* you came here to see me."

At the first syllable of Spanish, even while her own mind was lost in the seductive gentleness of his touch, Chase had shoved her behind him, his right hand automatically finding the grip of the gun. Almost before she realized what was happening, he had placed his body between hers and the mustached man who stood at the end of the narrow street.

Instead of staying where he'd put her, Samantha leaned far enough to the side that she could look around Chase's shoulder. She had thought she recognized the voice, and the hope that recognition engendered overrode any consideration for her own safety.

"It's him," she said to Chase. Even in the fading light she could see well enough to make the identification. "It's the man who took Mandy."

"Are you sure?" Chase asked. Together they watched

him walk toward them, unintimidated by the weapon Chase held trained on his midsection.

"It's him," she said again. "I'm sure."

There was no one else. Only this one man, still moving down the street toward them. It was so quiet that they could hear the sound of his boot heels striking against the hard-packed earth of the street.

"Why don't you stop right there, and we'll talk," Chase suggested.

The man smiled. The dark mustache that drooped around the corners of his mouth moved with the motion.

"Amanda's father," he said. It hadn't been phrased as a question, and Samantha felt sickness churn in her stomach at the sudden realization of what was about to happen.

"Mr. Kincaid hired me to bring the ransom down here," Chase said. "And to escort Amanda's mother. To deal with the details for her. To deal with you."

The dark eyes studied Chase's features, and then they moved to Samantha. She had no idea what her expression might reveal, but she tried to keep her emotions from being reflected in her face. She met his eyes with a silent entreaty. Sam had warned her this would happen.

Not like this, she found herself praying, *Not in this way. Please don't let Chase learn the truth from this man.*

Finally his gaze came back to Chase. "I think mine was a natural mistake, considering the...circumstances. But I'm confused as to why Miss Kincaid thinks she needs someone to deal with me." He looked at Samantha again and said calmly, "You have the money. I have the child. I fail to see what we need to talk about."

"The baby's here?" Chase asked.

Samantha held her breath, waiting.

"Nearby," the man with the mustache said simply. His eyes were still on hers, and she thought she could read the natural question in them. Or maybe that was just her guilt.

"You *did* bring the ransom, Miss Kincaid?" he asked.

That was the vital question, of course. One she wasn't

supposed to answer. That was Chase's job, and even as she thought it, he spoke. "We brought half a million dollars. It's all Mr. Kincaid could manage in the time you gave him."

The dark eyes moved back to focus on Chase's face, assessing him as the old man's had done. "That's why you were late?" he asked. "Because there was some trouble getting the money together?" There was silence for a heartbeat, and through it the man's gaze remained steady on Chase's face.

"We're late because somebody ambushed us," Chase admitted. "Somebody tried to kill us."

"An attempt to relieve you of what you were carrying," the kidnapper said, seeming to dismiss the attack as unimportant. "Is that the money?" he asked, pointing to the single suitcase on the ground beside their feet.

"Half a million dollars. A hell of a lot of money," Chase reminded him, "which will buy a lot of things. Whatever you want. Whatever you need."

"But still, it's only half of what I told you to bring, Miss Kincaid. I'm very disappointed. I thought you understood the requirements for getting your daughter back."

Samantha was biting the inside of her cheek, fighting the urge to speak, the urge to promise him anything. This was Chase's job, his area of expertise. This was what they had hired him to do, and she couldn't afford to screw the negotiations up by saying something stupid, not with Mandy's life at stake. Chase had said all along that they could probably cut a deal, and with only half the ransom, she knew they didn't have any choice but to try.

"She understood," Chase answered for her. "The problem was, as I've explained, it was impossible for Mr. Kincaid to raise that kind of money on such short notice. His assets are primarily in land, and that's not very liquid. Not in today's economy."

There was a short silence as the dark eyes again seemed to consider the accuracy of that. "And in some very prime livestock," the kidnapper suggested, "which could easily have been sold. As could the stocks and bonds. Or some of those extremely expensive horses. Mr. Kincaid also owns a bank in San Antonio and another in Austin, I believe. Could not one of his own banks have arranged a loan for Mr. Kincaid?"

So he *had* done his homework, Chase thought, reevaluating the situation. He had been wrong about that as well as about a lot of other things. Amateurs? He wasn't so sure anymore.

"Perhaps," Chase acknowledged. "If he had been given more time perhaps he could, but what we have with us now is $500,000 in U.S. currency. Unmarked. No effort will be made to trace it or you. A simple exchange is all that's needed. The quicker, the better. You know that as well as I do, especially considering that someone else down here is also aware that I'm carrying Mr. Kincaid's money."

"But that's not my fault, my friend," the man said calmly. "Or my problem."

"If whoever ambushed us followed us here, it might be."

"You weren't followed," he said with conviction. "You may be at rest on that account."

"The old man who brought us here? He works for you?"

The mustache moved slightly, again indicating amusement. "Your guide works for no one except his own people. We are simply…acquaintances."

"But that *is* how you knew we were here?"

"We've been waiting for you, watching the camp. After all, this is where we told you to come."

Chase didn't believe him, but he supposed it didn't matter. Nothing mattered now but doing the deal. Doing his job.

"Half a million dollars in exchange for the baby," he offered again. This was the important part. "Take the money, and it's all over and done. That's a big payoff for a few minutes' work."

The kidnapper's eyes focused again on Samantha. "Your father has a reputation for being a man of his word, a man of honor. It seems a shame that you haven't inherited that quality."

Chase laughed, the sound of it short, harsh, and deliberately mocking, but it prevented Samantha from having to formulate an answer. "That's a pretty ludicrous accusation from someone who steals babies for a living. A man of honor? I suppose you believe that's what you are?"

The dark eyes jerked back to Chase, and there was anger reflected in them for the first time. "Money's a tool. Something that can be used for many purposes, both good and bad. Perhaps I believe my purposes are more noble than Mr. Kincaid's. Or," he added, "that my needs are greater."

"Maybe so, but let's remember that Sam Kincaid *earned* this money. You're just stealing it. It's that simple. And it's not really a matter of honor at all."

"Nothing is *ever* simple, Mr. McCullar. Not in my country. Not now."

"Political," Chase said, letting his disgust show. "That's what this is all about. Antigovernment crap."

The dark man smiled again. "Pro-Mexico, perhaps."

"Whatever your *needs,* this is all we have to give you," Chase said. "Take it or leave it." He didn't bother to hide his contempt as he shoved the suitcase forward with his foot. He pushed too hard, and the case fell onto its side, a small fan of dust billowing out around the edges. "Do we have a deal?"

The dark eyes held Chase's for a moment, not reacting to the insults, and then they moved back to Samantha's face.

"When I have the money—the full ransom—you may have your daughter."

Still she held her tongue, waiting for Chase to respond. His job, she told herself. He knew what he was doing. Then, in disbelief at what was happening, she watched the Mexican turn and begin to walk toward the buildings on his right. He had just appeared out of the shadowed twilight, out of nowhere, and if he moved out of her sight, she was afraid he might disappear as easily.

"No!" she called and was infinitely grateful when he hesitated.

"Samantha," Chase warned, his voice very quiet. She couldn't tell what was in his tone. Probably fury. But she couldn't let the kidnapper walk away. She couldn't be this close and then—

"No *what*, Miss Kincaid?" the man said, turning back to face them.

"Just…no. Please, don't go. I'll get you the money. I'll bring the rest of it back down here. You have my word, but I need to have Mandy now. I need to take her home. She's just a little girl. She's bound to be frightened. She's never been away from home for this long before, and…with strangers, people she doesn't know and trust around her, she'll be afraid. You said you have a daughter." The last was a plea, a reminder, perhaps, of how he would feel. "You have to give me Mandy. I can't go back without her."

"You're suggesting that I should give you Amanda, and you will return with the rest of the ransom."

"Yes," she said. "I swear to you."

"I'll bring it," Chase interrupted, perhaps recognizing defeat now that Samantha had made the offer.

She knew he would be angry with her, but she couldn't help it. He was just going to let the man walk away, and she couldn't have allowed that to happen.

"You give us the baby now," Chase continued. "You tell me when and where, somewhere close to the border this time, no more of this wilderness run-around—and I'll personally deliver the rest of the money to you."

"And you, too, will give your word? On your honor, Mr. McCullar?"

There was a subtle challenge in the question, and she prayed Chase would agree. Anything to get Mandy back.

Promise him anything he wanted. She would see to it when they got home that the money was delivered. She just needed to get Mandy and get out of here before something else happened. Chase had warned her. If they didn't do it right the first time, they might not get a second chance.

"My word of honor," Chase agreed quietly, and she closed her eyes in relief.

"Perhaps it's lucky for us all that you, too, have a certain reputation, Mr. McCullar," the kidnapper said. "*Another man of honor.*" Then he turned to his right, to the direction in which he had been heading when Samantha stopped him, and he nodded.

Chapter Nine

It took a few seconds for Chase to figure it out. Maybe because what happened next had been so far from what he'd been expecting. Maybe because they had lied to him from the beginning. And now, of course, he understood why.

He hadn't ever had that much to do with kids—not enough to know how to judge their ages, but the little girl who stepped uncertainly into the narrow, dusty street and then began running toward them, her face full of joy, wasn't a baby. That much was certain. When he did the math in his head, he figured she must be four years old. At least close to that.

That calculation had come later. Even in the shadowed street where she appeared, there wasn't much doubt in his mind who Amanda was. Her eyes, wide with delight now at the sight of her mother, were blue—that clear, pale far-seeing blue of her Scots heritage. Her hair was fairer than Chase's, but his had been that color when he was little, that same towheaded blondness that would darken to wheat with age.

He could see a lot of Samantha there, too, of course. The delicate shaping of her nose, even the same dusting of freckles across it. The elegance of the bone structure that would become more pronounced, and more beautiful, as she grew up. And the translucent clarity of her skin.

But the strong McCullar genes marked this child as surely as they had always marked him and Mac. No one could ever doubt they were brothers or doubt they were their father's sons. That same heritage marked this little girl as surely as it had shown up so surprisingly in Rio's dark features, despite the strength and purity of his mother's criollo bloodlines.

The little girl running toward them was his. A McCullar. His blood. His daughter. There wasn't any doubt in his mind, but suddenly there was a hole in his gut. At least it felt that way. Like somebody had cut out the center of his body and left it empty, standing open to the cold, howling winds of shock and loss.

He couldn't even make himself watch as Samantha knelt to catch the small body that hurtled into her arms. He didn't listen to the sounds of their soft crying or to anything they said to each other. It wasn't that the vacuum that had surrounded him when he first saw Samantha again had reformed. It wasn't just shock. What he was feeling was anger. Sick fury. He had a daughter, a little girl who looked like Samantha, and he hadn't even known. They hadn't told him. The damn arrogant Kincaids hadn't intended that he should ever know.

Not good enough echoed over and over in his head as all the pieces that had been so puzzling about this kidnapping began to fall into place. Samantha's claim that there were no pictures of the baby. Their certainty that this wasn't about her husband trying to get custody. *"Believe me,"* Samantha had said, *"Amanda's father isn't interested."*

She was wrong about that. He would have been interested, Chase thought. He damn sure would have been interested in his own child. If he had only known... If he had been told. Five long years. All of them lost. Wasted. So damn much time out of her life was just...gone. Time out of his life. Time they should have known each other, have spent together. Time that couldn't ever be made up, a loss that couldn't ever be fixed.

"Would you bring me the money, Mr. McCullar?" the kidnapper asked, the words breaking into Chase's anger and desolation, into his sense of loss, and the realization that something infinitely precious had been stolen from him.

That was his job—just delivering the money. That was all Samantha Kincaid had wanted him for, he thought. Not to be a father to the little girl they'd created together. That realization also howled through the cold, empty place where his heart used to be.

He reached down for the handle of the suitcase and found that his hand was shaking. He couldn't seem to see the bag because his vision was blurred. He knew the case was there, somewhere just in front of him, lying in the dust of the street where he'd kicked it.

He closed his eyes, willing his brain to start functioning. He would have time for emotion later. Now he had to get them both out of here, he told himself. He had to get them both home safely. This was still dangerous territory, and he still had a job to do for Sam Kincaid. The job he'd been hired to do. *The hired help.*

He finally found the handle, groping for it almost like a blind man. He picked up the bag and began to walk toward the man with the mustache, trying not to think about Samantha and the little girl kneeling together behind him. Still excluding him.

"You tell me when and where you want the rest. Somewhere where nothing can interfere," he said to the kidnapper as he handed over the suitcase. The man's dark eyes were full of what looked like sympathy. Compassion maybe, Chase thought. Like Samantha's had been. Only he didn't need or want their damn compassion. He never had. Not from any of them.

"Acuña," the kidnapper suggested. "Saturday. Have a late dinner at Crosby's."

"Somebody's going to show up this time?" Chase asked.

The mustache moved again, and there was a flash of very white teeth beneath it. "It's so hard to get good help these days," he said, echoing that frequent above-the-border complaint.

"What went wrong?"

"Too many gringos," he said mockingly, and then the smile widened. "Kincaid's messenger should have been prominently out of place. Instead…" He shrugged.

"Tourists," Chase said. "Too many tourists there for the sale that day."

"My messenger approached three different people," he said, amusement still coloring his voice. "None of them knew anything about a ransom. The last time he tried to approach someone, the couple was praying. *Obviously,* he explained to me, he couldn't conduct a criminal activity in a church. He grew frustrated, and then he grew frightened that someone would call his activities to the attention of the authorities, so…he left." The kidnapper's voice mocked his helper's scruples.

"He wasn't the only one who was frustrated."

"My apologies. I will meet you personally on Saturday. You have *my* word. Nothing will go wrong."

"You're the one who called the hotel?"

"Of course. Things seemed to be falling apart. I couldn't take a chance on that. When my courier returned and explained what had happened, I made him describe the people who had been in town that day. I recognized you from his description. I suppose I should have known who Kincaid would send."

Another indication that what Samantha had suggested was true. Too many people now knew what he did down here. Too dangerous.

"Someone else recognized me," he said. "Someone who tried to stop us from reaching you. He took the other part of Sam's money."

"Then it was *not* a matter of difficulty in raising the ransom."

"No, you were right about that, of course. Sam Kincaid *is* a man of honor. A man of his word."

The man with the mustache nodded.

"I'd like to know who shot at us," Chase said. He could see the surprise in the dark eyes. "I know you had nothing to do with that, but... Whoever it was tried to kill us, and he didn't care about the possible consequences to...the child. He endangered all of us, and I'd like to know his name."

"I don't know who shot at you, Mr. McCullar."

"Maybe you could find out," Chase suggested. That request was what he'd been working up to. Apparently this man had connections in this part of the country. It was worth a shot.

The man's face didn't change. The pleasant smile had already faded at the mention of the attempted murder, and he seemed to be considering what Chase had asked of him.

"I'll see what I can do," he said finally. "I can ask some questions, talk to some people who might know."

"That's all I'm asking. I need a name."

"It seems to be important to you. Revenge?"

"A little girl's life was at stake. He didn't give a damn about putting her in danger. I'd just like to know his name."

The dark eyes held his, and then the man with the mustache and the beautiful smile nodded. "I, too, have a daughter," he said softly.

Then he cleared whatever emotion had been in his voice and pointed to the wall of the canyon beyond the end of the deserted town. "The border is due north, perhaps less than three miles on the other side of that ridge. The miners had a trail across it. That should make it easier for the three of you. There's a ferry two miles downriver that will take you across. You can be back in the States in a few hours tomorrow, even having to carry the child. I've left provisions for you in the last building.''

He turned and, the silver chains on his heels softly jingling, disappeared between the two buildings where Amanda had been waiting for his permission to join her mother. There would have been someone else waiting with her, Chase knew, but it didn't matter. The dealing was over. The negotiation. He had finished the business that had sent him into Mexico. Amanda was safe.

But he still had some *unfinished* business, Chase thought. There was a whole hell of a lot of unfinished business between him and Samantha Kincaid, and he knew that finishing it was probably going to be the most painful thing he'd ever done in his life.

SAMANTHA HAD WATCHED Chase give the Mexican the money. She had held Mandy's small, warm body safe against her heart and had seen him hand over the ransom to the kidnapper. That had been the easy part, she thought, watching the man with the mustache disappear. And now...

When Chase turned, she felt the tears well. His face was ravaged. She couldn't read any anger, although that had been what she'd anticipated. She had already acknowledged that he would have a right to be angry. She and Sam had tricked him. They had used him and played him for a fool all along, but until this moment she hadn't realized what this would do to him.

Nearly five years ago he had taken her virginity and then had never called her again. He had treated her like a one-night stand, and through all those years she had held on to her bitterness over that as her due. Now, for the first time, she realized that in doing what she had done, she had denied Chase the right to know his daughter. Denied him the right to the endless delight that having this little girl had been to her and even to Sam.

As angry as she had been with her father, as resentful as she had been over his continued interference in her life, she had never even considered doing to Sam what she had done to Chase. And only now, now that it was far too late to do anything to rectify that terrible mistake, did she realize exactly the extent of the wrong she had done him.

He walked back to where they were, but he didn't say anything. He just stood there, looking down at the two of them.

"Chase," she said softly, trying to think of something that might make a difference. There was nothing. No explanation or excuse for what she had done. Losing her daughter, even for a few days, had made her realize what he must be feeling right now.

Mandy was so like him. Too many times she had pushed that recognition aside, banishing any remembrance of Chase McCullar because she had been hurt by his indifference to what had happened between them. But what she had done wasn't right. There was no justification for denying this man, any man, the right to know he had fathered a child. There was no excuse she could make.

"This is Amanda," she offered softly. "Mandy, this is…Mr. McCullar."

"Hi," Mandy said, looking up into blue eyes that were a mirror of her own.

Chase swallowed, the effort of the motion visible and painful to watch, but he didn't speak. He nodded instead, a simple, wordless acknowledgment of the child's greeting.

When he didn't say anything else, Mandy turned back to Samantha. "I learned a new song," she said. "It's about a cat. I can teach you."

"Okay," Samantha agreed, but she wasn't looking at her daughter. Her focus was still on the face of the man standing before her, its harsh lines seemingly carved from granite.

"Why?" he asked. His voice was too soft.

There wasn't an answer, and she didn't attempt one.

"You told me…" he began and then he paused before

he went on, still gathering control. "That night… You told me it was taken care of."

"I know," she said. "I was afraid if I didn't, you'd send me away. And I guess…I just thought it wouldn't matter," she whispered. Finally they had been together, and if she had thought about consequences, it had not been with fear, but with joy at the possibility of a baby. Even Sam wouldn't stand in the way then, she remembered thinking. But nothing had worked out as she had thought it would.

"Wouldn't *matter?*" he repeated, his tone incredulous.

He hadn't understood. She didn't mean that having a child wouldn't matter, but that it wouldn't change anything. That night they had finally acknowledged what had always been between them. She had believed that after that, nothing could ever separate them, nothing could come between them. Except…it hadn't worked out that way. She had always believed that was because Chase hadn't wanted it to. Because he hadn't cared. He had meant what he'd said. Just satisfy the itch and then get on with their lives.

Now, so many things seemed to argue against that long-held belief. The way he had treated her this week. The way she would sometimes look up and find him watching her, the same look in his eyes that had been in them then. And now his reaction to Mandy.

"How could you have thought…this wouldn't *matter?*" he asked again.

"Because I thought we'd be together," she admitted softly.

He laughed, the sound of it as harsh and bitter as before, when she had told him that Jenny was dating someone. "I guess that's why you married someone else instead of telling me what was going on," he said. "Your choice or Sam's?"

"You don't understand," she whispered.

"You're damn straight about that. I *don't* understand. No matter what you and Sam felt about me, it seems I had a right to know—"

"Please, Chase," she begged. "Not now. Not here." Deliberately she glanced down at the little girl who was listening to this. Mandy wouldn't understand, of course, but she had sensed the tension. Her eyes were wide, moving from her mother's face to his.

Not in front of Amanda, Chase realized. She was right. As much as he wanted to scream out his outrage at what they had done, it couldn't be with their daughter listening.

"I'll find us a place to sleep," he said instead. Then he turned his back and walked away from them.

"Mama?" Mandy questioned.

"It's okay," she soothed, tugging gently on the nearest ponytail. "Everything's going to be okay, Cupcake. I promise you."

Wishful thinking. A promise she wouldn't be able to keep. Because watching Chase walk away from them made her know that without him, nothing in her life would ever be okay again.

THE KIDNAPPER HAD BEEN right about the miners' trail. It was still faintly visible and that made what they had to do possible. Chase carried the little girl, her soft arms locked trustingly around his neck. It would have been easier to carry her on his back, but his left shoulder was too bad now to manage that.

Instead he held her on his right hip, his arm around her bottom. He could smell the sweet, sun-touched fragrance of her hair, blond curls brushing against his face when she turned her head to watch her mother's progress.

Most of the time she sang, not singing to him, Chase gradually realized, but under her breath, entertaining herself. He recognized most of the usual children's songs, but some were new to him. Her favorite seemed to be a Spanish song about a cat. Her new friend with the mustache had taught her, she confided when he asked about it, and she was afraid she'd forget the words. Rosita would help her remember when they got back to Granddaddy Sam's.

Her natural faith in the goodness of people had not been damaged, it seemed, despite her ordeal. That trust came from the love that had always surrounded her, Chase knew. He would have to give the Kincaids credit for that, in spite of the fact they had decided that he should have no role in her life. Again he buried the bitterness and listened to his daughter's singing as he carried her back to the safe and secure world the Kincaid wealth had created for her.

WHEN THEY FINALLY reached civilization, Samantha called to give her father the good news that they had Mandy and to ask for his help in getting them the rest of the way home as quickly as possible. Sam dispatched one of the ranch's choppers to pick them up, and Jason Drake arrived less than an hour after Samantha had placed the call.

Judging by the quickly concealed shock in Drake's eyes when he saw them, she thought it was probably a good thing that her father hadn't come himself. She had known the three of them were the worse for wear and apparently they looked it. The mining camp might not have been far from the border, but the terrain they'd had to cross to reach the river would have been hard enough for experienced adults to manage traveling alone, much more so with the added burden of a four-year-old child.

Despite whatever was now obviously wrong with his shoulder, Chase had carried Amanda most of the way. He hadn't complained, of course, but she had been aware of the care he took when he had to move his left arm. She could only imagine the cost of carrying the little girl up and down the challenging rock face they'd crossed.

At least neither of them had had breath to spare for conversation. The explanation she had promised would have to wait until they'd reached the ranch. All the time she was physically struggling over the ridge and trudging stoically across the final stretch of grassland to the Rio Grande, her mind had also been struggling with what she could possibly say to Chase McCullar.

What words should come after *You have a daughter, bright and loving and beautiful, and I have kept her existence a secret from you?* What words could ever change the reality, the selfish cruelty, of that? None of the things she had felt about Chase's desertion seemed to amount to much in the face of what she had done. And it was no excuse, she acknowledged, that she truly hadn't realized what she had done until she had seen his face the day he learned he had fathered this child.

"Almost there, Mrs. Berkley," Drake said reassuringly.

"Thanks," she said, smiling at him. She had always admired Jason Drake for putting up with Sam's sometimes-irascible demands and peppery temper. Today she appreciated his calm efficiency and the care he was taking of them. A good man, she thought, and a good friend, just as her father had said.

Amanda was asleep in her arms, exhausted by the journey they'd made. She couldn't see Chase because he was sitting behind them. He hadn't said anything to her in the last eighteen hours. His conversation after they'd met up with Drake had been almost monosyllabic, definitely noncommunicative. She couldn't decide if that was from anger or exhaustion or pain. She would make Sam have a doctor look him over, she decided. Mandy, too, of course, just as a precaution.

She cupped her hand behind the head of her sleeping daughter and touched her lips to the smooth forehead, keeping the pressure of the kiss too light to chance waking her. She had Mandy back and that should mean all was right with her world. Only it wasn't—not anymore—and she knew why. She just didn't know what to do about it.

As they approached the ranch's landing strip, she saw that Sam was waiting for them, the hot afternoon wind blowing through his shock of white hair. He had one hand up to shade his eyes, watching as the helicopter began its descent. He was too stubborn to wear sunglasses, even in the strong Texas sun, even with the threat of cataracts. She waved at him, and he lifted his hand in response. Drake gave him a thumbs-up through the windshield. *All's well. Everyone safe.*

She didn't protest when Jason reached to take Amanda from her to carry her to where Sam was waiting for them. Her own knees felt weak, and she wasn't sure she was up to even that short journey carrying the sleeping child. Chase was obviously hurt, so it seemed to make sense to let Drake take Amanda.

But it had been another mistake, she realized when she met the coldness in Chase's eyes. Amanda was his daughter. He had carried her through the mountains despite his injury, and now Jason Drake was handing the little girl to Sam as if he'd had something to do with the rescue.

When Samantha reached her father, for the first time in years she had the urge to run into his arms. Sam must have sensed her unusual reaction. He was still holding Amanda, so he just pulled Samantha to him and squeezed her hard against his other side.

"You all right?" he asked.

She nodded, laying her cheek against the almost-forgotten starch-fragranced comfort of her father's plaid shirt. It felt good to be hugged. It had felt good to let someone else carry the burdens for a while, to handle the planning and see to all the details. Just as it had felt good to have Chase's quiet strength beside her while they searched for Mandy.

The irony was that this was what she had always fought against in the past—not being allowed to stand on her own feet. She found herself wondering why she had thought through all those years that she couldn't accept anyone's help. Now she felt only a deep sense of gratitude to the men who had cared for her and Mandy when they had needed them most. She was immensely grateful to *both* of them.

"Thank you," Sam echoed that gratitude, his voice directed over her shoulder. She turned, almost but not quite moving out of the circle of her father's arm, and found Chase watching them. "Thanks for bringing them home safe. A good job, McCullar. I want you to know I'm grateful. I don't forget those who do right by me and mine."

Chase said nothing for a moment, his eyes on the old man, and then he glanced at Samantha. The look was too brief to allow her to identify the flash of emotion that had been in the blue eyes before they moved back to Sam.

"I lost half your money, Mr. Kincaid. Half a million dollars. I let it be taken away from me, and then I had to promise the kidnapper I'd deliver another half million to him in order to get him to give us Amanda. I gave him your word that I'd bring the money. And my word," he added. The recital of events had been almost emotionless, as were his harsh features.

"Somebody ambushed us," Samantha said, trying to explain what had happened. The version Chase had told wasn't anywhere near the truth. Or maybe it was just the truth without the details, without all the mitigating circumstances. "They shot out the tire and the Land Rover went over a ravine, and then they tried to kill us. We had to leave part of the ransom and run or we *would* have been killed. What happened wasn't Chase's fault," she added. "And *I'm* the one who offered the kidnapper the money."

Sam nodded, his eyes still on the cold blue ones.

"I'll get the other half million," he said. "I'll get to work on gathering it up right away. And your fee, of course."

"No fee," Chase said. "That's for when I'm successful, not when the whole thing goes to hell."

Sam turned his head slightly, his chin touching against the blond curls of the sleeping child. "Seems like this qualifies as success. At least to me it does. It never mattered what it would cost to get her back. You knew that. And I always pay what I—"

"I don't want your money, Mr. Kincaid. I haven't earned it. Despite what your daughter said, this was a fiasco from the beginning. The only reason we got Amanda back is that we got lucky. That's all. Just sheer blind luck. There's no charge for luck.''

He nodded to Sam and then minutely to Samantha, his eyes again holding hers for only a second. He moved past them, walking across the tarmac in the direction Jason Drake was already moving in. They both turned to watch the two figures grow smaller, eventually swallowed up by the heat rising in distorted waves from the runway.

"What'd you tell him?" Sam asked.

She shook her head, still watching Chase. "Nothing," she said finally, her voice almost a whisper. "He didn't give me a chance to explain. I don't know what I would have said if he had. It seems you were right."

"Me?" Sam asked. "Right about what?"

"You told me a long time ago that he had a right to know. You said that any man would *want* to know, no matter what the circumstances were. That was one more time I should have listened to you. One of many, I guess."

"He gonna make trouble?" Sam asked. He shifted Mandy's limp body, settling her into a more secure position.

"Not the kind you mean," she said softly.

The trouble Chase McCullar represented had already happened, the same trouble he'd always represented for her, and it wasn't the legal kind. Not the kind Sam was worried about. Chase wouldn't try to take Mandy away from her. She didn't know why she was so sure about that, except maybe because she knew he hadn't changed at all. He was the same man she'd fallen in love with so long ago. A man of honor, she thought. A man who had never deserved what she had done to him.

Chapter Ten

Once Chase reached the Kincaid house, he didn't wait for Samantha and her father to arrive. He borrowed another vehicle, making his request to Sam's assistant. Drake hadn't asked any questions, his gray eyes this time full of something that looked almost like sympathy. The pickup he'd provided had a full tank of gas and a Texas road map in the pocket of the door.

Chase didn't need either. It wasn't until he was on McCullar land that he stopped the truck. He pulled his aching body out of the cab to look down on the sweep of barren earth that met the silver ribbon of the river, winding against the backdrop of the brown hills of Mexico. Like a hurt dog, he had run home with his tail between his legs.

He could see both McCullar houses from this vantage point. That was why he had come. A last look at what had once been his and Mac's—their heritage. The little house he had built didn't seem to have changed, at least not from up here. There were new outbuildings—stables, maybe—but the house itself appeared to be just the same.

He couldn't see enough detail of Mac's place to make any judgment about what had happened there, but there were changes, he knew. Thinking about Jenny living there with someone besides Mac was hard. That was change enough. Something he wasn't sure he could bear.

He remembered thinking how one event could change

your life. Like what had happened to Mac had changed his, changed it in ways he hadn't even known about until now. His determination to take care of his family, to make sure Rio paid for what he'd done, had cost him Samantha. And Amanda. Even now, he wasn't sure he could have done anything different, but he hadn't been given the chance to decide.

As it had in San Miguel del Norte, his vision blurred, the two houses almost disappearing behind the veil of stinging moisture. *No need crying over spilt milk,* his mother used to say. Or split lives, he guessed. It wouldn't change anything. He still had a couple of jobs to do. One for Sam Kincaid. And one for himself.

HE DIDN'T MAKE A conscious decision to end up at Doc Horn's any more than he had consciously decided to drive to the bluff that looked down on the river. He had just ended up there, operating on instinct, maybe.

Doc's little clinic treated everybody within a thirty-mile radius—people from both sides of the border, no questions asked. Chase had gotten stitched up here more times than he could count. Most had been because of minor accidents on the ranch. He'd come here once when he'd gotten thrown from a horse his daddy had told him not to ride. And after a fight or two. Even after the beating Sam Kincaid's rowdies had given him. Despite the rural setting, Doc did good work, as the faded white line on Chase's temple proved.

Chase was surprised when he staggered trying to get out of the truck and had to grab on to the door to keep from going down. He'd been running the last three days on pure nerve and adrenaline, and he guessed it was finally catching up with him. He'd get Doc to fix whatever was wrong with his shoulder and then he'd collapse in a bed somewhere for a couple of days before it was time to make the second delivery.

There were a few people ahead of him in the waiting

room. He sat down carefully in one of the cracked vinyl chairs and put his head back against the stained wall.

Even the slightly medicinal smell of the building was the same. And the same feeling was twisting in his gut that he'd had the other times he'd come here—the feeling that he'd screwed up and he had better be prepared to pay the consequences. He used to sit here dreading having to face his father's hair-trigger temper. This time he didn't know exactly what he was dreading, or at least he wasn't sure what he was dreading the most, he amended.

"Well, if it ain't my favorite patient," Doc said.

Chase opened his eyes and realized that the waiting room had emptied. He must have gone to sleep. God knew how much he needed it.

"Just your most profitable," he said.

Like Sam Kincaid's, Doc's hair had somehow turned to snow while Chase had been away. He was a little more bent, his face a little more deeply lined, but his eyes hadn't changed. Shrewd and kind, they were looking at him just as they had when he was about thirteen and had gotten himself mixed up in something they both knew his daddy would kill him for if he ever found out about it.

"Yeah," Doc agreed, "I been trying to figure out how I could make ends meet until you decided to come home."

That's exactly what it feels like, Chase thought. Coming home. It might not always be a pleasant experience, but at least you knew you were where you belonged.

"Come on in and let's see what you've managed to do to yourself this time," Doc suggested, pushing open the door of the small examination room.

DOC'S SOUND EFFECTS hadn't changed, Chase decided as he endured the examination. They were the same small humphs and sniffs he'd always made. Chase hadn't realized how bad his chest and shoulder looked because he hadn't changed clothes since he'd left Sam's place on Saturday morning. The bruising was pretty nasty, vividly colorful, although some of it was already starting to fade to yellow around the edges. As Doc examined him, Chase could smell the faint miasma of stale clothing and his own perspiration.

"I guess I should have grabbed a shower and a change of underwear before I came," he apologized.

"I've smelled worse in my day than a little honest sweat," Doc said, his fingers gently manipulating Chase's arm. "Most of my patients don't even own a change of clothing. They got nothing but what they're wearing when they get here and what they're wearing's usually still wet."

Doc treated a lot of illegals, some of whom didn't plan on returning to the other side of the shallow river. Chase couldn't blame them, although he knew that for most of the undocumented immigrants who came over the border, the States was no longer the land of milk and honey they'd anticipated. Too often they ended up working for wages American workers wouldn't accept in jobs that nobody else wanted because they were dirty or dangerous. But nobody could blame them for trying—not him and certainly not Doc.

He must have made some involuntary response to Doc's last torturing manipulation because finally the doctor stepped back from the table. "I'm going to give you a shot and take a couple of X rays. Maybe then we'll be able to figure out what to do. If it's any comfort, I don't think I'll have to shoot you."

Chase closed his eyes again when the old man left the room, lying back against the crackling white paper of the examination table. If Doc didn't hurry, he knew he wouldn't need a shot. He'd be out like a light without it. Maybe Doc would let him spend the night here.

He hadn't thought until now about where he was going to spend the night. There wasn't a motel around for miles, and he sure didn't anticipate being able to drive. He'd had some experience with Doc's idea of a little painkiller. Doc's shots were both fast and potent.

He decided he would worry about that later. Or let Doc.

Let somebody. Right now he didn't feel capable of making another decision. Not that he'd done too well lately making decisions. Like he'd confessed to Sam, the trip into Mexico had been a fiasco from the beginning.

After the old man slipped the needle into his arm, the rest of the examination drifted by in a pleasant haze of medicated unawareness. He wasn't completely out, just relaxed enough to feel free to cuss when it hurt. And it hurt pretty often. When he was through, Doc stepped back from the table again to look at his handiwork, which consisted of a cloth harness to immobilize his left arm.

"Shouldn't take more than a few days for that to start to heal. You'll be more comfortable with the support."

"I wish I'd gotten that shower before you hog-tied me."

"You can slip your arm out long enough for that. Removing a couple of layers of dirt'll probably help your feelings as much as that contraption. I expect what you could use most is a few hours of shut-eye. Jenny'll see to that."

"Jenny?" Chase questioned as Doc's hand steadied him down off the high table.

"I called her to come pick you up," Doc said.

"That's what family's for," Jenny said softly from the doorway of the examination room. "Picking up the pieces. I guess I'll just have to take Mac's place when it comes to you."

Chase's heart lurched, and he felt his eyes sting again, but he blinked the moisture away, hoping they'd believe it was just the effects of the medication.

She was still Jenny, small-boned and gently curved. She had none of Samantha's slender elegance. Her hair was cut short for convenience, with little regard for style. It was very dark, but the highlights, softly gleaming under the strong lamp of the examination room, were golden. Her eyes were wide and brown, surrounded by a fringe of impossibly long lashes. Her complexion was the smooth, flawlessly tanned perfection of a true brunette.

Because she was so small and brown, Mac used to call her his Jenny-Wren when he wanted to tease her, but there was nothing birdlike about her. She was as tough as her pioneer ancestors, a perfect match, he'd always thought, for Mac's quiet strength.

"'Lo, Jenny," he said.

"Looks like you could use a little help," she said.

Her own eyes were misty, but it had been almost a year since they'd seen each other. He'd phoned her, just to check on her, but lately he hadn't even done that. Too many exposed nerves.

"I thought maybe Doc would let me stay with him awhile."

"You're coming home with me, Chase McCullar," Jenny said. "I've got plenty of beds and you know it."

"But they've all got lavender sheets," he whispered.

He hadn't meant to say that out loud. The thought had just slipped past whatever control he had left. Maybe that was one reason he didn't come home anymore. And of course, because Jenny's house wasn't really home. Not without Mac.

He saw her glance at Doc, her dark eyes questioning. Maybe she'd just think the shot had made him loopy. Hell, maybe it had.

"I like lavender," he said, trying to fix it. That didn't make sense, either, he knew, but he couldn't think of anything else. Her lips began to tilt, and quick relief showed in her eyes.

"That's good," she said. She moved across the room to slip her small body under his good shoulder. "Let's get you home and into that bed, little cowpoke," she suggested, her voice gently teasing.

It was what Mac had called him when he was a kid, when he really wanted to get to Chase. Usually it drove him to throw a wild punch that his big brother blocked with the ease of practice and a longer reach. This wasn't going to work, he thought, feeling his eyes burn again. He had always known he couldn't come back.

"I can't," he said, stepping away from her, again almost staggering. "I still got Sam Kincaid's truck. I lost his money, but I still got his truck. Can't afford to lose that."

It was all perfectly clear in his head, but again the quick meeting of the eyes of the other two let him know he wasn't making much sense.

"Doc can take care of the truck," Jenny said. "You know you can't drive, Chase, and Doc hasn't got a bed that can hold you. You'll be better off at my house."

Not our house, he thought. Not hers and Mac's. *My* house. That was the reality. *Jenny's dating someone* flitted through his brain, but he couldn't think about that tonight. Maybe tomorrow he could deal with the idea that someone had already taken his brother's place.

"Come on, Chase," Doc said, putting his arm around his waist. "I'll take care of Sam's truck. I'll run it over to you in the morning. You let Jenny take care of you. From the looks of you, *somebody* needs to start taking care of you."

In the end it was easier just to let them do what they wanted, and that was how he ended up spending the night again on lavender-scented sheets in the narrow bed he'd slept in for most of his life.

AFTER HIS SHOWER, he had fallen into that bed and almost slept the clock around. When he finally woke, he found Jenny had laid some of Mac's clothes out on the foot of the bed. They weren't even too bad a fit, he realized with a trace of surprise. Apparently there wasn't as great a size difference between him and his brother as he'd always believed. Just part of that big-brother syndrome, he guessed. But then Mac had always seemed larger than life to him. He still did.

Jenny was in the kitchen when he walked in. He had

slipped his arm back into Doc's contraption, and he had to admit that it felt better that way.

"Hungry?" Jenny asked, wiping her hands on the towel that had been lying on the counter beside the sink where she'd been cutting up potatoes. She poured a cup of coffee from the metal pot that was always warming on the back of his grandmother's stove and set it down in front of him on the wooden table.

"Maybe," he said, easing down into the chair. He felt a little hungover, a little queasy, but he couldn't remember the last time he'd eaten. Maybe food *would* help.

"Breakfast or supper?" she asked. Her eyes had considered the care he'd taken sitting down, but she didn't ask how he was feeling. Jenny wasn't the mother-hen type.

"Whatever," he said.

"How about a sandwich?" she offered. "Just to tide you over till suppertime."

"That sounds good."

It was good, and he ate two before he quit. He didn't know whether the black coffee or the food was responsible, but both the nausea and the grogginess had gradually disappeared.

"Better?" Jenny asked, pouring him another cup and then putting the pot back on the stove.

"Thanks," he said.

"Doc brought the truck by a while ago. You want to tell me how you ended up with Sam's truck?" She pulled out the chair opposite his and sat down.

"I did a job for Mr. Kincaid."

"It was Sam last night."

"I was doped up last night. I guess I forgot my place." He hadn't meant for the bitterness to be there, but it was. Even he could hear it.

"But you *did* find Amanda," she said. It wasn't a question. Maybe he *was* still groggy because it took him a second to recognize the significance of that. Jenny knew what had been going on.

168 *Ransom My Heart*

"Yeah," he said, "we found her. How the hell did you know about that?"

"She's all right, isn't she?"

"She seemed to be fine. Well enough to sing some damn song about a cat in my ear for about five hours," he said.

He hadn't realized he was smiling. It was pleasant to remember that Mandy had held on to his neck, softly singing as he carried her. When he glanced up, Jenny's dark eyes were filled with that same look that had been in the kidnapper's. More compassion. He looked down at the coffee in front of him because he didn't want to see it.

"I don't think she was any the worse for what happened," he said.

"That's good."

"Of course, since I don't have any way of knowing what she was like before, I can't really say," he added. He allowed his eyes to move up to focus on hers. The accusation he hadn't voiced was in them.

"I'm sorry, Chase, but I gave Samantha my word."

"How long have you known?"

She hesitated, but Jenny hated deception, hated lying, so eventually she'd tell him the truth.

"Almost…from the first. Since Mandy was born, I guess."

"You didn't think you should mention it to me? The fact that I had a daughter?"

"I told you. I gave Samantha my word."

He nodded. That hurt like hell. Not only had the Kincaids chosen to shut him out of his daughter's life, but even Jenny had gone along with their decision, apparently accepting it as the right one.

"Thanks for the bed and the food," he said evenly, using his right hand to push himself up from the table.

"You're mad because I didn't tell you."

"I guess I'm just a little…confused, maybe, about why nobody felt I had a right to know. Especially you."

"Samantha said you never called her. Not after...that night. The night Mandy was conceived."

"You couldn't figure out why?" he asked. The bitterness was there again in his voice. He had done what he thought he had to do at the time. He had made those decisions based on the information available to him then. All Samantha had had to do was to tell him, and he'd have done what needed to be done there, too.

"Because of Mac," she agreed. "Because of Rio, maybe. But how did you think Samantha was going to react?"

"Damn it, I didn't know she was pregnant."

"If you *had* known, you'd have called her?"

"Of course," he said. "What the hell do you think I am, Jenny?"

She didn't say anything for a moment, but he saw the depth of the breath she took, and then her eyes lifted to his, and he was surprised to see anger there.

"What do I think you are, Chase McCullar? How about stupid? Is that simple enough language for you? Simple enough for even you to understand?" She pushed her own chair away from the table and went back to the sink, turning her back on him.

He had had it all fixed in his mind. He was the injured party. They had hidden his daughter's existence from him because they thought he wasn't good enough to be her father. But instead of being on his side, Jenny was raking him over the coals.

"If I had known—" he began again.

"Oh, I don't doubt that you'd have shown up if you'd known about the baby. I know you well enough not to have any question about that. Everybody, Samantha included, knows about that famous McCullar sense of responsibility. Always doing your damn duty. You all just have to do what's right, no matter the cost." There was bitterness in that and sarcasm, and it wasn't like Jenny to be sarcastic.

"What the hell's *that* supposed to mean?" Chase asked, finally feeling his own temper beginning to flare.

"It means that when a woman goes to bed with a man, she doesn't want the next time he shows up to be because he felt *obligated* to," Jenny said.

Finally she turned around to face him, and the anger he could hear in her voice was in her face, as well. "Just plain stupid," she said again. She threw the dishcloth she'd picked up back on the countertop.

"She told me she was protected."

"So if there's no possibility of a baby, you just don't see her again," Jenny jeered. "What's that called, Chase? One-night stand, maybe?" she suggested.

"That's not what I meant. You know what was going on. You, of all people, know what was going on then."

"That's no excuse. Not for what you did."

"What I *did* was take care of the things that had to be taken care of. I did what I had to do."

"And later?"

"You're the one who told me she was married. You made a point of telling me."

"Not until *months* after that night. Months after Mac's death," she challenged. "What about all that time in between? No phone call? No nothing? How do you explain that, Chase?"

"Damn it, Jenny, you know what I was doing. You, of all people—" He stopped the words, the accusation they contained. If Jenny couldn't understand, if he couldn't make *Jenny* understand what it had been like for him, then…

"It must get awfully crowded in there," she said into the silence.

"Crowded?" he repeated. He couldn't make any sense of that, not in the context of what they'd been discussing.

"Down in that grave with Mac," she said. "There must be barely enough room for the two of you, big as you are.

Or maybe you've been there so long you just don't notice the lack of room anymore.''

"Jenny." He whispered her name, too shocked and hurt to voice the aching protest. It wasn't fair. She didn't understand. Of all people...

"And the saddest thing is that Mac wouldn't want you there, Chase. You know that. Not you and not me. Mac wouldn't want it. Not any of it. He wouldn't have wanted you going after Rio. Or whatever happened between you and Samantha. He wouldn't have wanted you to lose Mandy. Not because of him. You can't use Mac as an excuse. It's not fair to the man he was."

Fair, he thought, despairing. Did she really still believe life was supposed to be fair? When had *any* of it been fair? Not what had happened to Mac. Not what the Kincaids had done.

"At least take responsibility for what you did. And for what you just plain *failed* to do," she finished and walked out the back door, letting the screen slam behind her.

Responsibility. That hurt, too, because that was exactly what he had thought he was doing five years ago. Taking responsibility, a responsibility he truly had never wanted.

Chase left through the front door, slamming it behind him. He got into Sam's truck and slammed its door, too. He stuck the key in the ignition and then found that he couldn't turn it, couldn't make his trembling fingers obey the command of his brain.

"It must get awfully crowded in there," Jenny had said. In the grave with Mac. He supposed there might be some truth in the accusation, except...

"Damn it, Jenny," he said aloud. "Damn it to hell." He put his good arm across the steering wheel and laid his forehead against it. He could feel the tears threatening again, and disgusted, he fought them. Who the hell did he think he was crying for? For Mac or Jenny or for himself? Or maybe for all three of them.

"Chase?" Jenny called.

He looked up and saw that she was standing on the porch, watching him. Compassion had replaced the anger that had been in her dark eyes. Seeing that released him. His fingers turned the key, even as he heard the endless echo of the explosion, saw again in his mind's eye the fireball reaching into the cold December night.

The engine roared to life as Jenny stepped off the porch. He threw the truck into reverse and pushed the gas pedal to the floor. The pickup skewed sideways as he spun the wheel, and then he accelerated, tires squealing and dust flying. Driving like a teenager, he thought in disgust. Only, when he *was* a teenager, he would never have pulled a stunt like that. His daddy wouldn't have put up with it.

By the time he'd calmed down enough to slow the truck to a reasonable speed, he was almost to the other McCullar house, almost to his place. *Hurt dog,* he thought again as the small house appeared out of the shimmer of late-afternoon heat. Coming home again, tail between his legs. Only, this wasn't home anymore. What had once been his, created by his own hands, now belonged to someone else.

The place looked almost deserted. It wasn't that things were neglected, but it seemed to be more than just hot-afternoon stillness, too. He stopped the truck under the old cottonwood tree in the yard and sat for a moment, looking it all over, letting the memories drift through his head, no longer trying to fight them.

There didn't seem to be anyone here that he might bother by taking a last look around, so he opened the door and crawled out, awkward because he was operating one-handed. Someone had hung a rope swing from the lowest branch of the cottonwood. He pulled back one side of the swing and then released it, watching the wooden seat sway crookedly back and forth over the bare patch of dirt beneath it. Finally he raised his eyes to the house.

There was a calico cat sitting on the porch railing, yellow eyes watching as he walked up to the steps. She was wary of him, but she didn't give ground. This was her place, her eyes seemed to say. She had the right to be here and he didn't. Right of ownership, he thought, stopping at the bottom of the two low wooden steps.

There was nowhere he could go, he realized, and be welcomed. Not back to Jenny's, not after what had been said, and not here. It seemed there was nothing left of what had once been home.

The screen door eased open.

"Hi," Mandy said softly. "I'm not supposed to come outside, but when I saw it was you..." She paused, seeming to be uncertain about exactly what she thought about his unexpected arrival.

"What are *you* doing here?" he asked. He found a smile for her from somewhere in the rubble Jenny had left of his soul. Her answering grin was quick, wide, and spontaneous, and he realized with a jolt around the region of his heart that she was glad to see him.

"Did you hurt your arm?" she asked, and then she pulled those big blue eyes away from their fascination with the harness Doc had fashioned and back to his face.

"A little bit," he said.

"Mama's asleep. I'm supposed to be, but I heard the truck."

"So you came out to investigate?" he suggested, squatting down until he was at eye level with her. *"Mama's asleep."* Inside? he wondered. What the hell was Samantha Kincaid doing asleep inside his house? Only...it wasn't his house, he reminded himself. He had sold it almost five years ago and now somebody else owned what had once been his. Somebody...

His eyes left his daughter's and made a quick inventory. Paddocks and stables. Horses. Kincaid. The natural progression of those words battered at his brain until he was forced to acknowledge what they all meant. "Stupid," Jenny had said. He guessed she was right.

Chapter Eleven

"You *live* here?" he asked, his gaze focusing again on the little girl. The tone of the question was too sharp, but he realized that only when he saw the shock in her face. One small bare foot twisted inward and then settled over the arch of the other. Both feet were a little dirty, Chase noticed. Playing-out-in-the-yard dirty. Just like his and Mac's used to be. Except there was a touch of pink polish on each of the tiny toenails. Little-girl toes.

"Yes, sir," she said softly, nervous now, maybe because his tone had seemed to imply that she had done something wrong.

"I used to live here," he said, working at making his voice calm and reassuring. "A long time ago."

She moved then, easing the screen door closed and walking across the porch on those small bare feet. She was wearing pink shorts and a sleeveless, flowered knit top. Her hair had been collected again into two ponytails, the soft blond curls almost touching her shoulders.

"Did you have a cat when you lived here?" she asked. She glanced at the calico, who was still watching warily from the railing.

"Never did. I always wanted one, but I guess I just couldn't find the right cat."

She nodded.

"Your mama bought you a toy cat in Mexico, but..."

Somehow we lost it, he thought. They didn't seem to be any good at holding on to things, him and Samantha. Not even the important ones.

"I know a song about a cat," she said into the painful silence.

"Yeah," Chase said, smiling at her again. "I know you do."

"I sang it too much, didn't I? Just about wore you *out,* listening to it."

"You didn't sing it *too* much," Chase denied.

"Just a lot," she suggested solemnly.

"A lot," he agreed, losing the battle not to smile. He watched her answering grin with the same squeeze of his heart he'd felt before.

"Mandy?" Samantha's voice drifted out through the screen door. Not anxious. Just a mother. Just trying to locate her child.

"I'm out on the porch," Mandy called.

Chase stood, knowing he wasn't ready for this. He wanted a chance to make it right, but he hadn't come up with any words he thought could explain what he'd done. And instead of trying, he'd spent the last forty-eight hours feeling sorry for himself because Sam Kincaid hadn't thought he was good enough to be his son-in-law. Except that shouldn't have been exactly a startling revelation for him, and what had been between him and Samantha had never had a whole lot to do with what Sam thought.

He could see her now, standing there behind the screen, looking out at the two of them. He couldn't tell anything about what she was thinking because it was too dark in the house. She stood there for what seemed like an eternity before she pushed the screen door open.

"Chase?" she said. "What are you doing here?"

"I used to live here," he said softly. "Remember?"

She nodded, emerald eyes suddenly washed with moisture, and then she looked down at her daughter. *Their* daughter, who had been conceived one cold December night in this small house.

"Why don't you go swing, Mandy, so Mama and Mr. McCullar can talk?" she suggested.

"Okay," the little girl agreed. She smiled at Chase as she went down the steps and by him. The cat leaped down from the railing, rubbed between Samantha's ankles and then, stepping almost daintily, followed the child down the wooden steps.

Chase waited until they were both at the cottonwood before he spoke. "You're living here now?" he asked.

There was a small flood of color into her cheeks and her mouth moved, her full bottom lip caught briefly by her teeth.

"Yes," she said finally.

"Why?"

"Because...this is McCullar land. I thought Mandy should have it."

He shook his head, slowly, fighting the emotional force of that. "Because she's mine?"

"Yes," she whispered.

"I wish I had known," he said.

There was no recrimination in the words. Jenny was right. What he had done had been stupid—maybe a lot of other things as well, but primarily stupid. Because he had finally realized that he had given Samantha no reason to think he would *want* to know about any results from that night. Stupid.

He lowered his eyes, trying to hide the impact of what she'd told him, the impact of what she had done to preserve Mandy's McCullar heritage. He noticed that Samantha's toenails had been painted with the same cotton-candy pink as her daughter's. Her feet were just as bare, but they were clean and slender and somehow elegant, even standing on the weathered boards of the narrow porch he had built.

"I wish you had, too," she said. Surprised, he looked

up into her eyes. "I wish... I've always wished Mandy could have known her daddy."

Their eyes held for a long time. The words he had wanted to say didn't seem important anymore. In spite of what had happened to Mac, there was no excuse for what he'd done. No rationale. No explanation he could give. Jenny was right about it all. At least about *almost* all of it. And the rest... He couldn't do anything about the rest.

"I'm so sorry," he said. "I thought..." He took a breath before he continued. "At the time I thought I was doing what was right."

"I guess that's what we all do. Just...what we think is right. Only...what I did was wrong. I know that now."

She wasn't blaming him, he realized, and a little of the guilt for throwing the precious years away eased in the hard tightness of his chest.

"Your father probably had something to do with it. I never was his ideal candidate for a son-in-law."

"It wasn't Sam's fault," she said. "He even told me it wasn't right to keep...the baby from you. He said you'd want to know. Any man would, he said, but...especially a man like you."

He wasn't sure exactly what Sam had meant by that, but he had sense enough to recognize, surprisingly, that whatever it was, it wasn't derogatory. That was evident from both the words and from her tone when she had said them.

"But he found you somebody else to marry," he reminded her, remembering again her father's role in all this. What Sam had said and what he had done seemed to be at odds with each other.

She hesitated, and he waited through a couple of thudding heartbeats.

"There wasn't anybody else," she admitted. "My...marriage was fake. A lie. I went along because it was important to him. Sam was trying to save face with the whole state of Texas, I guess. At the time, I really didn't care what he did. If he wanted me to say I was married, so all those people, all his friends, wouldn't know Sam Kincaid's daughter had been…sleeping around, I didn't see any reason not to make him happy. It didn't matter to me what he told them.''

Chase climbed the low steps and grabbed her arm, gripping the soft flesh above her elbow. He was so angry that he even shook her a little. ''What the hell does that mean—sleeping around. You weren't *sleeping* around.''

The words got louder with each repetition. They made him sick. She was his—had been his. *Only* his and he knew it. He wanted to kill whoever had said that.

''But that's what his friends would think,'' she said. ''Sam's seventy-four years old, and illegitimacy still carries a certain…stigma for his generation.''

''It carries a certain *stigma* for me, too,'' he said bitterly. ''Especially when it's my little girl—''

He stopped the words, but he couldn't prevent his eyes from moving to the child who was sitting in the swing. He could hear her singing, bare toes pushing against the dust under the seat of the swing. His gaze swung back to Samantha's.

''Why, damn it? Why didn't you just tell me?''

''You weren't ever here, for one thing. You were in San Antonio, making sure Rio got put into prison. You'd put the ranch up for sale. You just…weren't here.''

''Jenny could have reached me.''

''It wasn't a matter of *reaching* you, Chase. I thought you didn't *want* to be reached.''

He released her and turned around, leaning against the post, thinking about what Jenny had said. ''I never realized, not until Jenny told me…''

''What did Jenny tell you?'' Samantha asked from behind him when he hesitated. Admitting what Jenny had said was almost too painful.

''That I'd tried to crawl into the grave with Mac,'' he confessed finally.

''I always knew what you must have felt like when Mac

died," she said. "I even understood about Rio. I guess I was just too young and scared and...I didn't want Sam telling me what to do anymore. If he'd told me to stay away from you and not to ever let you find out about Mandy, I'd probably have *run* all the way to San Antonio to tell you."

"But that's not what he said?"

"'Any man deserves to know about his child,' he told me, 'but especially a man like Chase McCullar.'"

There didn't seem to be much more to say. Not everything had been said that would one day have to be said, but enough. It was a beginning.

"Watch me swing, Mr. McCullar!" Mandy called. She leaned back in the swing and pointed her toes toward the clear, blue desert sky. Small brown arms pulled at the ropes, sending the swing in a higher arch over the bare dirt beneath. "Watch me!" she prompted again.

"We're watching," Samantha called. "We're both watching you, Cupcake."

THEY ENDED UP AT twilight at the paddocks. The horses were obviously Kincaid stock and obviously well cared for. He wondered how much help Samantha had running the place.

"Sam give you a start?" he asked. They were leaning on the fence watching the newest addition to her stables bolt around on pipestem legs, occasionally shying from imaginary dangers. His mother stood nearby, placid as a sheep, but keeping an watchful eye on the colt's antics.

"He would have," Samantha said, and then she paused before she added, "if I'd been smart enough to let him."

Chase laughed at her tone.

"It would have been a lot easier," she admitted. She dropped her hand over the top rail, snapping her fingers, and the mare obediently ambled over for a visit.

"How'd you swing the ranch, if you didn't take anything from Sam?"

"I had a trust fund. My grandmother, bless her, thought

women should have something of their own. I already had
my own horses, the two mares and Lightfoot Harry. Sam
had given them to me as birthday presents through the
years, and I didn't have any qualms about bringing them
with me. Then he offered me a few mares at what were
rock-bottom prices, considering their bloodlines, and for
Mandy's sake, I swallowed my pride and accepted. I think
it's probably the first time anybody ever got the advantage
over Sam Kincaid in a horse deal.''

Chase laughed again, and eventually she joined him, the
tone of her laughter still slightly rueful. ''I picked up the
black at auction for almost nothing,'' she said, pointing to
a magnificent stallion.

''And you've been surviving by selling the offspring?''
he asked.

''Selling them without any trouble and for good money.
The breeding's prime, and everybody knows it. I had
planned to expand next spring, but now...''

''Now?'' Chase repeated when she didn't go on.

He wondered if that ''now'' could have anything to do
with him being back, and then he pushed that pleasant fantasy aside. Just because Samantha had admitted she wished
she had told him about Mandy, just because she'd said she
understood why he hadn't been here, where he should have
been, five years ago—none of that meant that she wanted
him here now. That was just more of his fantasy. More of
what *he* wanted.

''I don't know,'' she said softly. ''I just don't seem to
be able to plan right now.'' She patted the mare and then
pushed the reaching nose away with her hand, stepping
down from the bottom rail to look up at him. ''You want
to stay for supper? It'll be potluck, I'm afraid. Whatever I
can find in the kitchen. I don't usually take a nap in the
afternoon, but I can't seem to catch up.''

''I know. I slept the clock around at Jenny's.''

''Mandy seems to be the only one who's not been affected,'' Samantha said. Together they watched the little

girl climb up the fence rails to entice the mare to come to be rubbed by her small fingers. "Maybe we're just getting old," Samantha said, smiling at him.

"I feel old, about a thousand years or so, but I'm not sure it's entirely due to the trip."

"I know," she said.

"It seems that everything has changed."

"That's not necessarily bad."

He thought about that, his eyes on the child who had succeeded in getting the mare to do exactly what she wanted.

"Maybe not," Chase said finally. "But it may take some getting used to." He looked at her then, wondering if she could really understand what he was feeling.

She nodded, holding his eyes. And then she cleared the emotion from hers and asked, "When do you carry the rest of the money to the kidnapper?"

"Saturday. I'm meeting him at Crosby's."

"That seems...a little public."

Chase shrugged. "Keeping the arrangements under wraps didn't make it successful before. In and out. That's what I've always preferred."

"You be careful," she said.

The words moved in his memory. She had told him that the night he'd walked outside this house to find Rio waiting for him. The night Mac's truck had exploded.

"I will," he promised softly, just as he had before.

"How about supper?"

"Maybe some other time," he said, fighting the desire to stay. Fighting the need to walk into this house and make everything like it had been before. But that hadn't been what her invitation had implied. *"You got an itch, Chase?"* she had asked him tauntingly in the mountains.

He needed time to let her know that it was more than that. It always had been, of course, but he wasn't sure he was in control enough right now to make her understand.

He wanted her too badly, wanted them both too badly, to chance screwing it all up by a lack of control.

"I need to let Jenny know where I am," he said. "We had some words, and I left in kind of a…"

"A McCullar tantrum," she finished when he hesitated, and her voice was amused.

"Too much like my daddy, I guess."

"You don't have to be," she said gently.

"That's only as far as my temper's concerned, Samantha. I didn't mean anything else. I'm not like my father in anything else."

"He never made it right about Rio," she said.

Another illegitimate child who had grown up without a father. Had that been what had gone wrong in his half brother's life? Was that some part of the reason Rio had done what he'd done?

"When your mother died," she continued, "he could have married Rio's mother. There was no reason for him not to."

Chase shook his head. He had never found any resolution to his feelings about Rio, for the childish jealousy and the grief and anger for the pain his father's philandering had caused his dying mother. He didn't want to talk about his half brother. Maybe his thirst to make sure Rio paid for his part in what had been done to Mac was more what Jenny had meant. Crawling into the grave. Living in the past.

"I'm not like my father," he said again. "I promise you that, Samantha."

"I know," she said. "I know you're not."

"I want you to think about what we should do."

"Do?" she questioned.

"About Mandy. What's the best thing for her."

She nodded, eyes searching his face.

"And whatever you decide…" He took a breath before he said it, wanting to mean it, still wanting to do the right thing. "I'll go along with it. With whatever you think is best."

He turned away from the fence and began walking back to the yard where he'd parked Sam's truck. Mandy came running toward him and caught his hand. He stopped, standing there holding his daughter's tiny hand in his big one. *Just do what's right for her,* he thought again.

"Next time will you push me?" Mandy asked. "The next time you come? If your arm's all better?"

"The next time I come," he promised. His gaze lifted to find Samantha still by the fence, watching them. He squeezed Mandy's hand and then released it. He opened the door of the pickup and climbed inside.

"Bye, Mr. McCullar," Mandy said, waving to him, although he hadn't even started the truck. He fought the urge to get out and hold her, to settle the small warm body next to his as it had been during the crossing of the ridge behind the mining camp. To keep her safe. Instead, he lifted his right hand and then, taking a breath, he turned the key in the ignition. She was still waving when the dust trail the truck left behind obscured his vision. Or maybe that was something else.

SAMANTHA HAD ALREADY put Mandy to bed, tucking her between sun-dried sheets and reading *The Velveteen Rabbit* for about the millionth time. They both knew it by heart, but the familiar ritual was important, especially after the turmoil of the last few days. As far as Samantha could tell, the kidnapper had kept his word. *"As if she were my own daughter."* She found herself wondering about his child, about their relationship.

From there her thinking turned naturally to Chase. *"Whatever you decide... What's the best thing for her."* Because she knew Chase, she knew that whatever she decided was best for Mandy, he *would* agree to. A man of his word. A man of honor.

The kind of man she wanted Mandy's father to be. Maybe that was why there had never been anyone else. No one else had ever measured up to Chase McCullar. Not in her eyes. And, she admitted, no one ever would.

The best thing for Mandy? She knew what she believed that would be. Having a family, a real family. A mother and a father who lived together. And maybe later…

She realized that she had never before allowed herself to think about having other children, but now the images seemed to explode in her head, the feelings they evoked pushing under her heart, making her body too full as it had been when she had carried Mandy. Another baby. Chase's baby. And this time…

Except he had never said he wanted that or wanted her, she thought. Never *said* it, maybe, but in the mountains his body had betrayed his desire. *Healthy adult male* brushed like a warning through her mind, but she ignored it, and in response she felt the hot sweet ache move inside her own body. Never forgotten, those powerful feelings had deliberately been denied and buried in the routine of her busy life.

She remembered them now, allowed herself to remember. The caress of Chase's hands over her body. Slow. Unhurried and unhurrying. She shivered with the force of the memory and crossed her arms over her breasts, rubbing her hands up and down her upper arms.

She was still standing in the doorway of Mandy's room, staring unseeingly into its darkness. She could barely make out the small bulge of the sheet where Mandy lay, already asleep. Safe. Safe again, thanks to Chase.

She turned and walked out, pulling the door almost closed behind her, leaving only a crack so she could hear if her daughter called. She went into the kitchen and began taking the dishes she had used for their simple supper out of the drain tray and putting them back into the cabinets. Chase had built those, too. She touched the smooth surface of the door, feeling the solid strength of the oak under her fingers. Nothing fancy. Just strong and solid and dependable.

Except he hadn't been. One aberration out of all the years she had known him. She had told him the truth. She had known how Mac's death would affect him, but still... What he had done had been so out of character. Maybe Jenny had been right. Maybe for a little while Chase had died along with his brother.

She put the cup she was holding down on the counter and walked to her bedroom. She stood for a moment in that doorway, looking into the moon-touched darkness of the room, thinking about that night. Remembering. *Whatever you think is right...*

The phone interrupted, shrilling loudly enough into the stillness that she was afraid it would wake Mandy. She hurried into the living room and grabbed it before it could ring again.

"Hello," she said. It would be Sam, she had thought as she ran, calling to check on Amanda. But the voice that spoke to her wasn't her father's. It was familiar, its accented English almost as pleasant as the handsome face she was visualizing as she listened. Seeing him in her mind's eye just as she had last seen him, standing in the narrow street of the mining camp in the mountains of the Sierra del Carmen.

"Miss Kincaid?" he said.

"Yes." For some reason, her heart was pounding. Even knowing that Mandy was sleeping in the next room, she was still anxious, still frightened that this man should know her phone number, that his deep voice should speak her name.

"I would like for you to deliver a message," he said. He was still speaking English. Very good English, she realized.

"A message?" she repeated.

"For our...mutual friend."

Chase, she realized. Something about the exchange. The sick fear in her stomach eased. Nothing to do with Mandy. No threat. Just instructions for the exchange.

"All right," she said.

"Tell him…" The pleasant voice hesitated, seeming almost unsure of the message, and then finally he continued. "Tell him that the ambush was not what he thought. Not the man he thought."

She waited, thinking that there must be more, some explanation, some other meaning behind that cryptic phrasing. The "man he thought" would be the one who had recognized Chase in the shop that sold the painted animals—the other kidnapper. If he wasn't the ambusher…

"What does that mean?" she asked.

"The plan for the ambush originated on *your* side of the border," the voice said softly, almost as if he were afraid of being overheard.

"Our side? From the States? Someone up here?"

"Yes."

"Are you sure?" she asked, trying to think what that meant. It didn't make any sense. If it wasn't Mandy's kidnappers and not the man who had recognized Chase in Melchor Múzquiz, then who had lain in wait for them on the rock face overlooking that mountain road? Who had taken the rest of the ransom? "How can you be sure of that?" she questioned.

"As our friend realized, I know a great many people here, and I have…other contacts. Tell him what I said, Miss Kincaid. I believe he should be aware of the danger before he brings the rest of the money."

"Do you…"

She stopped because the connection had been broken. She stood for a moment, holding the dead receiver in her hand and then she reached out and placed it carefully back on the cradle.

Above the border. Someone *here* in Texas had arranged the ambush. But no one in the States had known anything about the payoff. Chase had insisted on that.

Except, she realized, someone obviously had. *If* the man who had just called was right. This was a warning given by someone who had a vested interest in seeing that Chase would be able to deliver the rest of the ransom. Why would the man with the mustache lie? Why would he even call unless he really believed what he had just told her?

Unconsciously, she shook her head. It couldn't be someone from up here. There *was* no one else. No one but the three of them had known about the arrangements. No one but the *three* of them, she repeated.

And thinking that, she picked up the phone again and began to punch in the familiar number.

Chapter Twelve

Jenny was on the phone when Chase walked into the kitchen. After he'd left Samantha and Mandy, he'd driven around for a while, trying to sort through all the emotions that had been stirred up this afternoon.

He'd ended up again on the bluff overlooking the river. From there he had watched darkness creep over what had once been McCullar land. It touched the low hills across the Rio Grande, painting them with purple shadows so that their harsh details softened and then eventually faded into the blue-black descent of night. He had watched the first stars come out and the lights in the two ranch houses come on, flickering faintly through the clear desert air.

He had tried to think about it all. About all of the people he loved or had loved. About his family. About his father's betrayal and about Rio's. Even about Sam Kincaid. There were no revelations about any of them. Or about himself, he guessed, but he felt better for trying to face some things that for years he had refused to think about.

When he drove into the yard at Jenny's, he cut off the engine and the lights and sat for a few minutes in the quiet darkness. He dreaded going in, dreaded facing Jenny, he guessed. There was nothing he could say to defend himself against the charge she'd made, no explanation he could offer as a defense.

Finally, he got out of the truck and walked up the back

steps and across the wooden porch. He knew she would hear him. The back door had been left unlocked, and he went through it and into the kitchen.

There was a plate with a cloth napkin spread over it on the back of the stove. That was where Jenny had always left Mac's supper when he was working late. Chase lifted the napkin, but his stomach roiled suddenly at the idea of eating. Mac's house, he thought again, and then he laid the cloth carefully back over the food Jenny had fixed for him tonight and went down the hall toward the den.

He could hear her voice, and he wondered for a second who had come to visit this late before he realized he was eavesdropping on his sister-in-law's telephone conversation. He had even taken a step away, intending to go on to his room and save the apologies he needed to make to her for the morning, when what he overheard stopped him.

"Because I didn't have a chance to tell him about us," Jenny said. "It wasn't the right time. We argued about his obsession with Mac's death, and then things just went…downhill from there."

Chase waited, trying to quell a resurgence of the nausea he'd felt in the kitchen.

"He's not home yet," she said after a few seconds. "But I'm not making any promises. You'll have to let me be the judge of when it's right to tell him."

There was another brief silence. Chase put his forehead against the wall, the pattern of the wallpaper his mother had chosen just before her death right in front of his eyes.

She had loved roses, but they had never flourished in the dry, too-alkaline soil of the ranch, despite her repeated efforts through the years. Finally she'd just given up—like she had given up on so many things—settling for the artificial blossoms that festooned the dark hallway in which he was standing. There his mother's beloved roses still bloomed in an almost-garish profusion of pinks and reds. Chase put his hand on one of them, long hard fingers tracing slowly over it as he listened.

"I have to go now," Jenny said softly. "I promise I'll call you tomorrow."

He heard her put the receiver back into the cradle and then he straightened.

"It's okay," Jenny said, her voice louder now, pitched to reach into the hallway where he was standing. "I know you're there."

Chase stepped into the doorway and into the light, but he didn't say anything. Her dark eyes met his without embarrassment and without apology. She didn't owe him either, he knew, but somehow he had thought she might not be quite so open about what was going on.

"That the new boyfriend?" he asked. He leaned his uninjured shoulder against the frame of the door.

"I'm not sure that's the right word," she said calmly.

"What is the right word?"

"For one thing he's not a boy," Jenny said. "But he *is* my friend. Right now that's all he is. He's been a good friend. Someone to depend on. Someone I've come to depend on."

Chase nodded, thinking of how long it had been since he'd been in touch. "Unlike your brother-in-law, I guess."

"I didn't mean that. I always knew you'd come if I needed you, Chase. And I've always understood why it was so hard for you to come back."

He gestured toward the phone beside her by moving his head in its direction. "That doesn't make it any easier, Jenny."

"I know that, too," she said. "But Mac's dead, and I'm still alive. There's nothing I can do to change that, Chase. And nothing you can do. No matter how much we might wish we could."

He nodded, remembering Samantha's words this afternoon about wishing. *"I've always wished Mandy could have known her daddy."* Maybe he couldn't do anything about what Jenny was doing, but he could still make that other wish come true. He still could influence that decision, the decision he had claimed he would leave up to Samantha. He still had a chance to change the way Mandy's life developed from here on out.

"Somebody I know?" he asked.

Jenny nodded, but she didn't offer the information.

"You're right," he said softly. "It's probably better if you don't tell me. Night, Jenny."

He turned and disappeared into the shadows of the rose-papered hallway.

"BECAUSE I DON'T believe you," Samantha said furiously. "I should have *known,* damn it. I should have figured it out, long before now."

"I had nothing to do with any of—"

"What if things hadn't turned out the way you planned?" Samantha interrupted, so angry she was almost spitting out the words, not even bothering to listen to her father's denials. His lying denials. "What if you'd gotten Mandy hurt?" she asked.

Only as she said it did she begin to realize exactly how dangerous the game her father had played might have been. "How could you do something like that, Sam? How could you play with people's lives like that? Just to get your own way. Just to manipulate us all."

"I told you I don't know what the hell you're talking about," Sam said stubbornly.

"You even said it to Mandy. She repeated it to me. What we need is a daddy. So you decided to make that happen, to get Chase back down here—"

"Now why the hell would I want Chase McCullar back in your life? Good riddance," he said. "I thought that five years ago. I *still* think it. You don't need McCullar."

"Except, for some reason you've decided that's not true. For some reason you've decided to play God with my life again. Controlling it, just like you've *always* tried to control me."

"I ain't gonna take a chance on Mandy being hurt. Or

you. You know better than that, baby. Thinking I had anything to do with all this is pure crazy, and you know it.''

"There was never any danger," she said. "You sent
somebody who can shoot out a tire from a mile away and
put a bullet through a jug of water. But then he can't hit
me or Chase, despite the fact that we're climbing hills without any cover? Maybe that was because he had orders *not*
to hit us, and you made sure he was a good enough shot
to do that.''

"And I could control how that car's gonna bounce? I
send my only child off the side of a ravine 'cause I want
to fix her up with a man I never have thought was good
enough for her? Does that make sense to you? Why would
I try to stop you from getting to Mandy, from getting her
back? Use your head, Samantha. You're smarter than this.''

It stopped the flow of invective for a second. She *did*
know Sam would never hurt her. Or Mandy. Which
meant...

"Just smarter than you, maybe. You set that up, too.
Mandy wasn't in any danger. Those were your men, your
kidnappers. The whole thing gave you a chance to call in
Chase and then to send us out into that godforsaken wilderness together. That was the whole point. To let Chase
know about Mandy. To get me and Chase back together.''

"You're the one who decided on going with him down
there. I had nothing to do with that. I even tried to talk you
out of it.''

Therefore guaranteeing that I'd go, she thought, recognizing her own familiar pattern of behavior in dealing with
her father. "You knew I wouldn't have any other choice.
Tell Chase about Mandy or go with him to make the payoff,
to identify my daughter. You *knew* that's how it would play
out.''

"You think I planned to send you into that country?
Without water?'' Sam said. "Without transportation?''

"*With* Chase McCullar. The best man for the job,'' she

said sarcastically. "You *knew* he'd get us out safely. You knew it, damn you. You were counting on it."

"You better remember a couple of things," Sam said, anger beginning to creep into his voice, too. "One, I'm not a fool. And two, I also know that country. I know what it can do to a man, even a good man. What if McCullar had broke his leg in that wreck? You really think I'd 'a planned on leaving the two of you out there in that situation? You think I'd hire men to put guns to my own grandbaby's head? To my daughter's?"

She didn't. Deep in her heart, she knew that he wouldn't do either of those things. Sam was ruthless and vindictive and hard as west Texas, but he loved Samantha and Mandy as he had loved her mother. However, she wasn't ready to dismiss the possibility that Sam was involved. It was just like him. Just like the old bastard.

"I'm sure you had a plan for that contingency, too," she said bitterly.

"Then why would I have him call you?" Sam asked. "You explain that to me, smart girl. If I set up the kidnapping, then why have that Mexican bastard tell you that the ambush had been set up in the States."

He was right. That made no sense, and if she hadn't been so furious with him, she would never have suggested it.

"Okay. Maybe he wasn't your man. Maybe you just decided to take advantage of the kidnapping to get me and Chase together. To give us a little time to discover..." She hesitated over revealing to him what she *had* discovered about her feelings for Chase McCullar.

"Exactly what did you all discover out there?" Sam asked.

Shrewd, conniving old bastard, she thought again, hearing the mockery in his voice. She felt a surge of guilt because this was her father she was thinking that about. But that was what he was, damn it. Everybody knew it. That was what Sam Kincaid had always been.

"What comes next?" she asked instead of telling him

what had occurred in the mountains. "You got something else planned for when Chase goes to deliver the rest of the money? I have to tell you that I'm not planning on going along this time."

"I don't know what you're talking about, Samantha. I had *nothing* to do with what went on before. I swear to you, I had nothing to do with that ambush."

"I don't want you pulling any more tricks, Sam. Whatever is between Chase and me is private. It's our business and not yours."

"You tell McCullar about the phone call, you hear me?" Sam said. "Maybe he can talk some sense into you. McCullar ain't no fool. He'll know I'd never do anything to put you or Mandy in danger. If somebody here did set up that ambush, McCullar better figure out who it was before he goes back. You tell him, you hear?"

Again Samantha found herself listening to the dial tone. This time she put the phone down with more force than she had before. Too much of what Sam said made sense. She didn't trust her father as far as she could throw him when it came to meddling in her life, but he loved Mandy. And he loved her.

As he had reminded her, if the kidnapper had been hired by Sam, then why would he warn her? But if he hadn't been, that still didn't mean that the shooter hadn't been Sam's man. There were plenty of people he could hire who had the kind of skill required for that job. The ambush had driven her and Chase into the mountains together and that still sounded to her like something that might have been on her father's agenda.

Exactly what Sam had hoped for had happened, she admitted. She had realized that nothing had changed about the way she had always felt about Chase. She had realized that Mandy had a right to her father's love. And she had realized that Chase McCullar still wanted her.

Shrewd manipulative old bastard, she thought again. Then she picked up the phone and dialed Jenny's number.

"IT'S FOR YOU," JENNY said, her voice coming from outside his bedroom door.

Chase had heard the phone ring, maybe an hour after he'd gone to bed, but no one knew he was here, so he had decided it couldn't be for him.

When Jenny had knocked on his door, he still hadn't responded. He had just been lying in the dark, trying not to think about the conversation he'd overheard. He thought if he didn't answer the knock, she would just go away. He sure as hell didn't want to talk to anyone tonight.

Somewhere inside he was afraid the person on the phone, the person who wanted to speak to him, might be the man she'd been talking to. Maybe wanting to tell him about their relationship, maybe wanting Chase's permission to court his sister-in-law. He didn't intend to listen to that request—not tonight, at least—so he had ignored the soft knock and Jenny's call.

He was surprised when she opened the door. He could see her silhouetted against the light from the hall. "It's Samantha," she said, when he didn't move.

Chase sat up. He had lain down on the bed still wearing his jeans, but he had slipped off Doc's harness and his shirt.

Jenny walked across the room and handed him the phone.

"What's wrong?" he asked, speaking quickly into the receiver. He might not be too bright when it came to his dealings with Samantha Kincaid, but he was smart enough to know that she wouldn't call him unless something had happened.

"I had a phone call from the kidnapper," Samantha said.

"And?" he prodded when she didn't go on.

"He said to tell you that the ambush originated up here."

Chase thought about what that meant, and as he did, he realized Jenny was still standing in the doorway, waiting. He put his hand over the phone and whispered, "It's all right. Nothing's wrong."

She nodded, and only then did she turn and leave, pulling

his bedroom door closed behind her and shutting off the light from the hall.

"Chase?" Samantha questioned the delay.

"Did he give you a name?"

"No name. Just that it was planned in the States and that you should know that before you carried the rest of the money down to him on Saturday."

"Okay," he said, still trying to decide the significance.

"I called Sam," she said.

He supposed that was inevitable, given that it was Sam's money he would be carrying and that she was Sam's daughter, but he wished she hadn't. The fewer people who knew anything, the fewer chances something could go wrong, but it was too late to change what had already been done.

"Sam said it wasn't him," Samantha said. "I still don't know whether to believe him or—"

"You think your *father* had something to do with that ambush?"

"It just…sounded like something he might do. Trying to manipulate the two of us."

"Why?" he asked.

She hesitated. "Because it put us back together," she said softly.

"What makes you think Sam would want that?" Chase asked. "He sure as hell has never wanted us together before."

"Maybe because there's been no one else," she said. There was a brief silence before she added, "And because he always wanted a grandson."

Chase eased a breath, trying to keep the sound of it from carrying over the line. A grandson, he thought, the images moving uncontrollably through his head. Suddenly, in response to those images, there were other reactions, just as uncontrollable.

"Not *my* son," he denied quietly.

"Then…not anybody else's," she said. "Sam's smart enough to have figured that out."

He wondered if that could possibly mean what it had sounded like, and then he buried the incredible thought in the necessity of dealing with the issue here.

"Sam wouldn't put you in danger," he advised.

"That's what he said."

"But you didn't believe him."

"Eventually. After I'd calmed down and thought about it."

"Which leaves us where?"

"I don't know. That's why I called you. The man who called said you needed to know before you brought the rest of the money."

"Yeah," Chase agreed. Damn straight he needed to know. He needed to figure out what was going on. To think about what Samantha had suggested about her father's motives, despite his denial. Could Sam have had any part in what had gone on down in Mexico? If not, then who else in the States would have reason to organize that ambush? When the answer to that brushed through his consciousness, his logic rejected it. Rio might hate him enough, but his half brother was still in prison.

"Are you still going?" she asked.

"I don't have a choice. I gave him my word. And Sam's."

"So what do we do?"

"Meet me at Sam's tomorrow. Call and tell him you're coming for lunch. I'll show up about one-thirty."

"Are you sure that's a good idea?"

"I need to hear Sam make that denial, to evaluate it, and then we need to talk to him about who else could possibly have known about the arrangements."

"Okay," she said. "What should I do about Mandy?"

"Bring her with you," he suggested. It was practical, of course. There would be plenty of people at the Kincaid ranch who could look after the little girl while they talked to Sam.

Maybe Rosita would help her with that damn song, he

thought, smiling in remembrance. But that wasn't why he had made that suggestion. He realized he wanted to see her again. He could admit that to himself now, even if he didn't tell her mother.

"All right."

"And don't say anything to anyone else about the call."

"Okay," she agreed.

"You're pretty damned agreeable tonight," he said, letting his voice relax into intimacy. He would worry about what the kidnapper had said later. Right now he just wanted to talk to her. To listen to her voice in the quiet, lavender-scented darkness that surrounded him.

"I worked out all my normal contrariness on Sam. Be glad I called him first."

He should be glad she had called him at all, Chase knew, given the mistakes he had made in the past. "How's Mandy?" he asked aloud.

"Mandy's...just Mandy. The same as always. Happy as a clam and totally undisturbed by what happened. At least from every indication."

"You've done a good job," he said. "A good job raising her. Especially having to do it by yourself."

There was a small silence, and he wondered if that had been the wrong thing to say, reminding her that he hadn't been around all those years. He had meant it as a compliment—a sincere one—but maybe it had backfired. Stupid, he thought again, listening to the silence.

"She mentioned you in her prayers tonight," Samantha said. He felt the hard pressure around his heart, a feeling that was happening often enough now to start being familiar. His daughter had prayed for him.

"You encourage that, sweetheart. I need all the prayers I can get."

"It's going to be all right, isn't it, Chase? Nothing else is going to—"

"It's going to be fine," he promised. "I'm not going to let anything else happen to Mandy."

"I wasn't worried about Mandy," she said.

Again something happened in his chest, making it hard to breathe.

"You're not worried about me, are you?" he asked softly, his tone deliberately belittling that concern.

"Ridiculous," she said, matching his mockery. "I know how tough all you McCullar men are."

He could tell from her voice that she had remembered even before she reached the end of the sentence.

"I'm sorry," she whispered, the terrible images that he lived with constantly, now in her voice.

"It's okay," he said. "I like you thinking that. Mac would have liked it."

Again the silence stretched across the distance between them.

"You be careful," she said finally. "I really *don't* want anything to happen to you."

He thought about that, about the promise it held. But he was afraid to respond to it.

"I'll see you at Sam's tomorrow afternoon. You and Mandy."

"Sleep tight," she said.

He held on to the phone for a long time after she had hung up, and for most of that time he wasn't even thinking about what the kidnapper had told Samantha. Other things took precedence. Other things that were far more important than figuring out who had planned the ambush.

He'd get around to that. Somebody had endangered Samantha and his daughter, and he hadn't forgotten it, hadn't forgotten the need to do something about it. That was still his job, he knew, and he also knew with absolute certainty that he was the best man to do it.

Chapter Thirteen

"Told her she was crazy," Sam said, looking up at Chase from under his thick white brows. He was sitting behind the rosewood desk, the three of them again in the room where they had discussed the trip into Mexico to pay the original ransom. The trip that had gone to hell in a handbasket.

"Who else knew the details?" Chase asked. He was leaning against the table along the wall. No suit this time. He was wearing a pair of Mac's jeans instead. It hadn't taken him long to get back into being more comfortable in the clothing he'd grown up in—far more appropriate for this area than what he had worn in California.

Samantha's eyes shifted from her father's face to his at the question.

"Nobody," Sam said.

"There are all kinds of ways people can find out information. Listening devices, phone taps…"

"I had 'em checked. The morning after Samantha called me, I had them do a sweep of the office. Phone's clean, intercom, everything. Nobody overheard what we talked about in here."

Then something or somebody else, Chase thought, some other direction. "Who brought the money to the ranch?" he asked, pursuing one of those possibilities.

"Dawson Sanders, president of the San Antonio bank.

Brought it personally as a courtesy to me. I told him to keep his mouth shut. Nobody at the bank knew who or what that money was for."

"But he did?"

"If Dawson wanted to steal from me, there are lots of ways for him to have done it before now. Safer and easier ways."

Which was true, Chase acknowledged. "Who saw the ransom note?"

"You and me," Sam said.

"What'd you do with it?"

"Put it in that safe right there." The old man nodded at the portrait of Samantha's mother hanging on the wall behind Chase.

"Would you check to see if it's still there?"

"Already did," Sam said. "It's there."

"Who else knows the combination?"

"Not a soul in this world. Not even Samantha."

Chase looked at her for confirmation, and she nodded. He should have known this would be pointless. Sam Kincaid wasn't a fool, and he wasn't careless. They were no closer to figuring out who might have planned the ambush than they had been before.

"And ideas?" Chase asked Sam. Why not take advantage of the old man's shrewdness and experience?

"I think you probably got some bad information."

"Why?"

"You said you asked the kidnapper to get the information for you because he has friends down there. Maybe he's protecting them."

That was another possibility, Chase realized. In his conversation with the Mexican, he had left little doubt that he was out for revenge. If the kidnapper knew the person who was responsible for the attack, he might choose this way to protect him, to throw Chase off.

"This is getting us nowhere," Samantha said.

"It's getting us further than thinking I'm the one," Sam said. "Damn fool idea."

Chase knew the old man was hurt that that had been Samantha's first thought. Having watched him with his granddaughter at the airstrip, Chase couldn't believe there was anything to that theory. The only problem was, he didn't have another one.

"So what do we do?" Samantha asked.

"I don't think there's anything else *to* do. Not until Saturday."

"And on Saturday?" she asked.

"I take the money down."

"Despite what he told us."

"If we can't figure out what's going on, then I don't know what else we can do. Maybe Sam's right. Maybe it's just a hoax."

"That's what you thought the first time."

"My instincts weren't entirely wrong then," he said, reminding them both that they had kept a couple of important things from him.

"I don't like it," Samantha said. "I talked to him. I thought he was telling the truth. I couldn't hear any deception in his voice."

"Maybe he was, but unless you have another suggestion, I don't know what else we can do."

"You can be careful," Sam said.

Chase's eyes came back to focus on the old man who had had surprisingly little to say during this session. That comment had been another surprise.

"I intend to," he said.

"I can arrange some protection for you," Sam offered. "We won't be taking a chance at scaring off the kidnapper this time. We got Mandy. We got nothing else to lose."

Nothing but a chance to flush out the person who had sent the shooter, Chase thought. "I think I'll provide my own security," he said aloud. "But thanks for the offer."

"You don't have to play hero," Samantha said, and he

looked at her again. There was a touch of color over each high cheekbone and her eyes were wide and very green. "Nobody expects you to get killed delivering that money."

"That's good," he said, smiling at her. "Because I don't intend to. There are still a couple of things I have to take care of."

She knew what he meant. The knowledge was suddenly there in her eyes. A couple of things to take care of, and this was part of it—looking after her and Amanda. Somebody had played a very dangerous game with his daughter's life and with that of the woman he loved. Chase McCullar didn't intend to let whoever that was get away with it.

SAMANTHA WALKED WITH him to the patio door. She waited until they were almost there before she asked.

"What did you think? Did you believe him?"

"Did you?"

"He's my father. I'm not very objective."

"Neither am I," Chase said.

"What does that mean?"

"Sam's never liked me. I can't see him trying to arrange for me to find out that Mandy's mine." *Or to be thrown together again with you,* he thought, but he didn't say it.

"I think he always…admired you more than you realized."

"Right," Chase said. "Admired me so much he had me beat to a pulp as a warning to stay away from you."

"That was years ago and even then, that's not why you stayed away. You did that because you gave him your word that you would. I think he admired you for that."

"I had good intentions," he said. Which had lasted about as long as it had taken her to unfasten the top button of her shirt that night.

"I don't think you ought to go Saturday. Not unless we can figure out what's going on."

"I don't have a choice, Samantha. I gave him my word."

"But it's possible that whoever knew about the first trip

may find out about this one. The temptation is still the same. Easy money.''

''We could do something about that. If you're willing to trust me again.''

''What do you mean?''

''We could try a little bait and switch, but I'd need your help to bring it off.''

''We made a pretty good team,'' she said, smiling at him.

''Which time?'' he asked softly, allowing the old memories to invade his eyes, allowing her to see them there.

''In the mountains,'' she whispered. Her smile had disappeared.

''Yeah,'' he agreed, his voice very low. ''I thought that must be the time you meant.''

She swallowed, the muscles in her throat moving and the soft color coming up through the translucent skin. ''Bait and switch?'' she asked, controlling the tremor in her voice.

''I'll call you,'' Chase said, and then grinning at her, he added, ''just as soon as I've figured it out.''

He opened the door, knowing that if he stayed any longer all his good intentions about giving her some time were also going straight to hell. He knew now why they said the road there was paved with them. All those good intentions.

''Mr. McCullar.''

He turned at the sound of his daughter's voice and watched Mandy come out of the kitchen door and run across the stone patio toward him. She was wearing a dress today, and he was a little disappointed that she was wearing shoes.

He had found himself thinking about those minute pink toenails at the strangest times, like after Samantha's phone call last night. Thinking about his daughter's toes and a lot of other things. He had remembered something his mother used to say to him when he was little. Something about taking the pigs to market, and he had found himself wondering if Mandy had heard it.

''Hi,'' he said, squatting down beside Sam's pickup. She

stopped just before she reached him, put the brakes on suddenly about two feet away from him. He could see her uncertainty about how to greet him in her eyes, even wondering, maybe, whether to hug him or not. "Did you come to see your granddaddy?" he asked, not wanting her to be uncomfortable about her relationship to him. That would come naturally, he thought, given time. If he were given enough time.

"Uh-huh," she said, nodding. "Rosita told me you were here."

He wondered why the housekeeper would do that, and then he remembered what Sam had said. Rosita had been with him since before Samantha's birth. She probably knew all the old secrets—including the one about Mandy's parentage.

"You tell Rosita I'm grateful," Chase said.

"She knew the song," Mandy said.

"About the cat?"

"Uh-huh."

"That's good. Now you won't forget it."

"Rosita said her mother sang it to her when she was a little girl. Just like me. Only she lived in Mexico then. I told her I'd been to Mexico."

He smiled at her before he asked carefully, "What else did you tell Rosita?"

"Just about my new friend."

"The man with the mustache."

She nodded. "But Rosita doesn't think she knows him."

"It's a big country," Chase said, thinking about the truth of that. "A lot of people live there. She probably doesn't."

"She said you were leaving."

"I'm going..." *Home.* He had almost said home, he realized. "To my sister-in-law's house."

"To my Aunt Jenny's," Mandy said, nodding. "Mama told me that's where you live. She's not really my aunt, but I stay with her sometimes. We live next door to her."

"That's right."

"Are you coming back to see our horses?"

"Not today, maybe, but soon."

"You promise?" she asked. She put her hand on his shoulder, resting it gently on top of the cloth harness.

"Cross my heart," Chase said. "I'm coming to see you."

"Okay," she agreed. She sounded like Samantha, Chase thought. She leaned toward him and kissed him on the corner of his mouth. A butterfly kiss. Baby soft and sweet.

"You be careful," Mandy ordered, and then she stepped back and watched him climb into Sam's pickup. In the rearview mirror, he saw Rosita come out the back door and stand, shading her eyes with one hand, as he drove away. Her other hand was resting on Amanda's shoulder.

THE MUSCLES IN CHASE'S neck were tight again on Saturday night as he headed to Ciudad Acuña. Lawman's instinct, premonition, or maybe just plain old fear. He hadn't been afraid of anything for a long time. Not until he'd had to climb out of that damn ravine in Mexico, he acknowledged, with Samantha up above him trying to provide some kind of cover fire.

All of that had changed. It had begun changing when he'd seen Samantha again. When Sam had said "divorced." When he'd realized that nothing was really different about the way he felt about her. After that, he'd been afraid to die, because he'd had something to live for—something to make right.

Now there was also Amanda. It seemed to him that all of a sudden he had a hell of a lot to live for, and yet here he was again, putting his neck into another noose. At least he was putting it there for his own reasons and not to rescue somebody else's loved one. And those reasons were worth dying for.

That's about as morbid as a mortician, he thought, shaking his head. That wasn't like him. He had the reputation of being cold and unfeeling. "Without a nerve in his body,'' someone had once said, meaning it as a compliment, he supposed. If that had ever really been true, it wasn't anymore. He wasn't looking forward to tonight, despite the fact that he wanted whoever had played with their lives, wanted him pretty badly.

He was still driving Sam's pickup. It didn't make much sense to change cars if his intent was to flush out the ambusher. If anybody *had* been keeping an eye on him, waiting for the additional payoff, then he wanted to make it easy for them.

He had pretty much discounted that possibility during the last two days. If the ambush had been directed from up here, that probably made it *less* likely that anyone could know about this second payoff. People in Mexico knew— the kidnapper and whoever he'd been working with—but Chase couldn't figure out how the ambusher could possibly know about his agreement to take another half-million of Sam Kincaid's money below the border. So he had believed his and Samantha's plan was probably another wild-goose chase. Until tonight.

He realized with surprise that he was almost to Del Rio. He had taken the road leading north from Eagle Pass, the highway that paralleled the river. He had made no effort at evasion or deception. That wasn't what this trip was about.

The headlights he'd been watching had been behind him for a pretty good stretch now. Close enough not to lose him and far enough away not to make him suspicious.

Whoever was following him didn't have much time now to play out whatever was going to happen. Pretty soon Chase would be into the lights of the small west Texas town and from then on, there wouldn't be any place on either side of the border to hit him before he kept his appointment. Like most border complexes, the two towns—Acuña and Del Rio—were in reality one community, separated only by the river and the bridges.

Even as he thought that, the headlights began moving up, gradually growing larger in the desert darkness. He glanced at the bag on the seat beside him and then back in the mirror. Definitely closer.

He could feel the adrenaline surging into his body, fighting the anxiety that had been there before. Now he just wanted this over. Wanted to be done with this job so he could get on with the other. The important one.

Although he had been expecting it, when it came, it all happened a little more quickly than he'd anticipated. Suddenly the Jeep was right beside him, running along with him in the eastbound lane, obviously not worrying about oncoming traffic, not on this isolated stretch of highway. He glanced to his left, but in the darkness he couldn't make out enough of the driver's features to attempt an identification. A man, he had decided, just before the Jeep sped up and veered in front of him.

Chase went off the road, just as the other driver had intended. That hadn't been his only option, of course. After all, he'd been prepared for the Jeep's move, or for something like it. Chase taught courses on defensive driving, gave seminars on how to avoid situations just like this. Only this time, avoiding wasn't what he'd intended.

The Jeep kept up the pressure, both vehicles bouncing along, still side by side, but well off the narrow road. Chase hit a couple of cactus plants, which appeared too quickly in the beams of his headlights.

Then both vehicles were into the wash—another site, carefully chosen. Chase had time to think before the wheels on the right side of the truck began climbing the rock wall. The Jeep didn't pull back, still edging him along, close enough that they'd bumped doors a couple of times.

Chase had slowed considerably, but between the incline of the wash and the Jeep's crowding, he didn't have much room to operate, not much room in case the truck spun out if he braked too abruptly.

Suddenly the Jeep dropped back, but before Chase had time to react, he ran into an outcropping. It wasn't big, but enough to turn the truck, sending it careening drunkenly on two wheels for a few seconds before the topography and the slope it had been following put an end to the ride. Almost in slow motion, the pickup lost the battle to remain upright and slammed over onto its side.

Chase felt the jar all the way to his spine, pain flaring like wildfire along the half-healed collarbone. Son of a bitch, he thought, gritting his teeth as he reached to douse the lights. The truck rolled on over onto the roof and before it had stopped moving, Chase had the door open and had slithered onto the ground.

The lights of the Jeep behind him were cut off abruptly, plunging the terrain around them into darkness. Chase used his elbows and knees, crawling quickly despite the rocks and plants, keeping his body low. As he moved, he heard the Jeep's door slam and even the footsteps of the approaching driver. Chase had managed to put maybe fifty feet of darkness between him and the man who had run him off the road.

"You okay in there?" the driver of the Jeep called, still standing a safe distance from the truck.

Trying to pretend that what had happened was an accident and he was just playing Good Samaritan? Chase wondered. Which meant he wasn't very bright. He was also carrying a flashlight, moving its beam slowly over the rough ground ahead of him, making himself a pretty good target.

They both waited through the desert silence that was the only answer to the shouted question. The questioner came closer to the truck, cautiously shining his flashlight around it. There was no movement, of course, from the overturned vehicle.

"Hello," he called.

Stupid, Chase thought again. The man couldn't assume Chase had been killed or injured in the wreck. He sure shouldn't assume Chase would believe it had all been an accident.

There had been something about the voice that was familiar. It had echoed in his memory, but Chase couldn't pin the recognition down, couldn't seem to remember where he had heard it before.

The Jeep driver moved closer. Still just man-shaped. That was all. Nothing he could recognize. From behind the outcropping, Chase could see the beam of light from the flashlight playing around the interior of the wreck now. Looking for him. And looking, of course, for what he'd been carrying.

Abruptly the flashlight was cut off. It seemed that the man holding it had finally reached the conclusion that if Chase wasn't in the truck, he had to be somewhere else, hiding somewhere in the darkness that surrounded him.

Then there were only sounds. As Chase listened to them, trying to identify each one, he backed quietly toward the place where the guy had left the Jeep parked, its motor still running, ready to move quickly out of the unforgiving territory they both knew so well.

Chase was careful, but the guy had probably been making enough noise himself that even in the stillness of the desert night he hadn't been aware that Chase was moving. When he came back toward the Jeep he was running. And he was carrying the canvas bag Chase had brought from Sam's.

By that time, Chase had put the Jeep between him and the man—a slight advantage, he hoped, when the shooting started.

"That's far enough," Chase warned. The .38 in his hand was directed steadily at the chest of the man carrying the bag. "Throw it down and put your hands over your head," he ordered.

Instead, before he had even finished speaking, the bag came hurtling toward him out of the darkness, quickly followed by a couple of shots seemingly directed at the spot where his voice had come from. Chase was no longer there, hadn't been there since he'd seen the bag coming.

He squeezed off a round of his own. He didn't think he

hit anything, but at least he would have a target he could see. And the guy had begun running again, only not toward the Jeep—which would have been the smarter thing maybe—but away from it. Toward too much open territory, too visible against the lighter darkness of the sky.

"Stop now," Chase commanded, "or you're a dead man."

Mac would have liked that line, gotten a good laugh out of the melodrama of it. He kind of liked it himself, Chase thought, his finger beginning to squeeze the trigger. He had given him fair warning, and if the bastard—

Then he realized, a little disappointed, that the guy *had* stopped, both arms lifting into the air. His first smart move, damn it. Chase forced himself to ease off the pressure on the trigger, and then he waited a second, just to make sure before he ordered, "Throw the gun. Pitch it forward toward the truck. And don't lower your hand below your ear when you do it."

He had time to count to three before the man obeyed, awkwardly sending the gun out into the darkness in front of him.

"Flashlight, too," Chase suggested.

"I left it in the truck. I couldn't carry everything." There was something plaintive about that. Almost asking for sympathy, Chase thought. Only he was fresh out. Not for a guy who put little girls with candy-pink toenails in danger.

Chase eased around to the front of the Jeep, to the driver's door. He shifted the revolver to his less-reliable left hand, knowing that the man he was holding pinned with its threat couldn't see him, couldn't see anything except the desert, stretching before him. Chase opened the Jeep's door and fumbled around until he found the switch for the headlights.

The man caught in their glare, silhouetted against the night sky was big, maybe as big as Mac. He was wearing jeans and a dark shirt, like just about every other inhabitant of south Texas, Chase thought.

"Turn around," Chase ordered.

There was a slight hesitation, and then, seeming to recognize that he had no choice, the man turned to face him.

Not bad information, Sam. You were wrong about that, Chase thought. *Pretty damn accurate, as a matter of fact.*

"Now what?" Jason Drake asked.

"Now we play Twenty Questions," Chase said, feeling anger at another betrayal blossom in his chest. *"My right-hand man,"* Sam had said. "I ask them and you answer them. And as you do, try to remember that I'm *not* real happy with you right now. There's a lot of goodwill down here that belonged to my brother. Somehow it's rubbed off on me. Nobody's going to give a damn if I shoot you. Nobody's even going to ask me to explain why."

"What do you want to know?" Jason Drake asked sullenly.

Chase laughed. "Everything," he said simply. "I want to know it all."

Chapter Fourteen

"Have a late dinner," the kidnapper had instructed. That was exactly what she'd been pretending to do for the last three hours, Samantha thought irritably, although she couldn't have named anything she'd eaten.

She recognized that her irritation, which had been increasing almost exponentially as she sat at the table in Crosby's, nursing a cup of decaf, wasn't really because she was having to wait. It was anxiety-based. Her mind and her heart were with Chase, who was supposed to be making his way here, traveling openly along the road to Del Rio.

He was the decoy, the intended target, and despite the fact that she had recognized the logic in his plan, she didn't like that aspect of it now any more than when he'd proposed it. She had only agreed because Chase hadn't given her a choice. He had reminded her that if their unidentified assailant had had any part in the original kidnapping, Amanda might possibly still be in danger.

So she had picked up the money at Sam's on Friday, using Mandy's weekend with her grandfather as a cover. Chase was to have gone to Sam's ranch tonight and without making any attempt to hide what he was there for, he would pick up another bag, only this one wouldn't contain any money. Bait and switch.

"May I join you?"

She looked up from her coffee at the question. Both

hands had been cupped around the white earthenware mug, maybe to still their trembling, or at least to make it less obvious. The man who had spoken to her was the one with the mustache, the one who had taken Mandy.

Neither of them seemed out of place in the popular restaurant, she realized, which was probably why he had chosen it as the rendezvous. There were some tourists scattered in the lively throng, and scores of natives and Texas border-hoppers jammed together among the crowded tables.

"Of course," she said politely.

He pulled out the chair across from hers and sat down. His dark eyes studied her face for a moment.

"Did you give our friend my message?"

"Yes," she said.

"I'm sorry I couldn't be more helpful."

"We appreciate what you did."

"Was it...profitable?"

Samantha hesitated. Of course, since it was almost midnight, whatever was going to happen had probably already happened, even while she had been sitting here, endlessly waiting.

"Not yet," she said. "At least, not as far as I know."

His eyes moved to survey the room, and she waited again until they came back to her face.

"Is that why you're alone?" he asked.

"My friend should be joining us soon."

"To deliver the package."

Again she hesitated, but this was, after all, why Chase had sent her. "I brought the package," she said.

She could read the surprise in his eyes, and then, as she watched, amusement touched their darkness. The soft mustache moved slightly as he smiled at her. "I think that makes you the...bagman?"

She laughed and was rewarded by a flash of very white teeth. "At least you didn't say bag lady," she said. "I think you've been watching too many bad American movies."

"Bad TV shows, all dubbed in Spanish," he agreed, still smiling.

"I guess technically you're right. I'm the bagman."

"Your friend believed that was safe? For you to come here?"

"He gave you his word—and my father's—that the delivery would be made. No one should have any reason to suspect that I'd be the one. I came the long way around. I crossed the border at Eagle Pass. I'm driving a rental."

"And you weren't afraid to carry that much money? You weren't afraid that someone might try to take it from you?"

She thought about Chase, deliberately making himself a target for whoever had shot at them. "It's only money," she said softly. That was the truth, of course—a truth she had always known.

"Spoken like a true Kincaid," the kidnapper said.

"What do you know about the Kincaids?" she asked. She resented his assumption about her and about her life, lumping her together with her rich father.

"Only that. Only the money. How much money you have."

"There's nothing wrong with having money. Nothing evil. Especially not if you've worked for it. My father *earned* what he has." She wondered why she was defending Sam, who certainly didn't need her defense.

"With a lot of help from his somewhat ruthless ancestors. Forgive me, Miss Kincaid. I didn't intend to express a disdain for your money. It is, as I told your friend, as I certainly have cause to know, a very valuable tool."

Samantha had fought her entire life against the implications of her family's wealth and against the easy judgments people made about her because of it. She understood, probably better than he did, all the things that money represented. More important, she even understood about the lack of it. She had known enough about that during the last five years. She knew that she would again.

"Whatever you feel about the Kincaids or about their

money," she said, "we've done what you asked. It's at an end. Whatever...use you have for the money you've stolen, I hope that it gives you some kind of pleasure," she said, not bothering now to hide her contempt.

Using her foot, she pushed the canvas bag she'd picked up at Sam's to his side of the table. Despite the noise that surrounded them, the dragging sound the bag made moving across the floor could clearly be heard, so she knew he'd been aware of what she was doing.

She stood. She took a ten out of her billfold, preparing to pay for her dinner and then leave. She was almost fumbling in her haste, suddenly needing to be out of here, needing to know about Chase, about what was taking him so long.

As she reached down to put the money on the table, the kidnapper's hand, his fingers long and brown and very strong, closed suddenly around her wrist. Startled, she looked up into his black eyes, filled now with the same anger she had seen in them only once before, when Chase had kicked over the suitcase in the dusty street of the mining camp.

"Pleasure?" he repeated softly, as if the word itself were an insult.

She didn't say anything, nor did she struggle to pull her wrist from his grasp.

"I hope *I'm* not interrupting something," Chase said.

He was standing almost beside the table. She hadn't been aware of his approach because her attention had been focused on the kidnapper's reaction and on the pain of his gripping fingers. Slowly he released her wrist, the marks his hand had made red against her pale skin, and his gaze flicked upward to Chase.

"Is something wrong?" Chase asked.

Samantha's eyes examined him also, checking to see if he was all right. In the dimness, his face looked strained, but he was here. At least he was here.

"I was getting a lecture on money," she said. "On its

uses. On being a Kincaid.'' There was a trace of bitterness in her tone, and Chase held her eyes for a second before he turned back to the kidnapper.

"You have your money," he said. "Consider yourself a lucky man, lucky to be alive. If I'd been with them the day you put a gun to my daughter's head and to hers, you wouldn't be. In the future, you stay the hell away from the people who belong to me."

The dark eyes that locked on his were unashamed and unafraid, just as they had been from the start, Chase realized.

"I'd like to show you something," the man said after he had held Chase's cold, angry gaze a long moment. "There's something I would like *both* of you to see."

"I don't think we have time to visit any tourist attractions," Chase said. "You ready?" he asked, turning to Samantha, deliberately breaking the compulsion that was in the kidnapper's black eyes.

"It won't take long," the man with the mustache said softly. "Five more minutes out of your lives, and *then* you may write an end to this. I swear to you on my mother's grave you will have no more dealings with me."

"We don't owe you five minutes," Chase said. "We don't owe you anything."

"Then my information didn't prove helpful in finding what you sought?"

There was silence for a moment, the crowd noises again intruding into the quiet circle the three of them made— unwillingly joined by danger and betrayal and honor. And by a little girl who was safer tonight because of what this man had told them.

"Five minutes," Chase said.

THE HOUSE HE LED THEM TO had been very close, within easy walking distance. It was in a mildly affluent area of the city, but Chase had wondered as they had followed the man through the dark streets what possible purpose this

could serve. Another wild-goose chase. At least it would
be the final one.

The woman who opened the door was obviously surprised that he had brought visitors. She was his sister, the
kidnapper explained, but he made no introductions. He said
something to her, the words too quietly spoken for them to
overhear, and they were aware that she argued with him,
shaking her head, but in the end she did as he had instructed.

The bedroom she led them to was very clean, its sparse
furnishings orderly. Against one wall was a child's bed,
hardly larger than a crib. The slight form that disturbed the
smoothness of the coverlet was visible in the dimness.

It was the kidnapper and not his sister who walked to
the table by the bed and lit the half-dozen candles in the
small shrine that occupied the top. At their sudden illumi-
nation, the sleeping child stirred, opening and then rubbing
her eyes, which seemed too large for her thin face.

"Papa?" the little girl said, questioning their presence in
her room in the middle of the night, but she didn't sit up.

"I have brought someone to meet you," the man with
the mustache said.

Her eyes focused on Samantha, who was standing now
almost beside the bed, drawn closer by the sight of the
child. She was near enough that the candles not only
brought to luminous life the gold threaded in the halo her
curling hair created but changed the translucent purity of
her skin to alabaster.

"An angel, Papa," the little girl whispered. "You've
brought me an angel."

"No," Samantha denied quickly, smiling at her.
"Only...a friend."

"You look like an angel," the child said. "Just like the
angels in my books."

"Thank you," Samantha whispered.

There was something wrong here, she realized. The girl
was tiny, only the size of a two-year-old, perhaps, but her

speech marked her as older. Turning away from the child and toward her father, Samantha asked very softly, speaking to him in English, "What's wrong with her?"

His dark eyes remained on the little girl, and his mouth beneath the soft mustache never lost its smile. "Unfortunately," he said, "my daughter was born with…some damage to her heart. A malformation. Easy to repair with the right surgeons, the right facility. Except…those are not here, not in my country, and they are not for people like us." His eyes moved to meet Samantha's briefly and then back to his daughter's, which were still shining with wonder at her unexpected visitors.

"Not an angel, little one, but a princess," he said, speaking to her again in Spanish. "A fairy princess who lives in a real castle."

"Does she have a magic wand?" the child asked.

The kidnapper looked again at Samantha before he nodded. "A very magic wand that can change lives. And she has loaned it to us for a little while."

There was silence now in the small dark bedroom. The only light was from the candles and from the twin stars of the child's dark eyes.

"No," Samantha said, smiling at the little girl. "She has *given* it to you. May it bring you great joy."

She turned to leave, fighting tears, hot stinging tears that welled because she knew he was right. Money was only a tool and it could be used for so many purposes. And she was also crying, she recognized, because her *own* daughter was safe, sleeping warm and healthy, protected in the house of her rich and powerful grandfather.

Chase had turned to follow Samantha out of the room when the kidnapper's question stopped him. "Would you steal to save your daughter's life, Mr. McCullar?" he asked. "Would you put a gun to someone's head if that was necessary to keep her alive?"

Chase turned back, looking at the little girl in the bed and seeing instead small, trusting fingers that had gripped

his hand. Soft lips moving to brush shyly against the corner
of his mouth. And toes, dusty from playing in the yard,
touched at their tips with pink polish.

"Yes," he said softly, knowing it was true, and then he
pushed by the man and somehow found his way out of the
small house.

Samantha was standing in the street. Without thinking
about it, acting on impulse alone, Chase put his good arm
around her and pulled her against his chest. She didn't resist, her slender arms automatically locking tightly around
his midsection.

"It's okay," he said, comforting. "Everything's okay.
It's all over."

"Let's go home," she said, her words muffled against
the front of his shirt. "I need to see Mandy. I just need…to
hold her. I need to keep her safe."

SAMANTHA DROVE WHILE Chase talked. His arm and shoulder had begun to hurt like hell, whether from tonight's accident or because he had left off Doc's contraption, he
didn't know, but having to tell Samantha what Jason Drake
had confessed to was a welcome distraction from the pain.

"When the kidnapper took Mandy, Drake thought he
saw an opportunity to make a fast buck, a whole hell of a
lot of unmarked and untraceable money, so he took it. To
hell with Sam. And even with Mandy."

"That rich bitch," Drake had said about Samantha, but
Chase didn't repeat those words. They were cruel and un-
true, and he saw no need to spread that venom. Maybe
Drake had been attracted, and Samantha had rebuffed him.
Chase didn't know and he didn't care. None of that would
be reason enough for Drake's betrayal.

"Sam trusted him," Samantha said. "He doesn't trust
many people, but I think that during the last couple of years
everything was getting to be…a little too much for him,
too much to manage. He needed some help, and he chose
Jason Drake. I thought it was all working out. I wasn't there

often, not often enough to see anything wrong. Sam's usually a pretty good judge of character.''

"Thanks," Chase said.

"I said *usually*." Samantha glanced over at him. His head was back against the headrest and his eyes were closed. "And eventually he figured you out," she added. *A man of honor,* she thought. Sam hadn't been wrong about Chase, no matter how faulty his judgment had been about the other man.

"You keep saying that. I haven't seen any reason to think anything's changed about Sam's opinion of me. Except maybe that I was better, somehow, when I was a lawman.''

"Sam liked Mac."

"Hell," Chase said, "*everybody* liked Mac."

"That doesn't mean he doesn't like you, too."

"I'm not trying to win any popularity contests with the old bastard." The old bastard who was her father, he realized. "Sorry," he said.

She smiled, her lips tilting in memory of how closely that echoed her own assessment. "*Conniving* old bastard," she corrected. And then, knowing he couldn't understand what had prompted that comment, she added, "Somehow that makes it even harder for me to understand how he could have so badly misjudged Jason Drake. That's not like Sam."

"You said it yourself. He's seventy-four years old. He needed some help. We all make mistakes about who to trust."

"How did Drake do it?"

"Since he's been working there he's just wormed his way into your father's confidence. He had access to almost everything. He'd even figured out the combination to the safe Sam was so careful about," he said. Then he told her, because for some reason it was surprising to him, even a little sad, to think about Sam Kincaid being sentimental, "The combination was based on the numbers of your mother's birthday. I guess everybody does stuff like that, even Sam."

"So Drake just took out the ransom note and read it."

"He was ahead of us all the way. He hired a Mexican shooter to go with him because the guy knew the country and because he worked cheap. They picked us up in Melchor Múzquiz and followed us when we left. Maybe that's why I kept feeling we were being watched. The shooter knew the back trails so they could get ahead of us once we'd given away our destination by making the turn to the west, to the mining camp."

"They intended to kill us?"

"They intended to get the money, but I don't think Drake put any limitations on how they did it. I don't think he cared."

"But the guy missed us. How could he miss us and hit everything else?"

"Good cover fire?" Chase suggested sarcastically. "Luck. Moving targets. Even the best hunters miss a lot of the time. And it's a lot harder to make yourself shoot people."

"And tonight? How did Drake know about tonight?"

"Because I told him," Chase said, sharp disgust in his voice.

"*You* told him?"

"At the airstrip. He was still standing around when I told Sam how bad I'd screwed up the original payoff and that the kidnapper wanted the additional half million. I wasn't thinking about who was around because I was so mad that you and Sam hadn't told me about Mandy. And because you let Drake carry her off the chopper."

"McCullar tantrum," she said, remembering Chase's eyes that day.

"When I came to the ranch tonight to pick up the bag that supposedly contained the money, all Drake had to do was follow."

"What did you do with him?"

"I called the sheriff on Drake's car phone. Turned him over to Val Verde County on an attempted-murder charge. That's what took me so long. Sam'll have to press charges for the other. You and I will have to testify."

"Poor Sam," she said.

"Because he trusted the wrong guy?"

"Because everyone will know. You know what they'll think. That he's past it. Just another senile old man, conned by a crook. God, he'll hate that."

"You don't have to be old to be conned," Chase said.

"I think it might make you feel more foolish if you are. At least...I think Sam will feel that way. Like everyone's laughing at him. That's always been so important to him."

They rode in silence for a while, the quiet miles slipping by in the darkness.

"Will you at least let me tell him?" she asked.

He turned his head, looking at the perfect line of her profile. "You think I'm going to gloat?" he asked.

"I just think I owe it to him," she said. "I'm his daughter. Sometimes...I forget that. Forget that *he* might need *me*. Forget what family's for."

"Picking up the pieces," Jenny had reminded him.

"You tell him," he agreed. "I won't even go in. I'll drop you off and go on back to Jenny's."

She turned to face him. "I didn't mean that," she said. "I *want* you to come home with me."

Only, Sam Kincaid's ranch wasn't home, he thought. Not by any stretch of the imagination. The only place that he and Samantha might consider home was the house he had built with his own hands. The house where she and his daughter were already living.

"Later," he said softly.

"You promise?" she asked, glancing at him again, uncertainty in her voice.

"I swear to you on my mother's grave," he said, thinking of Mandy's kidnapper. A man of honor. "And on Mac's," he added softly. For the first time since he'd been home, when he thought about Mac, his lips curved slightly, almost into a smile.

Chapter Fifteen

Chase realized only when the car had stopped that she had changed her mind. Judging by the poor quality of the roads, if by nothing else, he should have figured out a long time ago that they weren't headed to Sam's ranch, but he hadn't. The surfaces they'd been traveling on, both good and bad, had all felt like washboards to him.

After he'd told her about Drake, he'd just sat, eyes closed, cradling his left arm protectively against his body, his right hand cupping the elbow, trying to keep it from moving with the motion of the car. When Samantha had finally stopped the car, he opened his eyes and found they were parked in the moonlight next to the old cottonwood.

"I thought you were picking up Mandy," he said.

His heart had begun beating a little too fast, and he was trying to find some logical explanation for why she had brought him here. Some explanation other than the one that had immediately been there, full-blown in his consciousness, the one that had too much to do with his memories of what had happened in this house. Of being alone in it one night with Samantha Kincaid.

"I decided it's too late to wake them up. Mandy's fine, I know that, and it's the middle of the night. Why wake them up?" she asked reasonably.

It made sense, but it didn't really explain what *he* was doing here. Not unless... *Don't even think it,* he warned himself. Those were his fantasies, his dreams. They weren't necessarily hers, and he knew that they might not ever be hers again.

"You want me to take the car on to Jenny's?" he asked, holding his breath while he waited.

"Well, Chase," she said softly, "don't you think it's probably the middle of the night over there, too?"

There was a hint of amusement in her voice, and he knew she was looking at him. He could feel the force of her gaze in the quiet darkness. Finally he worked up enough courage to turn his head and meet her eyes.

"But your virtue's safe from me," she said. And then she added, "If you still want it to be."

Silence drifted between them again, but it wasn't like the other times. The quality of what was happening was different, and he couldn't decide why. Maybe because there was no longer any bitterness in the memories of what they had shared.

For him that bitterness had been replaced by the wonder of a little girl who was glad to see him whenever he showed up. And by Samantha's open acknowledgment that Mandy was his daughter and that she had always wanted her to know him.

But he couldn't explain why the bitterness had disappeared from the green eyes that were watching him now. Or why she had brought him here or why she had said what she had just said. He hadn't made much of an explanation about why he'd disappeared from their lives five years ago. At least not any that he could ever have hoped would be enough to overcome the pain of that desertion. But somehow, it seemed, he might have been wrong about that, too.

"I'm not sure I had much virtue to begin with," he said. "But whatever I've got, I'm not afraid to lose it."

"Okay," she said simply. "Think you can get out of the truck?"

He had to think about that, and as he did, he began to realize that he had set himself a damn difficult task. Not getting out of the truck. Hell, he could *fall* out of the truck. But managing the other? He wasn't so sure about his success at that. About how it would be for her.

"Maybe this isn't such a good idea," he suggested. That came from his brain. His body's response to what she had said had been just like always. Hard. Automatic. Samantha.

"You need some help?" she asked. "I can do that."

"I wasn't talking about getting out of the truck," he admitted.

"Neither was I," she said, and then she smiled at him.

"I'M STILL NOT SURE this is a good idea," Chase said.

He was standing in the same bedroom where Mandy had been conceived, standing in the same moon-touched darkness, surrounded again by the haunting fragrance of Samantha Kincaid's perfume. "This is not exactly..." He paused, then wondered how he was going to get out of finishing *that* one.

She folded the shirt she'd just helped him remove and laid it over the footboard of the bed before she looked back at him to ask, "Not exactly...?"

"What I've been imagining all these years," he whispered.

Her hands moved to the waistband of his jeans, her fingers brushing against the golden hair below his navel. Her hands were cool against his overheated skin and the muscles of his stomach flinched away from them. Again she looked up at him and smiled.

"I don't know why I always have to do all the work around here," she said, her voice teasing. "I swear, I don't know why I put up with it. Just working myself to death. Inviting you," she said, running the back of her hand slowly across his stomach, the tips of her fingers between the inside of his jeans and the ridged muscles. Her knuckles were as teasing as her voice.

"Undressing you." She bent her head and touched her

mouth to his chest. In contrast to her fingers, her lips were soft and warm, and his eyes closed suddenly.

"Seducing you," she whispered. Her mouth was close enough that he could feel the warmth of her breath as she said those words. It fluttered like a moth in the fair hair that matted his chest. "Everything, always, just left up to me to...handle," she finished softly.

She raised her head and met his eyes, her hands already beginning the task of unfastening the metal buttons of his fly. There was no answering amusement in his face. "Amused" wasn't any part of what he was feeling right now.

He lowered his head, bringing his lips down to hers. Her mouth lifted, opened. Her hands paused in what they had been doing, with maybe three or four of the buttons undone.

This was the first time he'd kissed her in almost five years, he realized. And nothing had changed about this, either. It was like a current moving between them. He couldn't think of anything else to compare it to. Circuit completed. Electricity arcing between hot wires. Jolting. Powerful.

Her hands left the buttons of his fly and moved again, slipping down into the waistband she'd loosened, into his briefs. Now her palms were moving against his skin. Her thumbs rubbed over his hipbones and then her hands shifted, coming together, centering on his body.

His lips pulled away from hers, gasping out his response to her touch. He shuddered, the impact of what she was doing moving through his whole body. Heat poured into him, igniting every nerve ending, running along them until the fire centered exactly where her hands were. Touching him, moving against his bare flesh, their coolness ravishing his heat. Not tempering it, but stoking, adding fuel to the flame that was already threatening to engulf him. To consume whatever shred of reason and restraint he had left.

"Please," he begged, the soft words almost a groan. "Oh, yes, sweetheart. Please."

Instead of obeying, her fingers moved back to the buttons, completing the task they had begun. Hurrying now. And then she was stripping the jeans off, pulling them down to the floor. She followed their fall, kneeling at his feet. He opened his eyes and looked down at her. Seeing her in the moonlight, he knew why the kidnapper's daughter had thought she was an angel. So damn beautiful. She always had been.

She reached up, and his briefs followed the jeans, dropping to pool around his feet. He put his right hand on her shoulder and stepped out of both garments. He was nude. Pretty blatantly nude, he realized, looking down at the slender figure at his feet.

He supposed he should be thinking about consequences. About what Sam would think about this. About something. Only his brain wasn't functioning too well right now. And if there were consequences...

"I didn't think it would matter," she had said about the first time. *He* would welcome another child. Another chance. One he probably didn't deserve, but one that Samantha was willing, apparently, to give him. Maybe tonight they'd make the grandson Sam had always wanted, he thought. Maybe tonight.

"This is going to be even tougher if you're planning on keeping your clothes on," he said.

She held up her left hand and he reached out and took it in his right. With its support, she stood. She seemed unembarrassed about his nudity—about the fact that he was undressed and she wasn't. Her eyes didn't avoid what was happening to his body. It would be pretty hard to avoid, he thought, but her eyes didn't reflect any coyness or hesitation. Her fingers found the hem of the short-sleeved silk-knit shell she was wearing, and arms crossed, she lifted it over her head and pulled it off.

Her hair fell back around her shoulders, a red-gold cloud around the beauty of her face, and then she reached behind her back to unhook her bra, quickly slipping the straps off her shoulders. She tossed the garments on top of his shirt that lay across the footboard.

"I should have been the one to do that," he said.

Only, he knew it would have happened much slower if he had. Taking his time. Touching his lips to the soft hollow at the top of her shoulder where the sweat-dampened sweetness of scent clung to her skin. Then moving to the flawless, slim perfection of her neck. And into the shadowed darkness between her breasts.

His eyes examined what she had revealed. Her breasts were fuller, of course, but they were high and firm, beautifully shaped. Tentatively, he put the fingers of his right hand against the outside of her breast. The skin there was like satin, incredibly white in contrast to the callused brown of his hand.

"What the hell happened to us?" he said softly. It wasn't really a question. Or if it was, he didn't expect her to answer it. She shook her head, but she caught his fingers in hers and held them for a moment, looking down at them. Finally she flattened her palm, allowing his big hand to rest, open and exposed, on hers.

"I'll never forget how you touched me that night."

"I wanted it to be perfect. I wanted you so much, had wanted you so long, that I was afraid… I was afraid I'd lose control. Scare you off," he said, his eyes on her down-turned head.

She looked up at that, and what had been in her eyes that night was there again. "You didn't scare me," she said. "It was…perfect. What I had always imagined it would be—the way I'd imagined you would be."

"Tonight…" he began, and then he hesitated.

"Tonight I show you."

"Show me what?" he asked, the question tinged with amusement.

"How I want to touch you. I want to show you what you gave me that night. What it feels like to have someone make love to you. So you don't have to think or plan or please. Just feel. Just let me make you feel.''

The thickness in his throat would probably have made speech impossible, but he truly didn't know what to say in response to that. Except suddenly he did. He knew exactly what to say. What he had wanted to say as he had worshiped her body that night five years ago. What he had wanted to say to her through the dozen long years he had felt it.

"I love you," Chase McCullar whispered.

Her eyes didn't change, didn't widen in shock or fill with tears. They rested steadily on his, accepting what he had said, accepting who and what he was. Just as they always had, he finally realized.

"I know you do," she said softly. "I think I've always known that you do."

HE WAS LYING BACK on her bed, still cradling his arm against his body, his trembling fingers locked around the elbow. Eyes still closed. Breathing in aching gasps.

But nothing was the same. Not like it had been in the car. The exquisite agony he was suffering was Samantha, moving above him in the darkness.

"I want to show you," she had said.

Then she had made that desire reality, touching his body in ways that were intimate beyond his wildest fantasies. *Her* hands had moved tonight in the scented darkness. Exploring. Sliding with deliberate slowness over his shivering skin. Her tongue flicking against his extended flesh, hot and sweet. More than his fantasies. Beyond any dream of her he had ever had. Until everything except her hands and her mouth and her tongue were forgotten, buried in the sensations that shook his frame, that shook the lonely isolation in which he had somehow existed without her. Not lived, but existed. He knew that now.

He opened his eyes. She was astride him, her head thrown back, exposing the slender column of her throat,

white against the blackness of the surrounding night. Her
hair was touched with moonlight, as the candles had
touched it. It floated as she moved, drifting over her shoulders, burnished with light.

He reached out, the tips of his fingers pressing against
the damp, shadowed hollow between her breasts and then
gliding downward, pulling against her skin, over her stomach, where she had carried his child, his seed. And then
lower still to where their bodies were joined. One. They
had always been one, but it seemed it had taken them a
very long time to realize that.

He almost sensed her reaction, the trembling response
beginning and then building as her body moved above his.
Then she arched backward, her breathing audible now,
gasping, echoing his own. Her fingers caught the hand with
which he touched her and tangled in his. Grasping tightly.
Holding on to him. Anchored by him.

When he felt her climax, her body out of her control, he
joined her, allowed himself to arch upward, his own body
exploding with convulsive power. Then again. And again.

It was not until those sensations eased, rippled into af-
tershock and then shimmered into slow heat that he was
aware again of the pain in his shoulder. Aware of the price
he would pay for even this semicontrolled movement.
Aware but uncaring. It had been worth whatever price he
would have to pay.

"You okay?" she asked softly. He opened his eyes to
find hers, wide and dark, looking down on him.

He laughed, the sound of it low in his throat, and he
watched the response of her mouth. Her smile a little too
generous. Eyetooth just the tiniest bit crooked. "I'm not
sure," he said truthfully. "Maybe we ought to give it another shot. Practice makes perfect."

"Are you saying that wasn't perfect?" she challenged.
"Is that what you're saying, Chase McCullar?" She put
her hands on either side of his stomach, palms down, and
leaned forward, almost threateningly, over his body.

"I'm not saying anything of the kind," Chase said. "I just always heard that the Kincaids demand the best."

"The best man for the job," she said gently, not tauntingly.

"If you're gonna start quoting Sam, then I'm going to sleep."

"Bet me," she whispered.

Chapter Sixteen

It was pretty late the next morning when the phone rang. Chase came awake to find himself alone in the bed they had shared the night before. Still nude. There had been a sheet somewhere, he remembered, but it seemed to have disappeared. He lay and listened to the morning, relaxed as a cat in the sunlight that was streaming into the bedroom.

Samantha must have been in the kitchen when the phone rang. He could smell coffee, and he could hear her footsteps over the wooden floor, hurrying to pick up before the phone could wake him.

She reached it before the third ring. Like the time at Jenny's, he didn't really intend to eavesdrop, but there wasn't anywhere to go to get out of hearing distance of the conversation. Besides, even if there had been somewhere to go, his aching body was too lethargic to drum up the energy to move. It was probably Sam, he thought, asking about last night.

Her father hadn't been thrilled about the role Samantha was supposed to play in what had gone on, but when Chase had called him to set it up, he had promised Sam that he'd see to it that nothing happened to Samantha. *"I'll keep her safe,"* he had said. *"On my honor, Mr. Kincaid."*

The old man had made no reply for a moment, and then surprisingly he'd agreed. *"You take care of my babies,*

McCullar,'' he had said just before he'd broken the connection. At least, that was what it had sounded like.

"No, of course, I'm pleased," Samantha was saying now, her voice coming to him clearly from the front of the house. Chase raised his head carefully and propped his bent right arm behind it, testing. He was sore—that was natural after last night's accident—but it would be bearable, he thought, until he could get back to Doc's.

"It's just that it happened a little sooner than I'd expected," Samantha continued.

Chase thought about that, trying to fit it into what she might tell Sam. She sure as hell wouldn't tell him *that*, he decided, grinning.

"How long do we have?" she asked, and he waited with her through the reply. "Well, I guess that's good. It may take me a little while to find somewhere. You did say he wants everything?" Another silence. "Okay. I'll come in Monday. Thanks for calling. I really appreciate you calling, taking time on a Sunday morning to let me know."

Chase heard her hang up and return to the kitchen.

"Samantha?" he called.

"In the kitchen," she said. "You ready for some coffee?"

Which meant she would probably bring him some, and he should start the process of sitting up. He unbent his right arm and used it to lift his body, easing his shoulders back against the headboard.

"Why don't you let me take you in to one of those twenty-four-hour things in San Antonio, one of those doc-in-a-box deals?" Samantha asked from the doorway. She held a mug in one hand. "Or better than that, to the emergency room?" she suggested.

"I'll go by Doc's when I leave here," he said.

"Doc doesn't have the latest equipment—"

"I promise you, sweetheart, what's wrong with me doesn't need the latest equipment to fix."

He held out his hand for the coffee and enjoyed watching

her walk across the room to bring it to him. She was wearing jeans and a tank top. She had probably been out to the stables already while he'd just lain here, sleeping like a dead man.

"And what would that be?" she asked, smiling at his tone. "Whatever's *wrong* with you this morning?"

"It feels a little like I've been rode hard and put away wet," he said.

Her hand hesitated, the mug just beyond his reach.

"Don't you pour that coffee on me," he warned, seeing the temptation in her eyes. "I swear I can't move fast enough to get out of the way."

"Is that what happened last night? You just couldn't move fast enough to get out of the way?"

"That's not *exactly* how I'd describe what happened last night," he said, and finally she put the mug into his outstretched hand and sat down beside him on the edge of the bed. She watched as he took the first swallow, rolling the heat and flavor of the coffee around in his mouth. "Was that Sam on the phone?" he asked.

He took another swallow, still savoring it. She didn't say anything, and finally he glanced up to see if he was missing something. The laughter that had been in her eyes was gone.

"It wasn't Sam," she said.

"Something wrong?"

"It was Blake Cunningham."

"You thinking about buying some more land?" he asked, smiling at her.

"Actually," she said softly, "I'm selling some."

It took a minute to penetrate, his brain overly relaxed by all the problems that had finally seemed on their way to resolution last night.

"I didn't know you owned any land but this place."

"I don't."

He didn't say anything for a moment, trying to figure it

out. "Why?" he asked. "You said you wanted Amanda to have the ranch, and I thought after last night—"

"Last night..." she interrupted, and then she hesitated before she completed it. "Last night didn't change anything about this."

His heart had stopped about halfway through that. "This?" he repeated carefully.

"I owe Sam a million and a half dollars. I don't have any other way to repay it. Even if we eventually get back what Drake took..." She shrugged. "Blake has found a buyer who wants it all. Everything that's here—lock, stock and barrel. I used to wonder when I was a little girl what that meant."

"You're selling the horses?"

She nodded, the cost of it in her eyes.

"Even Lightfoot Harry and your mares?"

"He wants it all."

"Damn, Samantha," he said. For the first time he looked away from her, thinking about the dreams that had crowded into his head this morning, waking up in this house, listening to her footsteps moving through the small rooms. The same stupid adolescent dreams he'd had before.

"He doesn't care if you pay it back," he said, and then wondered why he had bothered. They both understood that Sam didn't want the money. She was the one who cared. She was the one to whom the debt mattered.

She shook her head, not even trying to explain. This was part of the relationship she and her father shared. Chase might not understand why Samantha felt the way she did about accepting help from Sam, but he understood the ramifications of it.

"I'm sorry, Chase. I always wanted Mandy to have this. Something of yours. But...it's more important that we have Mandy back. That's the only reason I took Sam's money in the first place, and I'll never begrudge anything it costs to pay him back. Mandy's worth any sacrifice."

He nodded. She had said nothing about them. Nothing

about making plans together. *One-night stand?* he thought. Was that what last night was? Another one-night stand?

"I hope you won't begrudge it, either," she continued. "I know that you haven't really had time to get to know Mandy, but I think—"

"Don't say it," he warned her, his voice cold. "Don't even suggest that I might value this chunk of desert more than I value her."

"I know you don't. But I also know that this is your heritage. I know what that means."

"Mandy's my heritage, not rocks and sand. But you don't have to sell the horses. I'll take care of whatever's left after the land is sold."

"Sam said you made good money," she said.

That meant she was at least thinking about letting him handle part of the debt. But it also sounded like she was thinking he had salted away a good portion of what he'd made in the last few years.

"And I spent it about as fast as I made it," he confessed, not begrudging that, either. "But there's always more where that came from. Sam'll wait for his money."

"More trips into Mexico you mean," she said softly. "Negotiating. Carrying other people's money. Putting yourself at risk, a risk that increases each time."

"It's what I *do*, Samantha."

"It doesn't have to be."

He smiled at her. "We talked about this. Even if Buck Elkins needed a deputy, which I haven't heard he does, I can't go back to that. Or to the DEA."

"You could work for Sam."

He knew what she was thinking. She had said the old man needed some help, someone to see to things on the ranch that he no longer could handle himself.

"I don't think so." He hated to burst that particular bubble, but he couldn't see himself turning into Sam Kincaid's right-hand man.

She didn't argue the point. "The other's just so dangerous. You even admitted it. Too many people know you, know what you do.''

"I can't live off Sam Kincaid's charity any more than you can," he said.

She nodded and then the silence was back. The uncomfortable kind. He knew he needed to ask, even if the answer wasn't what he'd been dreaming about. He still needed to know.

"So where does that leave us?"

She looked up at him, her eyes quickly dilating. Shock, this time. She hadn't been expecting the question, he realized. And maybe that meant...

"Where do you want it to leave us?" she asked, her voice very low.

Fish or cut bait, his daddy used to say. Now was the time. No more years wasted on regret because he hadn't had sense enough to make it plain to her how he felt. He'd already done five years of that, a long enough sentence.

"Together," he said. "You, me, Mandy. Married. A family. A real family. And there's one job I'll be willing to do for Sam," he added. "Free of charge."

"What's that?" she asked, her lips beginning to curve.

"Make him that grandson he's always talking about."

THE WEDDING WOULD BE at Mount Ebenezer Baptist Church, the tiny wooden church the McCullars had always attended, where Chase and Mac had gone to Sunday school all those years ago. She and Chase didn't talk much about that decision. It just seemed right somehow.

She had told Sam that Sunday evening when she'd gone to the ranch to pick up Mandy and to tell him all that Chase had learned about Jason Drake's treachery. Her father hadn't said much, beyond the expected protest that she ought to be married at home, but he had offered her her mother's wedding dress. She had taken the veil and had even thought about wearing the beautiful silk-and-lace designer gown, but theirs wasn't going to be the kind of wedding Sam and her mother had had, with the cream of Texas society there to offer their blessings and good wishes.

The vows she and Chase would exchange were somehow too private for Sam's kind of show, the Kincaid kind. This wedding wasn't really a beginning, wasn't even a celebration. It was simply a culmination, maybe a maturing for them both. The church was big enough to hold their real friends, and in some way having the ceremony there would include Mac, too. She thought that might be important.

She had wondered how to tell Mandy, but in the end it had been far easier than she'd imagined. She had told her the truth—almost all of it. That Chase was really her daddy and that he'd had to go away for a long time, but now he was back and they were all going to live together.

"But where will we live?" Mandy had asked, a small worried crease forming between her deep blue McCullar eyes.

Samantha had mentioned nothing to her daughter about the sale of the small ranch, knowing that the loss of the horses would shadow even the joy of acquiring a daddy, so she hesitated, unsure what reassurance she should give.

"Will we have to go live at Aunt Jenny's?" Mandy prodded at that hesitation.

Samantha realized then that the question had nothing to do with the impending sale, only with her own explanation of where Chase lived.

"Maybe a new place," she suggested. "Don't you think that would be best? A brand-new place for the three of us. How do you think that would be, Cupcake?" she asked, holding her breath.

The blue eyes were still troubled at the thought of having to leave the only home she'd known, but Samantha knew her daughter was more adventuresome than she had been at that age. That quality came from Chase.

"Okay, but we'll have us a swing," she said decisively, "so Mr. McCullar can push me every day."

Samantha made no mention of the horses. Mandy

wouldn't be able to conceive that Samantha would leave them behind. She was finding it a little difficult to conceive of it herself, but despite Chase's offer, she knew it was the right thing to do—to sell the horses with the ranch. They were too valuable an asset not to. For some reason she couldn't stand to burden Chase with her debt any more than she could take Sam's money and not repay him.

During the next two weeks Mandy had helped her pack their belongings and had welcomed her father into the circle that had before included only the two of them. She delighted in his attention, and Chase was infinitely patient with four-year-old unanswerable questions and "supposes." Samantha often sat on the railing of the narrow porch, she and the calico cat together, watching while Chase pushed the swing, listening with serious attention to Amanda's chatter.

"Don't you get tired of it sometimes?" she had asked him one night, cuddled into the curve of his arm, as they lay together in the big bed while Mandy slept in the room down the hallway.

Chase always timed his arrival long after their daughter's bedtime, and he left in the predawn stillness of the desert night. She didn't know why that was so important to him, but she accepted that it was.

They both knew there would be gossip about their marriage, a lot of speculation. Chase had said he couldn't do anything about the fact that people would talk, but they weren't going to give them any further ammunition and they weren't going to take a chance on that talk hurting Amanda. But he couldn't seem to stay away and she didn't want him to, so for the weeks before the wedding neither of them ever got a full night's sleep, and neither of them cared.

"I mean, I love her better than my own life, but there are days..." Samantha said, moving her head slightly back and forth against his shoulder. "I have to confess there are days when I think I can't answer another one of those what-ifs."

"I have a lot of catching up to do. I owe her a lot of answers I missed being here to make during the last four years," Chase said. Then he put his lips against her temple, and she closed her eyes in anticipation of his touch. "I've missed so much—with both of you—that it's going to take me a lifetime to catch up," he whispered. "Even if I start now."

His hand moved downward to find the hem of the night-gown she wore. She wondered why she even bothered to put one on, as the fabric was pushed upward until his hand found what it sought, found and possessed with the sure, unquestioning confidence of ownership. Coming home.

IN SPITE OF EVERYTHING, Samantha thought, she had been expecting Sam to show up. And she wasn't entirely sure if it was the fact she was marrying Chase McCullar that was responsible for his absence. She really believed his feelings about Chase had changed. Maybe he hadn't come because of the betrayal of Jason Drake, because of the fear of what he would see in the eyes of those who knew about his misjudgment. Whatever the reason, as she stood in the back of the small church, she couldn't find that distinctive shock of white hair among the wedding guests, and the day was a little less perfect because of it.

She watched Mandy walk down the aisle, dropping rose petals one by one with serious concentration. It wasn't until the little girl looked up and spotted Chase standing before the altar that she relaxed. Eyes on her father, she began scattering the flowers with reckless abandon, evidently in a hurry to reach him. When she did, she took his hand, her tiny fingers reaching with confidence for his, despite the careful instructions Jenny had given her about where she should stand. Mandy had already decided where that should be.

Samantha's lips curved, watching them together. Finally

together. She was aware suddenly that the music that signaled her entrance had begun. Chase's eyes lifted from their contemplation of the pink-clad flower girl to find hers, and in their blue depths was the promise he had already made. *"Together. Me, you, Mandy. Married. A family."*

She would never remember her journey down that aisle or even the vows they repeated. Those words weren't necessary. They both knew that. It seemed that the ceremony lasted only a heartbeat, and then Chase was kissing her, his warm lips pressed over hers, his strong arm around her waist.

Cherishing and supporting. *To love, honor and obey. In sickness and in health. For richer or poorer. As long as we both shall live.* At least some of those words had lodged in her consciousness, she realized. The important ones.

When they turned to make their way back down the aisle, the three of them together this time, she saw that Sam was standing at the back of the church, his cream-colored Stetson held tightly in his big gnarled hand. She smiled at him, but he didn't respond, his lips slightly pursed and his eyes unreadable. He had turned away before they reached the double doors, and when they finally made their way outside, past the well-wishers, he had disappeared.

It was only later, at the reception where she and Chase had greeted what seemed to be the entire population of this part of south Texas, that she looked up to speak to their next guest and found her father standing before them. There was a moment of awkwardness, and then she put her arms around Sam's neck. His enclosed her, hugging her too tightly.

"I'm glad you came," she whispered. "I was hoping you would."

"You look like your mother," Sam said gruffly, pulling away a little so he could look into her face. "Only you ain't as pretty. Nobody was as pretty as your mama."

"I know," she said.

"I brought you a wedding present," he said. His eyes had skated to Chase.

"Thank you," Samantha said.

"Not you," Sam corrected. "You're probably too mule-headed to accept it. Him. I brought it for him. Maybe he's got sense enough."

"What is it?" Samantha asked, fighting a smile. Sam was probably right. She had never willingly taken anything from him, not after she'd reached adulthood. He certainly had ample reason to doubt that she would now—even a wedding present. Knowing Sam as she did, she guessed it would be something expensive and showy that he thought would impress everyone here.

Sam fished an envelope out of his pocket and handed it to Chase. Samantha held her breath, afraid that Chase's pride or his feelings that Sam still didn't find him good enough might get in the way of what appeared to be an attempt at a reconciliation.

Chase studied the old man's face for a moment and then he took the envelope. It wasn't sealed. Chase removed the single sheet it held. After only a cursory examination of what was printed there, his eyes lifted to his father-in-law's.

"What the hell is this supposed to mean?" Chase asked.

"You can see what it means. You're smart enough to figure it out."

"What is it?" Samantha asked, more than a little apprehensive at the tone of that exchange.

Instead of explaining, Chase handed her the sheet the envelope had held. As quickly as he had, she recognized what it was—the deed to Chase McCullar's land.

"How in the world did you get this?" she asked, trying to make sense of what it meant.

"The usual way," Sam said. "I bought the place. Lock, stock and barrel."

Her eyes lifted to his. "You were the buyer Blake found? But...why, Sam? Why would you do that? You must have known why I was selling the ranch."

"To pay me back. I knew. I figured all along you'd do something muleheaded like that."

"Then why..."

"Blake told me somebody else was real interested in the property."

"Who?" she asked.

"Trent Richardson."

"Senator Richardson? Why would he want—" She stopped because she had suddenly realized why. He was buying it for Jenny. To put the McCullar land back together for Jenny. She wondered if Chase knew about Richardson's determined pursuit of his sister-in-law, and then decided this wasn't the time to get into that. There never would be a good time for that revelation. Apparently Sam felt the same way, because he ignored her interrupted question.

"Besides, I like owning land," Sam said. "You know that. I hear this little bit can be a gold mine. Somebody's been raising some mighty fine horses down there. Everywhere I go, people tell me how good the breeding is. Those stables were just beginning to make a name for themselves, beginning to occasionally compete with Kincaid stock."

"I can't take this, Sam," she said softly. "I appreciate what you're trying to do, but I sold it all to get the money to pay you back."

"So pay me. The money's in your account—most of it, anyway. Enough of it. And my check's good," he said, mocking his own wealth.

"But...that defeats the whole purpose. If you buy the ranch and then give it back to me—"

"I ain't giving it to you, baby, much as I'd like to. I know you won't take it. Too much like me, I guess. But him," Sam said, gesturing with a movement of his head toward Chase, "I'm hoping he's got more sense than the two of us. Hoping he's less muleheaded. I'm giving this land to my son-in-law as a wedding present. Maybe a...welcome-to-the-family present."

Samantha looked down at the deed she held. Her father's

words made the print blur a little, but she managed to fold it up and hold it out to her husband. The slight vibration of the paper revealed that her hands were shaking.

"Maybe I ain't such a good judge of character," Sam continued, "but I usually don't make the same mistake twice."

It seemed an eternity as she waited, holding out the deed, watching both of them. She had no role in what was happening here, and she even understood that.

"We got us a daddy, Granddaddy Sam," Mandy said, materializing suddenly out of the crowd to latch on to Chase's leg. "Just like you told us to."

"I know you did, Cupcake," Sam said, but he didn't look down at her. His eyes were still locked on the other ones, the same McCullar blue. "Somebody who'll take care of you and your mama when I'm not around to do it anymore. I reckon you found the best man for that job."

"I know," Mandy said. "I helped Mama pick him out."

"Congratulations, McCullar," Sam said. "You got sense enough to realize what a lucky man you are?"

Another eternity passed before Chase's fingers closed over the paper Samantha held out to him. The deed to his heritage, his home, once more McCullar land—free and clear and in his name.

"Damn straight I do," Chase said softly, and then he smiled at Sam Kincaid.

Epilogue

The sound was something he had lived for for almost five years. He had fantasized about it through endless days in the worst prison in Texas, locked up for a crime he hadn't committed, for a murder he'd had no part in. Finally the gate of that hellhole had slammed shut behind him, and he was standing outside in the strong sunshine of a late-August afternoon.

The lines and angles of his dark, beautiful face were set and hard, almost rigid with the control that was second nature to him now. His cold eyes traced over the road that stretched in front of the gate.

There was nobody there to meet him, of course, but he hadn't been expecting anyone. Somehow the empty desolation of the landscape that surrounded him seemed appropriate. It matched the emptiness of his soul, a burned-out shell where once there had been the same feelings and dreams other men cherish.

But that was something he had learned quickly inside—not to have feelings. Not of any kind. Not about anything. And that dreams were what you clung to late at night when the lights were out and the familiar daytime noises had faded to the low, ever-present hum of hundreds of men existing together in a space that was too crowded and at the same time too empty.

He picked up the bag that contained his few belongings.

One of them was a bus ticket, compliments of the state of Texas. They take five years from your life and in exchange they give you a bus ticket. A one-way ticket home.

There would be no one waiting for him there, either. His mother was dead and his father had never even acknowledged his existence. He supposed people in that small south Texas community would question why he was coming back. Let them question and be damned, he thought bitterly. He didn't care what any of them thought anymore. That, too, had been burned out of him.

Rio Delgado was going home—not because he had any fond memories of the place and not because he had left anything there that he really wanted to go back to. He was going home for one reason and for one reason only. Because he had a score to settle with the man who had stolen the last five years of his life.

The three McCullar brothers once stood strong against the lawlessness on their ranches. Then the events of one fateful night shattered their bond and sent them far from home. But their hearts remained with the ranch—and the women—they left behind. And now all three are coming

HOME TO TEXAS

Gayle Wilson has written a romantic, emotional and suspenseful new trilogy and created characters who will touch your heart. Don't miss any of the cowboy McCullar brothers in:

#461 RANSOM MY HEART
April

#466 WHISPER MY LOVE
May

#469 REMEMBER MY TOUCH
June

These are three cowboys' stories you won't want to miss!

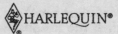

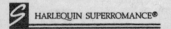

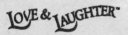

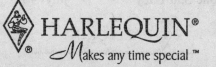

DEBBIE MACOMBER

invites you to the

⭐ ♥ HEART OF TEXAS ⭐

Join Debbie Macomber as she brings you the lives
and loves of the folks in the ranching community
of Promise, Texas.

If you loved Midnight Sons—don't miss
Heart of Texas! A brand-new six-book series
from Debbie Macomber.

Available in February 1998
at your favorite retail store.

Heart of Texas by Debbie Macomber

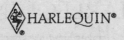
HARLEQUIN®

HPHRT1

MEN at WORK

All work and no play? Not these men!

April 1998

KNIGHT SPARKS by Mary Lynn Baxter

Sexy lawman Rance Knight made a career of arresting the bad guys. Somehow, though, he thought policewoman Carly Mitchum was framed. Once they'd uncovered the truth, could Rance let Carly go...or would he make a citizen's arrest?

MEN IN UNIFORM

May 1998

HOODWINKED by Diana Palmer

CEO Jake Edwards donned coveralls and went undercover as a mechanic to find the saboteur in his company. Nothing—or no one—would distract him, not even beautiful secretary Maureen Harris. Jake had to catch the thief—*and* the woman who'd stolen his heart!

MEN OF STEEL

June 1998

DEFYING GRAVITY by Rachel Lee

Tim O'Shaughnessy and his business partner, Liz Pennington, had always been close—but never *this* close. As the danger of their assignment escalated, so did their passion. When the job was over, could they ever go back to business as usual?

TALL, DARK AND SMART

MEN AT WORK™

Available at your favorite retail outlet!

 HARLEQUIN®   *Silhouette*®

Look us up on-line at: http://www.romance.net

PMAW1